CYBER THOUGHTS

Dima Zales

♠ Mozaika Publications ♠

Published by Mozaika Publications, an imprint of Mozaika LLC.
www.mozaikallc.com

Cover by Najla Qamber Designs
www.najlaqamberdesigns.com

e-ISBN: 978-1-63142-254-6
Print ISBN: 978-1-63142-255-3

CHAPTER ONE

I walk through Times Square with the unsubstantiated conviction that someone is following me. This has become an ongoing issue for me. Wherever I go, I think someone or something is there, lurking at the edge of my awareness.

It's like a canker sore you can't help but touch with your tongue. No matter what, I can't just chill and stop worrying about secret surveillance. The problem with this situation is that I know the name of the condition—paranoid schizophrenia—and the knowledge scares me more than my unseen stalkers.

I glance up at the flashy billboards, but the models in the ads aren't the culprits. Next, I look around and see thousands of happy tourists staring at the Naked Cowboy and taking selfies with all the unauthorized Disney and Marvel characters. I decide these aren't my mysterious followers either—which is fortunate. If I thought Mickey Mouse or Spider-Man were after me, I'd commit myself to an institution this very moment. Nor do I think it's any of the multitudes of annoyed New York natives who are following me, because all they want is to get through the hive of people and return to their offices.

Then I freeze in place because, for the first time since my paranoia began, I think I spot one of my stalkers.

It's a man whose face I can't discern. The only detail I can distinguish about this guy is that he's dressed in a perfectly tailored designer suit.

As soon as I spot one guy, I see a dozen more—all dressed in identical black suits.

When the Suits notice I'm aware of them, they abandon stealth and begin pushing through the crowd, eager and ready to grab me.

Since it will take too long to escape through the dense human fog on the street, I hurry toward the road instead. My walk quickly turns into a sprint toward 6th Avenue, and I push and elbow my way through to the car-beaten asphalt.

A black limo screeches to a stop, blocking my way. The limo window rolls down, revealing more Suits inside it.

Backing away, I glance in the direction of the traffic and spot a slew of cars descending on me—all driven by the Suits. I turn to look down the street and see an impenetrable traffic jam.

I turn back, only to face a wall of running Suits—except now I notice something about these men is horribly wrong.

As I attempt to register what I'm seeing, the ever-present bustle of Times Square quiets, creating the feeling that all the people and cars around me have frozen in place, perhaps as shocked by the Suits as I am.

There is a reason for that.

The Suits have no faces.

No, that's not exactly accurate.

They have no eyes, nose, or lips, and where the face should be, I see a smooth mirrored surface instead. Their hands are also reflective, as though their skin is made of aluminum and covered in glass.

What shocks me more is my reflection in their spherical mirrors. I look crazier than the homeless guy with Tourette's syndrome I often see on the ride to Techno's offices. My hair is long with a year's worth of grease in it. I'm missing teeth, my bloodshot eyes with the pupils the size of nickels are darting in random directions, and my face is concentration-camp thin.

The Suits approach me, and I have no choice but to assume a fighting stance.

Before I can land a single strike, however, strong arms grab me and throw me at the One Times Square building. As the impossible arc of my flight takes me toward the fortieth-story window, I again question my sanity—because every person in Times Square now lacks a face, their features replaced with smooth reflective surfaces.

I hit the window, and the glass shreds my skin with a million shards.

More Suits are waiting for me in the room.

They raise their hands, and mirrored blades eject from their fingers.

A dozen of them approach me.

I punch the nearest one in the stomach and wish Gogi were here to see the perfection of my movements, because he would be proud. Unfortunately, I don't have time to dwell on that for long. Instead of doubling over in pain like a normal human, the Suit slices my face with his shiny claws.

The pain is exquisite, and I realize something I should have long ago.

I'm having a nightmare. Again.

"You have been unconscious for four hours," Einstein reports somewhere in my groggy brain. "Current time is 4:37 a.m."

I'm about to mentally say something snarky to the AI but decide against it. I asked him to keep track of my brain awareness because I had a half-baked idea of dealing with my nightmares by asking Einstein a question along the lines of, "Einstein, am I sleeping right now?" The problem is that it's hard to remember about Einstein while inside a nightmare. Also, if my nightmare were extra creative, I could potentially dream up Einstein's answer.

My eyelids fly apart, and I'm faced with the pools of amber that are Ada's eyes.

"Another nightmare?" she whispers and cups my face in her hands, her delicate features contorted in a worried frown.

"*Da*," I whisper, trying to fight the grogginess. Then, realizing I just spoke Russian, I say in English, "Second one tonight. Must be some kind of a record."

"Are you being followed again, or did your dad try to kill you?" She sits up, and the sight of her perky upper body distracts me from the nightmare better than anything she could've said.

"Being followed." I force myself to refocus on her face. I know what she's about to say, but truth can be an annoying habit, so I also add, "I've been feeling like this a lot lately."

"Then will you finally go see a professional?" As she did during those few earlier pleading attempts, Ada uses the puppy-eyes tactic to make it extremely hard to say no.

"Shrinks did nothing for Mom when she needed help," I remind her. "Besides, what if I *am* being followed?" We've had this argument before, and it doesn't take enhanced intelligence to know I'm about to lose this battle.

"Gogi doesn't think you're being followed." Ada spikes her limp hair into a sad mockery of her usual Mohawk. "And the nightmares about your father are—"

"Fine," I say. On some level, I've been preparing to give in and see a shrink for a few days now. "I'll see him."

"Her," Ada corrects. "Dr. Golovasi."

"Of course that's her name." I snicker because the psychologist's name sounds like the Russian word *golova*, meaning *head*. "Your doctor is lucky she's not a proctologist."

Ada chuckles weakly. Her Russian has improved over the last five months, so she undoubtedly understood my joke. "Your appointment is at 11 a.m. later today. Now let's go back to sleep so you can get enough rest."

That she already has the appointment scheduled doesn't surprise me. She either just made it using her

AROS—Augmented Reality Operating System—interface, or, more likely, she made it earlier in the hope (or certainty) that she could convince me to go. In fact, she probably scheduled and rescheduled this appointment every day for months while she was chipping away at my reluctance.

We both yawn and get into our routine spooning position, her petite frame a perfect fit in my embrace.

As though on cue, I feel a small, warm body cozy up to me from behind my neck. It's Mr. Spock. He's peacefully grinding his teeth in a monster bruxing session, which tells me he's in rat nirvana. I launch the new version of the EmoRat app, and it allows me to feel what my furry friend is feeling—a blissful, in-the-moment calmness that us humans, at least the New York types, can only envy. He's happy to be in bed with us and his fellow rats for the night, though the others are cozying up in front of Ada.

"Good night," I say. I almost add, "I love you," but I stop myself.

Before moving in together, Ada and I said we loved each other, the first time either of us has felt this way about someone. Sadly, I also learned that Ada is peculiar when it comes to the L word. She wants to see actions that show love rather than hear the constant repetition of those words. For some unfathomable reason, she finds them corny. I suspect this whole issue is something *she* should see a shrink about, but if she doesn't want to hear me wear out the phrase, I'll play along. This way, when I do say it on some auspicious occasion, like our twentieth anniversary, it'll feel more powerful—and I think that might be Ada's point.

Feeling more relaxed, I focus on breathing evenly, and after about thirty more inhales of Ada's coconut-scented hair, I fall asleep.

If I have any more nightmares that night, I don't remember them.

CHAPTER TWO

"Dr. Golovasi will see you in a moment." The plump receptionist blows a bubble with her chewing gum. "Fill these out for now."

I take the forms, but before I fill them out, I locate the Wi-Fi and switch over from the slower cell connection. My whole world brightens, and I inwardly sigh at yet another confirmation that I've become as reliant on Wi-Fi (and connectivity in general) as a severely nearsighted person on their glasses. It's gotten to the point where I would've canceled this visit if they didn't have Wi-Fi—a purely hypothetical scenario since Ada made the appointment and she has the same quirks in this regard. Plus, this is a doctor in Manhattan, so Wi-Fi is pretty much guaranteed.

I mentally instruct Mr. Spock to stay in my pocket in case they don't allow pets at this office, and then I make quick work of the paperwork and hand it back. Once I'm back in my chair, I take out two Rubik's cubes and busy myself by speed-solving both puzzles simultaneously. Once I solve and mix the cubes a few times, I try the same feat blindfolded, after first memorizing the state of colors on both cubes. This second way of solving the Rubik's cubes is more interesting, but it only keeps me busy for a few minutes, plus the receptionist gives me weird looks. Bored with the physical world, I remove the blindfold, close my eyes, and launch the Telepathy app.

Ada's pride and joy, the Telepathy app is like a text messenger on steroids and amphetamines. The app uses Brainocytes to activate the areas in the brain that give the message receivers the eerie feeling that the thought they're getting from the sender is making an audible sound in their head. The sender can also imbue the thought with a range of preconfigured emotions—like emoticons, but way cooler since you can feel them. On top of that, Mitya, Ada, Muhomor, and I developed a statistically optimized language to express ourselves quicker and more effectively via electronic communications, and that includes the Telepathy app.

We call the new language Zik, short for *yazik*—Russian for *language*. Zik is as terse as we could get away with, so, like in Russian, articles such as "a," "an," and "the" don't exist in Zik. The Zik alphabet, if you can even call it that, is simply numbers in base two, also known as binary. We took the most commonly used words in Russian and English and represented them using binary numbers according to usage. The least commonly used words get bigger numbers, and thus longer strings of binary, while the most commonly used words get smaller numbers, and thus shorter representations. For example, the word "have," statistically the ninth word in our usage, is simply the binary for nine—1001. Something like "ossify" (turn into bone), though relatively short in English, becomes the binary for thirty thousand (111010100110000) in Zik. The number would be higher if it weren't for Mitya's penchant for boner puns raising the odds of that word getting used. Just for contrast, the original English "have," when represented in ASCII form (one of the ways the alphabet can be encoded in computers) is a whopping 01101000 01100001 01110110 01100101. It might not seem like a big deal to a layperson, but using smaller binary numbers greatly speeds up communication for people with a brain boost.

In any case, now that we have Zik, speaking with people in the outdated verbal manner is a chore. I'm constantly tempted to interrupt the slow-motion speech of my investors because I usually know what the person will say thirty percent into their sentence.

"Hey, sweetie," Ada greets me telepathically in Zik. A warm, fuzzy emotion that's the Telepathy app's equivalent of the smiley face emoji (with the little heart emoji thrown in) accompanies her words.

Emojis are also numbers in Zik. That might sound cold, until you remember the standard smiley face emoji everyone texts to each other is merely the characters ":" and ")" or the number 00111010 00101001 in binary. In fact, in Zik, we can add intensity to our emojis, allowing for a wide range of subtlety in the emotional subtext we use.

"Hi, babe," I reply, imbuing my message with the Zik equivalent of a confident wink. "I'm here at the shrink's office, in case you thought I'd flake out at the last minute."

Ada's avatar appears in the air in front of me. She opted to look like a mischievous imp, so it must be another Monday.

"Do you mind sharing?" she asks and waves her hand around her body.

She's requesting that I launch the relatively new app we call Share. When running, this app allows Ada to see what I see and hear what I hear—not unlike the rat version she developed for Mr. Spock and his kin.

I activate the app, and the imp looks around the room.

"You're not in the office yet." Ada's voice rings throughout the waiting room. Obviously, her speech isn't really here; it's merely the Brainocytes stimulating the auditory center of my brain. More specifically, it's a Zik message that our newly advanced version of the Teleconference app converts into speech experience. This is how we now "speak," even when within earshot of each other and not in public. In public, we speak out loud so people don't think we're a couple of weird mutes who don't even use sign language.

"The appointment is for eleven. It's 10:58 on the clock here." I nod toward the digital wall clock. On Ada's end of the conversation, my avatar looks like Misha, the Russian Bear mascot of the 1980 Summer Olympics in Moscow and my namesake. "I guess the doctor is punctual."

"Awesome, we have two minutes to kill. Time enough for a chat," Ada says out loud, but she must've also used the Telepathy app, because I receive an emotion that's probably smugness. I'm still not as adept as Ada at interpreting emotional subtext.

With our current brain boosts, two minutes is plenty of time to have an actual conversation, albeit a light one. In the past five months, Mitya has stripped several of his companies of high-end servers in order to throw these resources at the brain boost project. This has given us all cognitive capabilities we're still learning to exploit. We accepted Mitya's servers because making money with boosted intelligence has become so easy for us that we can easily compensate the affected companies. And even without that, the companies will be better off because we used our boosted intelligence to design replacement servers that will be head and shoulders above the ones we've borrowed. In fact, many of these super servers are currently in the pipeline at major manufacturers. Among the new hardware available today, the highlight is probably the Braino servers, built with IBM's custom and highly experimental neurosynaptic computer chips. Then again, if you asked Muhomor, he'd probably say the best hardware we have is the Qecho. The 100-qubit quantum computer isn't yet used for brain boosts, per se, but it does help us solve several important and difficult problems, including encryption and decryption of secured messages—a branch of computer science that gives Muhomor the equivalent of what normal guys would call an erection.

"Yeah, we can chat," I tell Ada. "I was getting bored anyway."

"Oh?" Ada's avatar looks extra impish. "You're not multitasking?"

"Of course I am. I'm pair programming with Mitya right now."

One of the coolest benefits of having extra brainpower is the ability to split my attention in a way that wouldn't be possible unenhanced. That's what allows me to virtually observe Mitya's coding and provide him with feedback on the app he's writing while sitting here and talking to Ada. Mitya's app will allow someone with Brainocytes to move the latest model of the Roomba cleaning robot with their mind. Pair programming and my brain boost are how I've gotten way better at coding, though I've mostly concentrated on helping open-source projects online instead of writing Brainocyte-ware.

"Let me know if you want me to take over for you." Ada sends this telepathically, but her lips move as though she's speaking. "Talking to the doctor might require your full attention."

"I might take you up on that," I reply. "I could use the time to brush up some more on psychology."

The other day, when I started suspecting Ada would win our "see a shrink" argument, I read a bunch of psychology textbooks, but it's a big field and I could be better prepared.

"Just don't be a wise-ass." Ada's face looks too serious for an imp. "According to Google, she's the best in NYC."

"Fine, but I'm still skeptical," I mentally reply. "How much can I tell her? From what I know about doctor-patient privilege, anything short of planning a crime is protected, but you know how complicated it is with—"

"Tell her as much as you need to so she can do her job."
Ada's avatar flies closer.

"But that might include mentioning the Brainocytes
Club," I warn.

Brainocytes Club is what Mitya, Ada, Muhomor, and I
call ourselves. Like in *Fight Club*, the first rule of Brainocytes
Club is you don't talk about Brainocytes Club—a rule that's
easy to follow since we use the Telepathy app instead.

"If you need to, I think it would be worth telling her
about Brainocytes," Ada replies telepathically. "Then again,
if it doesn't come up, don't mention it."

"Just in case, I have a non-disclosure agreement that
Kadvosky drafted." I pull the paper out of my back pocket
and examine the legalese that even the intelligence boost
has trouble deciphering.

The Kadvosky law firm is the most famous and, not
coincidentally, most expensive law firm in the world. Mr.
Kadvosky is the best of the best, and Mitya put in a good
word for me with them, resulting in me being able to use
Kadvosky whenever I need legal counsel. When I asked
for this non-disclosure agreement, I learned more than I
needed to know about my default protections in the eyes of
the law, plus the extra protection this document provides.

"That might be overkill, and she may not want to work
with you." The imp avatar crosses her arms and narrows
her eyes. She doesn't want me to sabotage this appointment. "Promise you'll do your best to make this part go
smoothly."

The receptionist pops her gum. "Dr. Golovasi will see
you now."

"Saved by the bell," Ada mumbles.

I get up and approach the office door with a disproportionate amount of anxiety. I feel as though I'm seeing a dentist instead of a shrink. I debate launching BraveChill, the anti-anxiety app Ada and I collaborated on. It works with neural networks that connect the cerebral cortex to the adrenal medulla—the inner part of the adrenal gland located above each kidney, an organ responsible for the body's rapid response to stressful situations. Then I chide myself. Using BraveChill in this circumstance would be like launching ballistic missiles as fireworks. App-medicating can be as addictive as using meds, and the last thing I need is an addiction.

Taking the natural route, I draw in a deep breath, release it, and walk into the room where Dr. Golovasi lurks.

CHAPTER THREE

When I'm this nervous, I automatically stop multitasking and focus my full attention on my environment because I've been known to trip on objects around me. Once, I nearly stepped on man's true best friend—a rat.

Being this focused gives me an unnaturally complete snapshot of the room around me. I observe details that would normally take ten minutes of careful examination to glean. I guess the age and make of every piece of furniture, and I estimate when the central air filter will need a change. I figure out when the room was last dusted, and since dust is mostly made up of dead skin cells, I calculate how many patients the shrink has seen since the last cleanup. Last but not least, I take in the antique redwood bookshelves surrounding the office and mentally catalog each title to look up later. I also spot the article the doctor was reading in the *New York Times* on the small table, then get around to taking a good look at the doctor herself—and feel instant relief.

If my first schoolteacher, Lydia Petrovna, mated with Mary Poppins and Mrs. Doubtfire, that odd hybrid child would look just like Dr. Golovasi after she reached menopause. Instead of anxiety, I suddenly feel like I should eat my vegetables and study geometry—and this in turn makes me smile at her. It's weird how hard it is to feel nervous when confronted by such a kind sparkle in someone's eyes.

Dr. Golovasi notices my smile and gives me one in return. Her teeth are so toilet-white I bet they'd shine bright purple under a black light. She stands up and offers me her hand. "Nice to meet you, Mr. Cohen."

"Nice to meet you, Dr. Golovasi." Her hand is as warm as her face. "Please, call me Mike."

"Okay, Mike. Please call me Jane." She gestures at the plush, overstuffed couch.

"Sure, ma'am," I reply as I sit down and wonder why I have such a hard time picturing myself calling her Jane. In the Russian tradition, calling an older doctor Jane instead of by her full name with the patronymic would be the equivalent of not addressing her by the plural "you." Both cases are breaches of protocol and feel wrong, especially in light of her resemblance to my first-grade teacher.

The doctor sits back in her chair, her gaze enveloping me like a warm blanket.

"I—Before we begin… err… I'd like you to sign a non-disclosure agreement," I say and get back up, rustling the paper in my hands. I feel like a complete idiot. "I know this might not be orthodox, but I'm an extremely private person, and if you don't mind…"

Dr. Golovasi's eyebrows rise. "This is a safe place. Anything you tell me in here is already privileged."

"I get that," I say, feeling even more of an ass. "But this document should reinforce the seriousness of my need for discretion. This way, I can take civil action should—"

I don't finish my thought because I see a miniscule frown creep into the corners of the doctor's eyes.

"Good going." Ada's telepathic message is chock-full of sarcasm. "You just threatened a nice old lady."

Whatever doubts Dr. Golovasi might have, they disappear from her face and she says, "Please, let me have a look at that."

I hand her the paper and amble back to the cushy couch.

Dr. Golovasi puts on the pair of reading glasses hanging from her neck. That reminds me of the second nicest person I knew as a kid—a lady librarian who'd always save the newest science fiction releases for me in middle school.

Since I have some time while the doctor reads, I code-review Mitya's app, write a function for the open-source project I've been helping out on, balance my checkbook, do some light shopping on Amazon, research a couple of companies for my fund's portfolio, skim the ebook versions of the more interesting books I spotted on Dr. Golovasi's shelf, read a couple of articles in the *IEEE Journal on Selected Areas in Communication*, read an article in *Advances in Physics*, and write down an idea that occurred to me.

"Hey, Ada," I mentally say. "Check out my write-up. I think I figured out how we can make a transistor that can scavenge energy from its environment. If my back-of-the-head calculations are correct, that would lead to ultra-low power consumption."

"She's done." Ada's voice is so loud I get the illusion my ears are ringing. "Focus on your visit for now. The transistors can wait."

"Okay, Mike." Dr. Golovasi pushes her glasses higher on her nose, pulls out a pen, and signs the non-disclosure agreement. "Hopefully, this will make you feel safe here."

I retrieve the paper, sit back down, and look at the doctor.

"Though it might seem redundant, I must go over your usual patient privileges," she says and goes into an explanation that boils down to her being ethically, professionally, and legally obligated to not disclose anything I tell her, except something like me planning to hurt myself or others. She finishes with, "Do you have any questions about this?"

"No, Dr. Golovasi, I understand." What I don't add is that my non-disclosure would probably cover me in the unlikely event that I told her I was planning on hurting someone.

"Please, call me Jane," she says and takes off her glasses.

"Okay, ma'am," I reply and mentally send to Ada, "No offense, but this is where I bid you farewell."

"Good luck," Ada says without any hurt in her tone.

I turn off my Share app and Mr. Spock's equivalent (since Ada can and does access him), and say out loud, "Is this the part where I lie down and get in touch with my feelings?"

"If that makes you more comfortable." Dr. Golovasi gives me a wry smile. "To start, why don't you tell me what brought you here?"

"I'm not actually sure I even need to be here." I decide I prefer sitting after all.

She reaches for a notepad and pen. "The mere fact you came here proves you need to be here," she says gently.

To me, it's the fact that I don't call her out on that zany Hallmark-card wisdom that proves I indeed need to be here, but I don't say that. Instead, I choose to go with a more careful, "My biggest concern is trouble sleeping."

She asks for clarification, and I admit I've had really bad nightmares every night for months.

"We'll come back to that shortly." She scribbles something down, probably, *Yep, a nut job*, before looking up again. "Is anything else bothering you?"

"I've been getting anxious much too easily lately," I admit. "Sometimes, it happens for no reason, but I think it's just the effect of poor sleep. I also feel jumpy and easily irritated, and my girlfriend thinks I exaggerate the negative aspects of my life. But all these things can also be caused by insomnia."

I stop talking, but Dr. Golovasi looks at me expectantly, her patience reminiscent of a Buddhist monk's. Her posture says, *Okay, that's a good start, but now tell me the really juicy details.*

I stay silent for a few more beats, then decide to just come out with it. "I also relive certain horrible events that happened to me recently. I feel a lot of guilt, though I think it's a justifiable response."

Dr. Golovasi's left eyebrow rises slightly, as though saying, *Okay, I'll definitely need to hear about these horrible events, but it seems like you're still holding out on me.*

I take a breath and continue. "I guess the biggest issue is that I often feel like I'm being followed," I say.

This breaks through her calm facade. "Why do you say that?" she asks avidly, leaning forward—something I take as a bad sign.

Seeming to realize she's betrayed too much emotion, the doctor steeples her fingers in front of her face in a gesture that might've fooled someone whose brain wasn't as overclocked as mine. "Why do you say this feeling of being followed is your biggest issue?" she clarifies.

"Well, to start, no one believes I'm being followed," I say, wishing we could converse in Zik so I could add a big dose of hesitation to my words, as well as speed this whole thing up.

"You've told people close to you about these feelings?" There appears to be approval in her tone. "But you're not happy with their reaction?"

"I just told my bodyguard and my girlfriend," I say. "And yes, it sucks that they don't believe me."

She must have other patients with bodyguards, because she just looks at me expectantly again, her countenance saying, *Get on with it already.*

"Okay, I didn't even tell this to my mom." I inhale some extra air and breathe it out. "The thing is, I recently learned that my half-sister suffers from paranoid schizophrenia."

As soon as the words leave my mouth, I realize I never admitted this truth to myself. I never dared to connect the feeling of being followed with my research on my half-siblings—the kids my deceased father had with his wife of forty years. After the events in Russia, I learned I have a half-brother named Konstantin, or Kostya, and a half-sister named Masha. Kostya turned out to be one of the so-called New Russians. He made a lot of money in the oil industry, then invested in an internet startup that later exploded in growth. He's unmarried, likely because he spends considerable time and money on psychiatric care for Masha.

My half-sister believes poltergeists are after her. I learned that when Muhomor hacked the computers at the clinic where Kostya keeps her. In Masha's defense, there was a time in the eighties when many Russians believed in poltergeists, perhaps in part because Russian folklore contains a mystical creature called *Domovoi*, an often mischievous but friendly house spirit. The spirits my half-sister believes stalk her are more frightening than the relatively benign Domovoi, though. Last year, Masha tried to take her own life, but she said it was the spirits. This was her sixth suicide attempt. When Kostya shared the fate of our father with her, Masha scratched Kostya's face to the point of leaving permanent scars.

So yeah, my biggest fear is that the stressful events that led to my father's death triggered something in me, something like what poor Masha is going through.

After all, we share a quarter of our DNA.

"I can see there's a story behind all this," Dr. Golovasi says, taking me out of my reverie. "Do you feel comfortable sharing any of it?"

"It's a really long story…"

"The purpose of the first session is for me to learn more about you," Dr. Golovasi says. "I'm here for you to tell me long stories."

I sigh and do my best to tell her what happened five months ago. I explain how I enrolled Mom into the Brainocytes study and describe the kidnapping of Mom and the other patients, our trip to Russia, the rescue, and all the violence and death I witnessed along the way. I sugarcoat some of it—especially the murders my cousin Joe and his minions committed—and I don't mention my Brainocytes.

"I read about your mother's kidnapping in *The Times*." Dr. Golovasi shifts in her seat. "Your story sounds like it would cause anyone to have trouble sleeping."

I'm tempted to say that Joe sleeps like a psychotic little baby, but instead, I lamely mumble, "Yeah, it was pretty rough."

"At least you made new friends in the process. This Gogi and Muhomor sound like interesting individuals."

I nod. "True, though Gogi treats me like a client half the time, while Muhomor is just Muhomor."

"Oh?" She leans toward me again. "What do you mean?"

"Muhomor was brilliant even before—" I was about to say, "before Brainocytes," but I change it to, "Before he took a bunch of computer courses here in the States. Now his ego doesn't fit through most doors."

"But you guys can bond on a work level?" She tilts her head quizzically.

"Not really. Cryptography, Muhomor's passion, isn't my favorite branch of computer science. So we're not exactly bonding over that. If anything, he and Mitya might be getting close, and I wish I was above feeling jealous, but I'm not."

She looks so uncharacteristically interested in my words that I wonder if this bromance jealousy is something she wrote her PhD on.

"What do you think they do together that you don't do with Muhomor?" she asks, confirming my suspicions that she's latched on to this topic.

"Muhomor developed an ingenious cryptosystem that only Mitya can truly appreciate," I say with a shrug. "My girlfriend doesn't care about the subject, and neither do I, really."

What I don't mention is that, unlike Ada, I tried to understand Muhomor's work, and it was too dense for me—one of the few things to challenge me intellectually in a long time. It literally made my brain hurt.

Instead of her eyes glazing over at the word "cryptosystem," Dr. Golovasi looks like she just shot espresso into her eyeballs. I recall that we've decided to keep Tema—short for the Russian word "kryptosystema"—on the hush-hush, so I say, "Anyway, I think I got sidetracked a little."

"You're right." She fiddles with her pen as though unsure if she should write a note in her pad. "Tell me, what have you done to cope with all this stress?"

"Right. Stress management." I prepared for this question to the point where I can demonstratively fold over a finger for each activity. "I've been keeping busy helping Mom recover, I picked up a couple of new hobbies, I make sure to get pet therapy from my rat, and I've started a new exercise routine."

"Those are great, especially the exercise," Dr. Golovasi says, but I get the feeling she's holding back some questions, such as, *Did you just say rat?*

"Yes and no," I reply. "My hobbies involve coding, which can be frustrating at times. I also started learning how to shoot. Though it's therapeutic, it isn't your typical calm hobby."

"I see." She steeples her fingers again. "Then I urge you to consider things like yoga, meditation, and massages. Keep spending time with your pet." She stops, then adds, "Intimacy is also a crucial stress reliever."

I consider her words. Continuing pet therapy is easy. I feel Mr. Spock against my pocket as we speak, and I sense happy thoughts coming from him while the little guy munches on a piece of dry mango. Regarding meditation, we recently developed an app that helps us concentrate, and Mitya claims it's done wonders for *his* ability to meditate, so maybe I'll try that. I had an ex who tried to get me into yoga, and Ada goes to yoga as well, so I might join her. I hate massages, but for the sake of my sanity, I'm willing to give it a shot. Perhaps I'll start with a foot rub?

Thankfully, intimacy is one aspect of my life I have completely covered. Ada and I have so much sex that running out of condoms has become a real hassle, though I'm not sure I want to discuss this with this older woman, who's also a complete stranger.

As though psychic, Dr. Golovasi says, "I completely understand if you're not comfortable talking about your romantic relationship with me at this time. Just know it's an important part of your life, and we're bound to discuss it eventually."

"No, I don't mind," I lie, as much to myself as to her. Double-checking that the Share app is off, I tell the doctor, "There's not much to say. On my end, I think the relationship is great. I love her. I think she's amazing, caring, brilliant, and gorgeous. She gets me like no friend or girlfriend ever has. She loves me, though she doesn't like saying it. The intimacy, especially the sex, is beyond my wildest dreams… I just worry she'll get tired of my problems someday."

"What makes you think she will?"

"Nothing." I cross my arms over my chest. "If anything, she's extremely supportive. For example, she's the one who made this appointment for me. She cares about me and wants me to be well. It's just that, well, it goes back to that feeling of being followed."

What I don't mention is that Ada has been acting more than a little strange lately, and this change in behavior terrifies me. I hope I'm just being as irrationally paranoid about Ada's weird behavior as I am about being followed. Still, I can't shake the feeling that Ada wants to have a big talk with me about something, and when girls want to have a big talk, it's never good news. But I don't want to go into any of this with the shrink. I really am not comfortable with her yet.

Realizing I won't add anything more to this subject, Dr. Golovasi says, "Are you worried she'd terminate the relationship if you developed the same condition as your half-sister?"

I look down at the Persian rug, glad I killed the Share app when I did. "That's one of my biggest fears, yes."

"Maybe I can put your mind at ease, then," Dr. Golovasi says, and her voice turns exaggeratingly soothing. "Given what I've heard, and speaking with you like this, I doubt you're schizophrenic. If I had to diagnose you—and I don't yet—in the worst case, I would say you might be suffering from post-traumatic stress disorder. It's more likely, though, that you're having a normal reaction to a horrific situation—if the word 'normal' can have any meaning in this context. I think more sessions will allow us to sort through all this in more detail, but I don't think you should worry about becoming like your sister."

I exhale in relief. "Okay. So what do you recommend I do?"

"Let's start by having you come see me once a week. We'll do talk therapy like today and try cognitive therapy to control your negative thoughts. I'll also teach you some relaxation techniques that will help you cope with stressful situations. Your homework for today is to reduce the stress in your life as much as possible. Consider spending more time with your friends and family. Continue to exercise.

Research meditation—though it's also something I would be happy to teach you down the line. Develop healthy sleep habits by only using the bedroom for sleep and sex, not TV, and go to bed at a regular time. Don't drink caffeinated drinks or other stimulants. And make sure your bedroom is dark and free of unwanted sounds."

"Okay." I store my ongoing recording of everything I just heard and saw during the last hour to the data servers in case I want to replay what the doctor said at a later date. Then I mentally text Gogi my desire to have a training session today, since it's what the doctor ordered. I also text Mom, telling her I'll come visit today, and call a meeting of the Brainocytes Club for later in the day, since that's also in the doctor's prescription.

Thinking of Mom reminds me of a joke I've been itching to tell the doctor, so I say, "You know, Dr. Golovasi, it's been nearly an hour and we still haven't blamed my mother for anything."

"As a mother, I find that stereotype insulting," the doc replies, her eyes crinkling into laugh lines.

"My mom is amazing," I say to make sure she knows I was kidding. "If I'm messed up, it's either my own fault or by random chance."

"As far as I'm concerned, when you can excel at your job, have fulfilling relationships with friends and family, and maintain a romantic relationship, you're not formally 'messed up,'" the doctor assures me. "If I were to use a car metaphor, I'd say you just need a little tuning, that's all."

I smile and shake my head. "Normal people don't need to see a shrink."

"Everyone should get therapy," she retorts. "I visit a therapist myself, as does my son."

"Forgive me if I remain skeptical when a professional tells me everyone should use their services," I say, but my tone is light.

A soft alarm sounds, and Dr. Golovasi looks at her watch. "I'm afraid this is the end of our session. We should have more time in our next session."

"That wasn't so bad," I tell her and realize it really wasn't. I know it's probably pure placebo, but I already feel somewhat better. I read about this in one of the psychology books I studied for this appointment. The act of making changes in your life makes you feel more in control of your destiny and often provides noticeable relief. I wonder if I'll feel like someone is following me at any point during the rest of the day.

"To make the next appointment, please speak with Monika." Dr. Golovasi gets up and offers me her hand.

"Thanks, Dr. Golovasi," I say and give her a firm handshake.

"Please, call me Jane."

"Of course, ma'am." I'm guessing if we continue this, in a year or so, I'll be able to address her so informally. "See you next week."

CHAPTER FOUR

"Begin," Gogi says and throws a punch at my shoulder.

I dodge and telepathically tell Ada, "Given that I didn't feel like anyone was watching me on my way to the pet sitter and here to the gym, I'd say therapy is already working."

"That's encouraging," she replies, her thoughts imbued with happiness. "I do wish you'd stop these brutal sessions, though."

There's a lot of hippie in Ada, and that includes a deep dislike of violence. She refuses to watch overly violent movies, even though some of them are awesome. So it's not a huge surprise that she hates my trips to the gun range and worries about Gogi's lessons. Trying to keep any defensiveness out of my mental reply, I send, "The doctor approved this. Actually, she suggested I exercise more."

"Yes, but if the good doctor saw this so-called training, I bet she'd recommend simple cardio, or lifting weights, or, my favorite, resistance band exercises."

"You mean the exercises my mom does?" I reply.

What I leave unsaid is that those puny resistance bands aren't necessarily Ada's favorite exercise, given how fond she is of dancing on that stripper pole in her bedroom. I don't feel comfortable even thinking about that in front of Gogi, lest he sniff out my thoughts and make a comment over which I'd have to kick his ass for real.

"Just because your mother does it doesn't make it less cool," Ada counters, though we both know she lost this round. Deciding to fight dirty, she plays the girlfriend card. "I just can't watch you get hurt."

"I can disable Share," I warn her and fling my fist at Gogi's solar plexus. "Or you can stop looking."

"Someone will need to call the ambulance when you eventually cripple each other," she says out loud in my head.

"Suit yourself. Now, if you don't mind, I'm going to focus on this. I think the warm-up is over."

"I'm just a fly on the wall," Ada says, and I feel a mental disconnect, telling me she shut down her Telepathy connection.

I try to focus, but my thoughts scatter, as often happens when I first bring all my attention to my physical surroundings. The white-floored dojo looks brighter and the mirrors on the walls shinier.

To get myself more in the mood, I use the Music app to play Metallica in shuffle mode. As with everything Brainocytes, the music is only in my head. That's fortunate, because if I blasted my tunes this loud in the real world, the dojo would shake, and Gogi and I would have permanent ear damage.

As though in sync with the frantic drumbeat in my head, Gogi chops at my neck, but I step back just in time.

Unbeknownst to Gogi, I decide to expand the scope of our session and enable the new app I named after its designer—the Muhomor app.

The room appears subtly different, and I get a strange set of synesthetic sensations that are part of this app's user interface. I see the Wi-Fi networks that permeate this space as slightly colorful shimmers in the air. In addition to the colors, these networks possess qualities reminiscent of something between taste and smell.

Gogi blocks my punch with his elbow and counters, so I keep most of my attention on him, but I also allow the Muhomor app to hack into the Wi-Fi it feels is the "tastiest," for lack of a better term. The app makes short work of whatever security the Wi-Fi possessed, and once I'm on it, I see a web of connected devices as Augmented Reality. Like the Wi-Fi, each device has a sensory perception associated with it. The brightest one is the security camera behind Gogi, my target from the get-go. A moment later, I can see his movements through the camera.

Someday soon, I'll have to convince Gogi to let me fight him blindfolded so I can look like a cool character from those old kung fu movies where the master hones the pupil's senses that way. For now, I use the camera feedback as an extra pair of eyes. The trick helps. I find it much easier to watch Gogi's legs from this vantage point, and I jump away from a shin kick in time. Gogi rewards the accomplishment with a grudging grunt.

As per my research, the majority of Gogi's moves come from a Russian martial art called *Systema*. If what I read about it is true, it's a pretty lethal system with plenty of creative ways for hurting people, which is ironic given how uncreative the title of the fighting style is. Systema means "the system" in Russian. Gogi definitely has his own take on Systema, though, with some influences from *Chidaoba*—a form of Georgian wrestling. These influences are apparent when Gogi gets his opponent (typically me) on the floor. Gogi also occasionally utilizes a move or two inspired by *Khridoli*—an eclectic, traditional set of Georgian martial arts that is so old and comprehensive it includes fencing and archery—as well as moves from Greek wrestling that he likely picked up from the late Nadejda.

I dodge Gogi's attempt to seize my elbow and realize I'll eventually need to hurt Gogi's feelings by getting another trainer. The intelligence boost helps me learn how to fight nearly as fast as any other activity, so I've made great progress in these few months of training. Once I learn everything I can from Gogi—likely in another couple of months—I won't want to limit myself to his style. Like Bruce Lee and many others before and after him, my long-term ambition is to form my own fighting style, something I'll get around to after I get a good sample of existing martial arts.

Daydreaming about my own style doesn't lower my battle awareness, so when I see an unusually fortuitous opening, I take great pleasure in kicking Gogi in the groin. Though he's wearing a protective cup, his face contorts in genuine pain, and I realize I applied too much force for a friendly sparring session.

Gogi's face reddens, and I can tell things are about to get serious. Everything about Gogi screams, *No more Mr. Nice Georgian.*

He chops at my neck, and I twist away to avoid getting my clavicle shattered. Then I barely dodge a frantic array of punches. Keeping me on the defensive, Gogi goes in for my right knee. Only my camera view allows me to catch his intention and step back in time.

Grunting something that I think means "good" in Georgian, Gogi leaps at me and grabs me by the shoulders.

I try to break his grip but realize my error a moment too late.

Gogi grabs me by the waist and does a maneuver he probably learned from Nadejda. Before I register the how of it, I'm flying toward the mat at a speed that's hard for even my enhanced mind to estimate.

"Careful!" Ada screams, as though I can control my flight in this fraction of a second.

I land on my side, and Gogi lands on top of me, causing me to lose what little air was still in my lungs.

I debate whether I should surrender, but something stubborn drives me onward.

If there's one part of Gogi's fighting style I haven't mastered yet, it's wrestling.

The Russians have a strong stereotype about Georgians. They think Georgians are horny all the time and swing both ways, leading to a whole genre of anecdotes (what Russians call jokes). Coincidentally, the butt of these Georgian jokes is almost always a guy named Gogi. I hate labels and discrimination of any kind, and it's not like I've done any statistical analysis on the behavior of the typical Georgian male, but this limited sample of one Georgian, Gogi, fits the Russian stereotype eerily well. He seems to enjoy this wrestling part of our training on a level I'm somewhat uncomfortable with—especially when, like now, I feel something poking me in the back. I hope it's Gogi's gun, or a Sharpie marker, or anything but him being too happy to be wrestling me.

Trying my best to convince myself of the educational value of wrestling on the ground, I decide to put in an effort and grab for Gogi's ankle.

My reward is a light kick to the face.

Before I even understand what happened, my face is under Gogi's armpit—a horrific place—and I can't see much with my eyes.

Struggling for air, I look at us via the camera feed. Though it looks like we're having rough, kinky sex, I'm in too much pain to find any humor in the situation. Instead, I tap the mat in surrender.

This is when I notice Joe standing at the dojo's entrance.

"Not this again," Ada's voice intrudes. "Just run away. Now."

"Remember what we agreed last time?" I remind her. "You just overstepped your bounds, and I'm turning off the Share app." Before Ada can object, I terminate all the communication apps.

My true reason for breaking contact with her is the very real chance that I might embarrass myself. I don't want my girlfriend witnessing my humiliation.

For good measure, I even get rid of the EmoRat app. The latest version of the software has created an almost empathic link between me and Mr. Spock, a feature that lets me know how the little guy is doing and lets him know when his behavior is upsetting me. It rarely does. Not for the first time, I wonder if you can say "he's such a good boy" about a rat? In any case, EmoRat might make him aware of my anxiety, and there's no reason for that. He's probably playing with his two friends, Kiki and Boss, at the pet sitter's place. Kiki and Boss are two strangely rat-friendly Chihuahua brothers that the owners of the Furry Ritz have vouched for. I think the Chihuahuas decided that Mr. Spock is a runt of a dog from their breed, or maybe they formed an alliance with the rat based on the age-old logic that the enemy of my enemy—cats—is my friend.

Getting up, I dust myself off and prepare to leave the mat as though Joe isn't there at all.

"Show me what you've learned." My cousin is already on the mat, standing in a fighting stance.

"I'm good, Joe," I say, though I know full well it won't work. "I already got my blood pumping today." With faint hope, I try a lie that appeals to Joe's sense of professionalism. "I've got to hurry to get to an investor meeting in Midtown."

Instead of replying, Joe interlaces his fingers and stretches his arms so that his fingers produce a loud, painful crack.

Then he approaches me with the inevitability of the *Titanic* iceberg.

CHAPTER FIVE

Behind my cousin's back, Gogi gives me a thumbs up that seems to say, *Hey, I think you can handle him this time, but if not, better you as his punching bag than me.*

"Einstein," I mentally command. "Please monitor my vitals. If I break something or pass out, I need you to call an ambulance immediately."

"You got it, boss," replies Einstein, and even though he uses Zik, he somehow still has a German accent. "Your blood pressure is already elevated. Your adrenaline levels are above normal. Your caffeine level is too high. You're—"

"Einstein, please don't use ongoing commentary," I say and feel a bit guilty for interrupting him. Then I feel silly about the guilt since, being my AI personal assistant, Einstein has no feelings to hurt. If Einstein had feelings, I wouldn't want to piss him off because he has a lot of information on me via a bunch of "lab on a chip" biosensors imbedded in my body. After spending two years in development at Mitya's BioInfo company, the sensors can detect increased levels of hormones, as well as the presence of alcohol and other pharmaceutical or illegal drugs, and they can even diagnose some diseases.

Seeing a blur of movement, I focus both my biological eyes and the camera on Joe. If the intensity of a stare could hypnotize a person, Joe would surely go into a trance. I turn off my music and debate disabling the camera view as Joe strikes with a speed a cobra would be jealous of.

If I wasn't watching his back muscles through the camera, I would now have a broken jaw. As is, I block with my left forearm (even though my physical therapist suggested I leave it alone for a month), and it explodes in pain.

Ignoring the nauseating sensation, I smoothly transition from the block into a right forearm strike. To my surprise, I graze Joe's face.

This is the first time I've made any contact with Joe, and a smidge of elation penetrates my deep dread.

The look in Joe's lizard-like eyes turns sixty shades icier than their usual emotionless abyss. Yet—and I could be having an adrenaline-induced delusion—there's something like pride in those eyes as well. I've been wondering why Joe does this to me, and the most generous conclusion I've reached is that perhaps these torture sessions are his way of showing me a type of cousinly tough love. Like maybe he's making sure I'm ready to defend myself should a psychopath attack me—and what better way to prepare for that scenario than fighting him?

Pride or not, Joe's counterattack is brutal. I duck just in time to avoid a broken nose. Then I shift to the side, taking a hard hit to my pectoral instead of my neck, but then I falter and get punched in the middle of my chest.

I'm still trying to remember how to breathe when Joe performs a throw I don't recall learning, and the room blurs in front of my eyes. Through the camera, I watch myself fly toward the mat and land on my back.

"This is an ambiguous situation," Einstein says. "Your oxygen levels are critical, but you're still conscious."

It takes all my willpower to mentally tell Einstein I don't need the ambulance yet.

Four hands help me up from the mat, and I dazedly comprehend that two of them must belong to Joe, who's never helped me up in the past.

I'm led to a bench and dumped there to come to my senses.

Dazedly, I hear Gogi and Joe discuss my progress in Russian, as though I'm not there.

"The kid is a quick learner," Gogi says. "Must be your good genes."

I can't decipher Joe's response through the frantic pulsing in my ears.

"You there? Can you speak?" Gogi walks over to me and waves his hand in front of my face as if I'm drunk. "Do you need my services today?"

"Maybe later," I half gasp, half grunt. "Going to the gun range next. I'll text you after."

Gogi loses interest in me and walks back to Joe. I hear him say, "Let's go smoke a joint. It's my treat."

I'm not sure what my cousin replies with, but they leave.

I spend the next half hour stabilizing my breathing so I can use an app to summon my new car, Zapo 2. Even in my condition, it's not hard to get the car to leave the parking lot and meet me by the door. The hard part is walking to the car, but I manage that too.

"Einstein," I mentally order when the car door closes. "Drive me to the gun range."

"You know you go to the gun range too often when the gun range people know your name, what gun you carry, and exactly how many bullets you'd like to buy," Ada says.

Despite her general anti-gun rhetoric, Ada chose a Lara-Croft-inspired avatar to talk to me, one with two guns sitting in sexy hip holsters.

"I need to focus, babe," I say and put a bullet in the head of the big target. "It's a miracle I made that shot while talking to you and looking at that outfit."

"That *was* a pretty good shot." Ada's avatar dissipates. "And you made it without the aim-assist app and while being distracted."

I grunt in satisfaction and do another warm-up shot, this time aiming for the target's heart. I hit it dead on, and Ada claps, though without visual cues, it's hard to tell if she's showing support or being sarcastic.

Next, I enable my newest app for the gun range, and the usual AROS interface gives way to a heads-up display (HUD) where I see the world as though through a sci-fi helmet inspired by my favorite video games, particularly *Halo* and *Metroid Prime*. The HUD keeps track of bullets in my gun and my hit stats, and it has a sobriety indicator along with other goodies. It also lets me put an overlay on the target I'm shooting at. Today, that happens to be a picture of Joe's face, but it could easily be anyone from Osama bin Laden to Barney the Dinosaur. Once Joe's illusion is in place, I pull the trigger, and the HUD shows a nice animation of my cousin's head exploding when I hit the center of his forehead.

"Very mature," Ada says when I restore the fake Joe and shoot him in the forehead again. "All you need to do is refuse to fight him next time."

Instead of answering, I hack into the gun range's security camera and close my eyes.

Shooting in this mode is something I still need to master. I shoot, and all that happens is my already sore arms hurt a little more from the recoil.

I adjust my aim and shoot again. The bullet doesn't even hit the side of the paper target.

"Maybe it's too soon?" I ask Ada rhetorically and enable the aim-assist app in a special camera-view mode Mitya helped me design.

In the camera view, I see a line of magical-looking light going from my gun to the target. Aiming becomes a matter of moving my arm around until the line touches the desired part of the paper target.

I align everything and shoot. This time, I hit the bull's-eye—something I'm hoping to learn to do without the aim-assist as well.

"I'm visiting Mom after this. Do you want to join me?" I telepathically ask Ada as I reload my gun.

"Yeah, definitely," she replies. "I think that's where JC is, so he shouldn't bitch too much about me taking a longer lunch."

Her mention of her boss, the CEO at Techno, reminds me that I haven't checked my corporate email today, so I mentally read and reply to emails as I squeeze out a couple more rounds of ammo. Work has become something I do remotely, with a small percentage of my attention dedicated to it. I had to hire a few more people to cover for me when it comes to routine matters, and I made it crystal clear to everyone to only include me in meetings that would have existential consequences to the fund. Those types of issues come up about once every couple of weeks. In any case, given my Brainocytes-assisted ability to pick good companies for the fund, my people probably think I sold what was left of my soul to the devil, and they're happy to communicate with me however I want, so long as my picks continue making us obscene amounts of money.

"Your lunch might be extra long," I remind Ada. "We're going to the Brainocytes Club meeting after."

"I can join that virtually, like Mitya. I'll dedicate part of my attention to the meeting while I sit in my office at work."

"No, please. I need you there. If Muhomor and I are the only ones present physically, he'll take it as a chance to bond." That wouldn't be a bad thing, except for Muhomor, that means talking about his collection of zero-day exploits and telling me how many hackers couldn't crack his unbreakable Tema. Or worse, making me an accomplice to a federal crime by sharing with me the latest highly secure network he got into just for kicks.

"Fine. I'll strongly consider your preference," Ada replies telepathically, and I learn that there's a way to make a message sound noncommittal in this mode of communication. "Bear in mind, I've been working remotely so much that my minions pulled JC into a couple of meetings, and he's more than a little peeved with me about it."

I tsk-tsk. "Yeah, pulling the boss into a meeting should be considered cause for dismissal."

For my last bullet, I shoot blindfolded without the app and again miss. Figuring Ada will do as she wants in regard to the club meeting, I change the topic and ask, "Would you mind picking up Mr. Spock from the Furry Ritz on your way to Mom's?"

I approach Mom's new apartment and ring the doorbell.

It took all of my boosted intellect to convince her to let me buy this place. Now she lives much closer to my pad and, as a small side effect, close enough for JC to visit on his lunch break. Ada was right: he *is* visiting Mom today—either that, or someone else in this neighborhood drives a red Tesla with a lucky four-leaf clover pendant hanging from the mirror and plates that spell TECHNO.

As I walk into the downstairs lobby, I smell Mom's *borscht*. That she can go out and locate a store in a new neighborhood, remember to buy all the borscht ingredients, and recall that her new and younger boyfriend, JC, likes borscht for lunch is but a small part of the outstanding improvements brought about by Brainocytes. Mom is completely back to normal—and above normal in many ways, since she can do some of the same things as the Brainocytes Club. Because she's one of Techno's success stories, we are keeping her brain loaded with official Techno applications only, but as soon as her official treatment is over in a few months, we plan to extend her an offer to join the Club and take advantage of everything we've developed.

"Hi, kitten." Mom kisses my cheek excitedly and adds, "JC is here." She makes JC sound like "Jessy," but her boyfriend doesn't seem to mind.

When I walk into the room, I see Techno's redheaded CEO holding a piece of dark bread that Mom buys from a local Ukrainian store, and adding spoon after spoon of farmer's market sour cream into his large bowl of borscht.

In the middle of the table is a big chessboard. Leave it to my mother to play physical board games, and chess no less. I can see that the whites—probably JC's—will be toast in four more moves. That Mom can play chess again is yet another heartwarming sign of her improvement.

JC looks at me, and I reluctantly smile. I guess as long as he doesn't make jokes such as, "Call me Dad," our relationship can stay fairly cordial.

"Please tell me Adachka is coming," Mom says.

Before I can reply yes, the intercom rings.

I scan the kitchen and notice Ada-safe food in the form of potato-filled dumplings, pea-filled pirogi, and a huge salad. The sight of boiled cow tongue with mashed potatoes throws me for a loop; then, with a sinking feeling, I recall whom Mom makes this for. Confirming my suspicions, I hear Mom scream from the door, "Abrashen'ka, Josen'ka, please take off your shoes."

It's Uncle Abe, whom I'm happy to see, and his son Joe.

When they enter the kitchen, Uncle Abe shakes JC's hand, but Joe gives the older man a look that says, *If my aunt so much as says one wrong word about you, in lieu of a cow tongue, it will be yours that gets boiled next time—and it will be attached to you during the cooking process.*

Joe then turns his attention to me, looking me up and down. "How did the investor meeting go?" If he's upset about me not inviting him to join us for lunch, he hides it well. "Everything is cool, right?"

"All good," I reply. I wonder if this is Joe's roundabout way of forbidding me from telling Mom and his father about our earlier fight, or checking how I'm feeling.

"JC, let's call it a draw," Mom says, and I'm pretty sure she's just pretending not to see her eminent victory. "Next time, I play whites."

I help Mom clear the chessboard from the table, and we set more plates down.

The intercom rings again, and I go open it this time, since it can only be Ada.

"Hi, honey," Ada says and kisses me on each cheek. "Here's someone else who wants a kiss."

She takes out Mr. Spock, and he looks at me with the warmest expression a rat is capable of. Giving me a dog-like wiggle of his tail, Mr. Spock washes his whiskers with his little paws and scurries over to my hand. Before Mom can catch sight of him and possibly faint, I give Mr. Spock a little smooch and mentally ask him to hide in my inner jacket pocket—a request he's happy to comply with, as always.

We enter the spacious kitchen, and Ada gives Joe a narrow-eyed stare.

Unsurprisingly, her telepathic message is full of annoyance as she states, "What, the gym wasn't enough? He's here too?"

"Part of the family," I mentally reply. "In his defense, Mom is happy to see him."

Happy might be an understatement. Mom is practically beaming with contentment after everyone sits down and she tells us about the food options.

"This is amazing, sis, as usual." My uncle ceremoniously places a bottle of Stolichnaya vodka he brought for the occasion in the center of the table.

"A toast," JC says, quickly realizing he *will* have to drink vodka on his lunch break. "To Nina's amazing recovery."

To match his words, JC looks at Mom with such warmth that I grudgingly pick up my shot glass and clink it against his. Uncle Abe grunts approvingly and clinks glasses with JC, and even my cousin looks slightly less eager to stab JC with his fork.

I feel guilty that Gogi isn't here. He loves being the *tamada*—a type of Georgian toastmaster—at a table with drinks, and his long toasts are legendary. I've told him many times that if he left the bodyguard business, he could always turn his toasts into Hallmark holiday cards.

"Gogi," I text to appease my conscience. "I have an important meeting taking place at Kharcho in a bit. I could use your protection."

I don't really need his protection during the Brainocytes Club meeting, but if I offered to buy him lunch just for the heck of it, he might refuse. Kharcho is an authentic Georgian restaurant owned by Gogi's distant relative, so I'm not surprised when my bodyguard eagerly replies that he'll be there.

Everyone eats Mom's food and drinks another round of vodka shots, courtesy of Uncle Abe's typical Russian peer pressure. Ada is the only person without vodka in her belly, and this is because my uncle gave up trying to convince her to drink vodka months ago. I think Uncle Abe gave up on Ada in general when he learned she's vegan. We had to painstakingly enumerate a list of what vegans do not consume for him, and I think he still has a hard time with the "no ham" part. To Uncle Abe, Ada's dislike of vodka is almost normal compared to her veganism, and he probably erroneously thinks that Ada considers alcohol an animal product—and hey, sometimes, there are worms in tequila.

"So, how are things going between you two?" Mom asks, her words slightly slurred from the alcohol. She asks the question in English, though Ada's Russian is now good enough that she would've understood it.

"Things are great," Ada says after an awkward pause. "Why do you ask?"

That pause makes me worry. This is yet another example of strange behavior on Ada's part that I should've discussed with the shrink. Language aside, Ada probably doesn't realize this is Mom's roundabout way of asking when she'll be a grandmother, so there's no reason for my girlfriend to feel weird about the question.

"I think you make the most wonderful couple." Mom smiles at us and plops another serving of mashed potatoes on Ada's plate.

"You really do," my uncle says. "Let me say a toast to you."

He orates the equivalent of an epic poem dedicated to our health and vitality and about how lucky we are to have each other.

I don't let my uncle's words go to my head. To consume extra vodka, Russians will happily drink in celebration of anyone's health, including dead leaders like Lenin, and use any holiday as an excuse to drink, even something as uneventful as National Doughnut Day or Dress Like a Pirate Day.

"We should leave before dessert," I mentally tell Ada after she explains to Mom how full she is. "JC is too drunk to worry about your lunch time."

As though to support my secret message, JC gulps down another shot, his nose already turning a deeper shade of red. Until recently, I thought JC had Irish blood, but now I'm less certain. When it comes to drinking with the Russians, JC definitely doesn't live up to the Irish stereotype of being able to handle large amounts of liquor—not that I believe in stereotypes.

"Blood alcohol level is unsafe to drive," Einstein informs me after I swallow my final shot.

"Noted," I mentally reply. "When we get inside Zapo 2, you're driving, no matter what I say, and Ada can even sit behind the wheel."

CHAPTER SIX

Ada and I hold hands as we walk from the parking spot to the restaurant where we're meeting the rest of the Brainocytes Club.

Unfortunately, as the vodka buzz begins to dissipate, the annoying feeling of being followed returns. I wonder if the shrink's effect was indeed a placebo, and a short-lived one at that. I almost feel as though I'm being followed by a new group of people. This is odd, and not just because I have no clue who was following me before, besides figments of my imagination.

Gogi is already at the restaurant, and Muhomor promises to arrive in a couple of minutes. The day is extremely nice for November, so we decide to get a table outside and order our drinks—vodka for Gogi, a glass of famous Borjomi water (a mineral-rich water of volcanic origins that's over fifteen thousand years old) for Ada, and tea for me.

When Muhomor arrives, we order food and wait for Mitya to get in touch with us remotely.

Ada and I get *gozinaki*, a confection made of caramelized walnuts fried in honey, and I get an extra piece for Mr. Spock. Since we're the only guests at the restaurant at the moment, and because the server knows us, I allow Mr. Spock to sit on the table, next to my plate.

Gogi comments that we ordered a treat that's traditionally eaten on New Year's and thus incongruous in the middle of fall, especially on such a warm day. We point out that it was on the menu, so his gripe is with Nikolozi, his fourth-removed cousin and owner of this place. Gogi orders *kharcho*, the signature Georgian soup from which the restaurant got its name, and *shashlik*, a Georgian version of a shish kebab.

"Lots of vegan-safe dishes," Ada says wistfully as she scans the menu. "I'd like to try the beetroot *pkhali* with walnuts, but I'm too full."

"I'll bring you here on an empty stomach tomorrow," I promise. "Also, Mom knows how to make some Georgian dishes since they've made their way into Russian cuisine, so I'll tell her to make something for you next time."

"Are we ready for the meeting?" Muhomor sends Mitya, Ada, and me an invite from the Teleconference app.

"I'm ready." Mitya shows up as a see-through holographic image in one of the empty seats at the table, making our meeting look like the Jedi Council gathering from *Star Wars*.

"Let's begin, then," Muhomor says in Zik via the Teleconference app and uses the Augmented Reality interface to give himself giant ram horns that humorously complement his usual pajamas.

"Speaking of you being horny," Ada says to him in Zik. "Mike told me Lyuba is in town."

"Lyuba's vacationing in the US, yes." Muhomor looks confused. "What does that have to do with my horns?"

I almost choke on my tea, and Ada bursts into laugher, probably getting Borjomi water into her nose. Of course, the way-too-normal and gorgeous Lyuba isn't Muhomor's girlfriend. Ada now owes me a beer and a sexual favor since we made a bet on this topic earlier. She was sure Lyuba and Muhomor were in a long-distance relationship, and I said that wasn't possible. Mitya and I call Muhomor bisexual behind his back, only the "bi" is short for "binary code." The guy eats, sleeps, and dreams cryptography, hacking, and coding, and he doesn't have any interest in either gender when it comes to sex. Two weeks ago, one of my investors invited us to his bachelor party. Muhomor came with us and proceeded to hack the stripper's phone instead of getting a lap dance or even looking at the girl. He also hacked the website of the club where the event was taking place.

"Whose turn is it to speak?" I ask. I opt not to spruce up my avatar today, beyond putting a gun holster on the outside of my jacket in the Augmented Reality. In the real world, my unlicensed Glock 19 from the gun range is hidden right behind the virtual one inside my blazer. After Russia, I can't bear to walk around unarmed—another issue I should probably work on with the shrink.

"Ladies first, as usual?" Mitya winks at no one in particular.

"Isn't that reverse sexism?" Muhomor complains.

"I don't have much to share anyway." Ada ignores Nikolozi as he brings out a tray with food and starts putting it on the table. "I've worked out a method to mass-produce nanomembranes, and Mike has helped me set up a company that will fabricate an ultra-rapid water filtration system by the end of next year. The prices should be low enough for anyone to afford it, and it will be easy for a philanthropist"—she gives Mitya and me a pointed look—"to make a huge dent in solving the world's clean drinking water problem."

We nod approvingly, and Ada shares a couple more things she's developed, all with the theme of bringing global abundance and prosperity.

"What about Brainocytes development?" Mitya asks when Ada pauses to mentally take a breath and sip her real-world water. "Did you put together any interesting apps?"

"I have," Ada replies and examines her glass. "Mike and I pair programmed it and plan to test it out, but I'm not ready to disclose the details yet."

Ada likes to be mysterious, and in this case, I'm glad she is. From what I understand from observing Ada coding it, the app does something like the Vulcan mind meld, only in real time. The two individuals who use this app together will have their brains temporarily connected. The sex applications are so obvious that I'm glad Ada doesn't give my friends any new fodder with which to tease us for being a couple. When it comes to this topic, Mitya and Muhomor have the maturity of fourth graders in detention.

"Fine." Mitya bites into a Snickers bar, and I assume he does it for real since I see no reason for him to fake it using Augmented Reality. With mock grumpiness, he adds, "Is that all?"

Ada shakes her head. "I also figured out an extremely efficient technique that will allow us to convert atmospheric carbon dioxide into carbon nanotubes." In the real world, Ada tells Nikolozi that she's not interested in more dessert, while at the same time, in Zik, she says, "The nanotubes can be used as batteries or even as the water filters I mentioned. That's what sparked that idea in the first place."

"And?" Muhomor makes sure Ada can see him bite into his pork shashlik. He knows she doesn't like the idea of pigs being killed for food. She thinks pigs are cuter than and as smart as dogs—not that this argument would work on Muhomor. He'd probably eat dog shashlik if it were on the menu.

"Dude." I send Muhomor a private telepathic message imbued with a touch of anger. "Don't piss off my girlfriend. Besides, Georgian food is famous for lamb, not pork shashlik."

I also tell Ada to ignore Muhomor's shenanigans.

"You think Ada prefers baby sheep as food?" Muhomor replies and, as usual, makes the telepathic message disproportionally snarky. "You realize Georgians believe in having the whole sheep family watch the killing."

"They do not," I counter, but then realize I'm doing exactly what I warned Ada against—paying attention to

Muhomor's crap. Still, I can't resist adding, "In any case, in America, lamb doesn't always mean baby sheep."

"And that's it," Ada says in conclusion, not looking at Muhomor or his food. She clearly took my advice of not rising to Muhomor's bait better than I did.

"Perhaps I can go next?" Mitya is now drinking a Red Bull, another item inconsistent with our Georgian cuisine. "Ada's given me a nice segue, because my 'benefit for humanity' idea would provide those batteries she mentioned with cheap energy."

"Yes, go." I sip my tea and, not for the first time, wonder how crazy we must look to Gogi, Nikolozi, and even Mr. Spock. The whole meeting is happening virtually, in our heads, so to them, with maybe the exception of Mr. Spock, we must look like we're sitting there, eating in silence. Ada, Muhomor, and I can multitask by talking to Gogi while keeping the meeting going, but Gogi doesn't seem to mind the silence today.

"Fusion," Mitya says triumphantly. "Specifically, 'star in a jar' technology that will provide nearly limitless energy in two years, or thereabouts."

Everyone looks at Mitya with a mixture of wonder and skepticism.

He smirks and says, "I'm sending you the details, but to sum up, I invented a three-dimensional shape that will allow us to cheaply confine plasma inside a powerful magnetic field."

"Hold on," Muhomor says after a moment. "You're talking about a *tokamak*—technology Soviet scientists invented back in the fifties."

I look up "tokamak" and find that the idea has indeed been around.

"Sure." Mitya grins. "That was the inspiration, of course, but unlike all the early designs and plans, mine *will* be built, *will* be cheap, and *will* change the world more than anything we've come up with thus far."

We all let our imaginations run wild at the thought of what limitless energy could do for the world.

The purpose of the Brainocytes Club, or one of its purposes, is to benefit humanity. More accurately, we figured we owe it to the world to use our enhanced brainpower for its betterment. And if our various contributions toward that goal were a contest, Mitya would be winning. I guess it shouldn't be a big surprise; the guy always had grand visions, and the brain boost only multiplied his talents many times over.

"Anything else?" Muhomor asks sarcastically and with obvious jealousy. "Did you figure out how to have world peace and save all the kittens from starving? Oh, wait, that's Ada's thing."

"I respect Ada's endeavors." Mitya gives Ada a good-natured thumbs-up. "Since you asked, though, why yes, I do have something else. Several things, actually. A few things I've saved for last. A) I've gotten us more server space, B) I've designed another set of brain regions we can simulate, C) I've designed a way of caching access to the servers, resulting in faster performance, and last but not least, D) I've optimized our overall brain boost allocation algorithms while still keeping it as max-min fair as I could." Mitya stops and notices that the second part of his statement wasn't fully understood, even by Ada. "In other words," he clarifies, "we're ready for brain boost v9."

Ada claps in excitement, Muhomor almost chokes on his meat in glee, and I have a hard time suppressing my grin. Every time we've boosted our intellect, the gains have exceeded all of our lofty expectations, and with each boost, our expectations have grown higher and higher. The only downside, and it's a tiny one, is that each boost triggers side effects in the beginning. Still, the worst side effect so far has been dream-like pre-cog moments. I'll never forget the one that scared me so much during Mom's rescue. Nowadays, though, we've figured out a way to cope with these deceptively realistic hallucinations by remaining vigilant during our boost upgrade times and asking ourselves, "Is this really happening?" more often than a normal person would. So far, we've all reported that asking ourselves that question short-circuits the pre-cog moments—if that's what's happening. Pre-cog moments are different from dreams, in that I have asked myself, "Is this really happening?" during a nightmare, and it didn't wake me up.

"I take it you want me to launch it." Mitya looks too smug for his pseudo-Jedi avatar. "It's ready to go."

"Of course you should launch it," we scream, almost in unison. Muhomor actually says it out loud in the real world, and Gogi raises his unibrow at him.

"Okay then." Mitya's avatar pushes the big red button that appeared next to him. "Get ready to be smarter."

CHAPTER SEVEN

Unlike with the other brain-boost upgrades, I feel a difference in my perception. It's as though I took a drug that makes the world around me slow down. The feeling is reminiscent of how everything seems in moments of extreme duress—something I experienced quite a bit during the trip to Russia.

"Wow," Ada says, probably experiencing the same effects as me.

"You rock." Muhomor salutes Mitya's hologram with his glass and gulps down the wine. "I feel like Mike should speak next, since Mitya's work is impossible to follow up."

"Fine, I'll go." I pick up Mr. Spock and scratch his chin like the EmoRat app told me he wanted me to. I don't care if my friends make snide remarks about me looking like a movie villain with my pet rat. "I've been pair coding with all of you, as well as writing code for various open-source projects. I now feel confident enough to write Brainocyte apps on my own, so unless someone objects, that's what I'll start doing." I give them a moment to object, but they seem to agree that I'm ready, making me feel warm on the inside—though Mr. Spock's bruxing is helping with that too. "When it comes to my big idea, I'm still obsessed with giving Brainocytes to the whole world. I think we should make it open source right now, if Muhomor finally agrees."

I've been arguing that Brainocytes should be widely available, even if it means Techno, and by extension Mitya and I, makes less money in the process. If the mere four of us have begun to noticeably change the world for the better, what would happen if millions or billions of people like us existed? Surprisingly, it's Muhomor who objects, and we try to run the Brainocytes Club through unanimous votes.

"I'm still not ready." In the real world, Muhomor asks Nikolozi for *pakhlava*, a dessert similar to Turkish baklava and one of my favorites. "But now that I've finally made Brainocytes traffic secure, we're closer than ever to being able to release this technology without plunging the world into a dystopian surveillance state where the government can read your thoughts."

"Hey, you're taking someone else's turn to talk about your agenda." As usual, Ada is acting as the moderator of the Club meeting. "We'll come back to you in a second. Let Mike finish. I happen to know he has more to say."

"Thanks, Ada." I bend down to put Mr. Spock on the pavement, as the little guy wants to go to the bathroom by a tree. "One of the things preventing wide Brainocytes adoption is the lack of a way to mass-produce some of the nanoparticles required for Brainocytes. So, I've developed a way to do just that. How much do you guys know about microfluidics—a way of manipulating tiny droplets of fluid in a narrow channel?"

Everyone gives me a look that says, *Are you kidding? We know all.*

"Right, okay." I spot a cat far in the distance and use the EmoRat to alert Mr. Spock. "My idea should reduce the cost of Brainocytes development from obscene to less ridiculous levels. Of course, there's still a ton of work that needs to happen in the manufacturing space, but I think once the incentives are there and more people are looking at the Brainocyte designs, the costs will drop further. This is yet another reason to release the technology into the world."

"I agree," Ada says. "That's what always happens when you make technology open: costs go down."

"Especially technologies susceptible to Moore's Law, which the Brainocytes are," I add as I feel Mr. Spock run up my pant leg and jump back onto the table.

"Okay, I've been sold on sharing Brainocytes with the world for a while." Mitya must've gotten bored of his avatar, because he's replaced his regular visage with a gray, faceless blob. "Send me the specs for the microfluidics idea. I think it might be an interesting read."

"Me too." Ada steals the saucer from under my teacup, pours water into it, and pushes it toward Mr. Spock.

"Me third," Muhomor echoes and takes a piece of pistachio from the top of his dessert and throws it in my rat's general direction. "Maybe you'll impress me enough for me to stop vetoing this Brainocyte-sharing idea."

"That's it for me," I say. "Muhomor, the baton is yours. Go ahead and spew your security-related wisdom at us."

"Before I start, has anyone cracked Tema?" The hacker looks challengingly at Mitya, the only person he deems capable of even coming close to such a feat.

"No." The gray blob that Mitya chose as his new avatar looks down, as if in shame. "And not for the lack of trying, believe me. You can rest assured, Big Brother doesn't stand a chance."

I also tried cracking Muhomor's cryptosystem—mainly to wipe that smirk off Muhomor's face—but alas, I had no luck. Ada also failed, and she likes annoying Muhomor more than I do. It's safe to say the Tema cryptosystem is unbreakable, but none of us will admit this to Muhomor. He's already too arrogant to let live.

"I doubt any of you can crack my baby," Muhomor says and grabs a cup with his honey-sticky fingers. "Did you do as I asked and rewrite all the AROS apps to use Tema?"

"Yes," Mitya and Ada say, as I knew they would since I was looking on while they made the necessary code changes to all our communication apps.

"What about EmoRat?" Muhomor points at Mr. Spock, who decided to munch on what's left of my gozinaki. "The rat is happy right now, isn't it? It wants to jump into your pocket soon, right?"

"Unlike you, Mr. Spock is a he, not an it." I know Muhomor didn't simply guess Mr. Spock's EmoRat messages to me, but rather hacked my connection with the little guy. The hack was possible because the app must not be encrypted with Tema. "I'll fix the app now."

I open the AROS integrated development environment, aka AROS IDE, to work on the code in question.

"Outside of Tema," Muhomor continues, "I developed a way to use Brainocytes as a biometric authentication system—a sort of brain print as it were. Emailing you all the deets."

I skim the specifications Muhomor sends and exchange glances with Mitya. I think we're both wondering if it's worth boosting Muhomor's already enormous ego yet again. Ada must not share our qualms, because she turns to Muhomor and says out loud in the real world, "Muhomor, this is brilliant. I wish I'd come up with this."

Gogi raises his unibrow even higher—aiming it at Ada.

"I try." Muhomor looks like he might have an aneurism from pride. "Once Brainocytes are widespread, people can start using my brain-print technology and not bother with passwords, since most people can't create a strong-enough password to save their bank accounts. The final thing I want to report is my success in penetrating the IARPA systems."

Short for Intelligence Advanced Research Projects Activity, IARPA is a government agency that does high-risk/high-payoff research for the US government intelligence community. So naturally, the mood at the meeting grows solemn, and Mitya speaks for everyone when he says, "Dude, how many times do we have to ask you to stop doing illegal stuff? You're in the US on my H1B visa. If you get caught, I'll be guilty by association."

"I was cautious." Muhomor runs his fingers through his anime haircut and scratches his skull. "What I found was worth it. IARPA is working on reverse engineering the human brain's algorithms. Can you think of anyone interested in those results?"

"They'll eventually publish their research to the public," Mitya says, but the idea of reading whatever Muhomor stole seems to have mollified him. "I guess what's done is done. Let's see the papers. I know you're dying to share."

Ada and I aren't so easily placated. I'm about to give Muhomor a piece of my mind, when the paranoid feeling of being followed returns and then gets multiplied a thousand-fold.

I focus all my attention on the strange feeling, and as though from a distance, I hear Ada complain about Muhomor's hacking escapades.

Something tells me it's not paranoia this time, though I guess that's how paranoid people always feel. That same something tells me there are people stalking me more openly, and that same instinct insists I *was* being followed before.

Unsure whether I should go along with my delusion, I decide to prove the feeling wrong by showing myself that the street is as empty as it appears at first glance. It's fortunate there are no pedestrians and cars, because that will help me provide my neurosis with irrefutable evidence. Diligently, I examine every inch of the dead-end street and don't see anyone, only a row of parked cars.

Next, I look for people inside the surrounding businesses, and that yields no results either. I can't even see the owners inside. Since not much happens on this street on weekdays around 3:30 p.m., I don't take the empty street as a sinister sign. Unfortunately, despite the input from my eyes, something in my brain insists people are hiding somewhere.

Determined to try another route and working almost on instinct, I launch the Muhomor app, and the software does what it usually does, allowing me to sense the invisible electromagnetic waves all around us.

I see the bluish, cherry-scented Wi-Fi network of our restaurant. Muhomor's Brainocytes and phone, Mr. Spock's Brainocytes, Ada's Brainocytes and phone, and Gogi's phone are all connected to this cherry-scented Wi-Fi, which makes sense. I also experience colors, tastes, and smells from the Wi-Fi networks of the other businesses on the street, but I still have no clue as to the nature of my concern.

Figuring Wi-Fi is useless, I switch the app to focus on cell phone traffic instead of Wi-Fi. Luckily, the app can detect a wide range of signals, including AM/FM radio, TV signals, Bluetooth, and a slew of other options that would only interest Muhomor.

Cell phone coverage is an almost imperceptible shimmer, like the heat haze you see on a hot day above a desert road. It takes concentration to tell Verizon apart from say, AT&T, but around each cell phone, I can make out the colors that indicate its cell phone provider, and akin to Wi-Fi, I can smell and taste these connections, giving me an idea of whether I can hack them.

I close my eyes and focus on the cell phone colors around me. Predictably, there's a bunch around the table and a couple inside some of the businesses. All those are as I expected.

What I didn't expect, though, are the shimmers behind a couple of the parked cars down the street.

At first, I tell myself people might've forgotten their cell phones inside their cars. But when I open my eyes, I verify with ever-increasing dread that the shimmer is coming from outside the cars, not inside. Then I see one of the shimmers move and catch a glimpse of sunlight reflecting off one of the lurker's sunglasses.

Trying my best not to panic, I frantically switch back to Wi-Fi mode and seek a camera to look through. I hit jackpot when I get on the pawnshop's mint-scented Wi-Fi, located just to the left of the spot where I spotted the reflection. The security camera is basic, but I still make out the one chilling detail I was missing.

The man wearing those shades is holding a gun with an elongated barrel ending with a silencer.

What's worse is that I see more people with guns. This isn't that big of a surprise, since each man is attached to the cell phones I detected earlier.

My racing heartbeat reminds me of the sounds the engine in Mitya's Bugatti Veyron made the day we drove through the Nevada desert at 250 miles per hour.

I wasn't being paranoid before—and now that I know I'm not crazy, I almost wish I were.

CHAPTER EIGHT

As before, when I was in those gray-hair-inducing situations in Russia, the stress combines with the brain boost to drastically slow down time. The sunglasses-clad man in the camera seems to move as though through molasses as he signals his conspirators.

I leap into mental action. In panicky Zik, I inform my friends about my discovery and then deal with their reactions, which start off as incredulity but quickly turn to terror. At the same time, I craft a text to Gogi. "We're being ambushed. Here's a link to a camera feed. Don't show any alarm yet. We want them to think they still have the element of surprise."

"Who are they?" Mitya demands.

"What do they want?" Ada grabs my elbow, her small hand like an icicle. "Do we have time to call the police?"

"Mitya, get in touch with the cops first and Joe second, in that order," I mentally send instead of answering their questions. "Muhomor, I can't hack their phones, but I suspect you might succeed where I've failed."

As my friends start on their tasks, I notice Gogi hasn't checked his phone yet, and a whole microsecond has already passed.

I kick Gogi's foot under the table, and when I catch his gaze, I pointedly look at his phone. Since it isn't clear whether Gogi understood my intent, I use EmoRat to give instructions to Mr. Spock. The rat scurries down the table to get within Gogi's eyesight, freezes, and then glares at the phone. He lifts his paw and points his nose at the phone—a rat's version of a posture I usually associate with hunting dogs.

"I'm in their phones," Muhomor says. "Sending you all the information on their identities."

Continuing to multitask, I read our assailants' profiles while trying to devise a plan.

The men ambushing us are former military personnel, with a dash of penal system alumni, and they're all extremely dangerous. They have something else in common as well—they work for a security agency that sounds eerily like Joe's. A man called Vincent Williams spearheads the agency, and his resume makes my cousin look like a boy scout.

Viewing images of Vincent Williams, I shudder. He reminds me of this documentary about chimpanzees I recently saw. In the documentary, there was an extremely violent, cannibalistic chimpanzee named Scar, and Vincent wears that same expression, the one that says, *I'll kill you and then I'll eat you.* Like the ape, Vincent also has a scar on his face, and like the ape, Vincent is impossibly big for his species. I suspect Vincent has been working out and taking steroids since high school, an impression that strengthens as I mentally flip through his dossier. On his social media, he posted pics where he's posing like a bodybuilder, so I gather he might be into that sport. His muscles look like giant tumors in some places, and I suspect the ginormous latissimus dorsi muscles in his back are growing their own sets of muscles at this point—and those muscles might also have muscles.

After what feels like millennia—though I suspect it took less than a second—Gogi looks at his freaking phone. Ever so slowly, he clicks my link, and I watch in real time as blood leaves his face. Then his jaw muscles tighten, and his Stalin mustache twitches.

"Ada, take Mr. Spock in an unsuspicious manner, like you want to pet him," I mentally order. "And be prepared to do exactly as I instruct. Same goes for you, Muhomor."

"Police and your cousin have been notified," Mitya reports.

Almost instantly, the texting app notifies me that I have a message from Joe. It states, "Do not engage Williams. I'm too far away from your location. Run."

I see that Gogi has received the same not-so-useful advice from Joe, and he's probably thinking the same thing I am. How are we supposed to run? Problem one is that we're on a dead-end block with the bad guys blocking our exit. Problem two is that if we get up, the hidden assailants will become open assailants. Our only option is to use the restaurant's back door—assuming it has one.

"Muhomor, get us schematics for the buildings on this block," I say urgently. "We're looking for back doors. Hack City Hall if you need to, but get it now."

In the back of my mind, I wonder if this whole attack is Williams's attempts to settle a score with Joe? Alternatively, is it possible an enemy of mine hired this goon? If so, who? Did my half-brother, Kostya, learn of my role in our father's death and decide to take revenge? I decide to tackle this question later, in the unlikely event that we survive.

"Your stress levels are abnormal," Einstein chimes in. "If I might recommend—"

"No audio feedback until I command otherwise," I mentally snap at the poor AI. "If you want to be useful, launch the Batmobile app for me."

The Batmobile app is what I've been calling an app Mitya wrote a few weeks back. It allows me to remotely drive Zapo 2 and lets Mitya control a couple of the high-end limousines that he owns in every major city. I rarely use the app because I usually ask Einstein to auto-deliver the car—a task the latest version of Einstein can easily do, thanks in part to Mitya's brain-boosted coding prowess. Automating and controlling vehicles remotely is one of my friend's obsessions.

In any case, with the various sensors embedded throughout Zapo 2, I can see the road on all sides of the vehicle. Using the app to start the engine, I carefully pull the car out of the parking spot and cruise it at five miles an hour down the street toward Vincent Williams and his pals.

"Schematics," Muhomor says and uses the Teleconference app to pull up the necessary screens for all of us to see. "Also, more camera views." Footage of our attackers shows up from different vantages. Some of the camera views seem to be from the culprits' own phones. If we survive, I'll risk boosting Muhomor's ego by telling him how awesome he is.

"No back exits that I can see," Mitya mumbles. "There are windows facing the other street. Maybe if you break them—"

"And assuming they aren't coming from that way too," Muhomor interrupts.

As I drive the car and confirm Mitya's analysis of the schematics, I also examine the weapons the bad guys possess while battling a heavy feeling settling in my stomach. "I can crash Zapo 2 into them. In the commotion, we can try escaping through the window Mitya mentioned," I think half to myself and half to my friends. "Or I can move the car closer. We can jump in and—"

"Get sprayed with bullets on our way out of the block," Muhomor cuts in. "I don't think your windows are bulletproof, so jumping in won't work."

"Don't tell us what *won't* work without offering your own suggestions," Mitya counters.

"Fine," Muhomor says tersely. "How about—"

In that moment, Nikolozi comes out of the restaurant with the check.

Through the camera views, I see frantic movement happening behind the cars.

"Shit," Mitya says somewhere in the distance. "He spooked the lurkers."

I feel like my consciousness splits into two. One me speaks out loud while the other me sends mental messages. Mentally, I say, "Ada, run into the restaurant and hide in the refrigerated room here." I highlight the spot on the schematic. "Muhomor, try to be useful. Mitya, if you haven't already, report shots fired to the cops." Out loud and at the same time as my mental messages, I bark, "Gogi, we're being attacked."

I then jump to my feet and turn over the table in front of us the way I've seen heroes do in movies.

Our adversaries no longer bother with stealth; their heads are now visible to the naked eye from behind the cars.

Blood pumps in my ears, and the world around me seems to move even slower—as though it was shot with an impossibly fast camera, or like I'm seeing everything in bullet-time, a la *The Matrix*. Then Williams fires his gun, and the fact that I don't see the bullet mid-flight breaks the illusion.

A soul-piercing scream reverberates through the air.

CHAPTER NINE

Worry for Ada rips at me like a rabid bear, as it's her voice I just heard. Without turning, I scan my surroundings through the restaurant's security camera.

A body hits the ground behind us with a thump.

My breath whooshes out in a mix of horror and relief. The victim is not Ada, who must've been screaming in horror; it's Nikolozi. The head wound I see in the camera leaves no room to doubt as to his horrific fate—not unless someone knows how to put parts of his brain back in his head.

Trying to keep my hand as steady as on the gun range, I aim the Glock. Part of me registers that Gogi is doing the same. I enable the HUD and the target-assist app. I'm now surrounded by small views into every camera I have access to, as well as some helpful gun stats, including the number of bullets in my gun—ten. I also have a virtual assist line that makes it nearly impossible to miss.

Cursing myself for not carrying extra ammo, I aim for the bad guys' leader's shoulder, but then I spot Gogi aiming for him as well. I change my target from Williams to Jason—a man who's aiming at Gogi's forehead. As I place the aim-assist line on Jason's shoulder, I note that Ada is hurrying toward the restaurant. *Good.*

I pull the trigger.

Without the gun range's earmuffs, the gunshot smacks my eardrums like a brick and creates the illusion that the recoil of my Glock is stronger than usual. My reward is the sight of Jason's right shoulder turning into a bloody steak as he falls to the ground.

Gogi must've fired at the same time, but instead of hitting Williams, his target, the bullet hits the back of Ethan Madison, who, according to his dossier, is a new recruit in Williams's crew. Ethan must've decided to take the bullet for his boss. Unless he's wearing a bulletproof vest—a possibility to take into account—the decision just cost him his life. Ethan falls on top of Williams in a murder-scene-body-outline heap that tells me he wasn't wearing a vest after all.

As I aim at my next target, I notice Muhomor running behind Ada. Despite the apparent cowardice of this move, I'm relieved, as he's blocking Ada with his body.

Kevin, the next man I shoot in the shoulder, cries out, and Gogi takes his second shot. A man who used to be called Bob Young falls to the ground with a bullet in his cheekbone. Somehow, despite his scream, Kevin—the guy I shot—is still standing, so I waste another bullet, this time going for his right shoulder. This shot does the trick. Kevin slumps to the ground and screams like a detainee in the Abu Ghraib prison.

Ada and Muhomor are almost through the door. To give Ada the best cover I can, I mentally floor the gas of the Batmobile app and point Zapo 2 at the gap between two parked cars, where the majority of the remaining attackers are hiding. For good measure, I activate the nitro system, inspired by something I first saw in the *Fast and the Furious* movies. Sven, the guy who installed the nitro, warned me I could only use that feature twice before needing a refill, and more importantly, that Zapo's tricked-out engine could easily get shot to shit from a single nitro use. But I think Sven would agree that if there was ever a time to risk the engine, this would be it.

Through Zapo's microphones, as well as with my own ears, I hear the brain-shattering screech of metal and plastic tearing each other asunder. Through the cameras, I see Zapo rip through the back and front bumpers of the cars parked in its way. A couple of the assailants manage to jump out of the way, but two aren't so lucky. One of them, Logan, is left lying on the asphalt, with a chunk of bone sticking out of his right leg like an ancient arrow tip and his blood gushing in a stomach-turning geyser. Another guy, nicknamed Deaf John, got hit with Zapo's left mirror and is on the ground as well, hopefully knocked unconscious for a long time.

Though I'm flooring the mental brake pedal to spare the car any unnecessary damage, poor Zapo continues its unfortunate trajectory for another couple of feet, straight into the laundromat's front window. I cringe when I hear the shattering sounds coming from the laundromat—sounds I perceive both through my real-world ears and from what Zapo's microphones deliver to my brain's hearing center. Then I needlessly blink my real-world eyes as the cameras show me Zapo hit the coin machine. The four front-facing cameras blink out of existence, but the side and back cameras still work, allowing me to see car parts and quarters fly in every direction.

"I fear Zapo 2 might've joined its predecessor in car heaven," Mitya says from somewhere, but I ignore him.

Ada is inside the restaurant, but Muhomor is acting like a complete idiot. He turns around to see what the big bad noise was about.

"Go in!" I mentally shout at him. "Make sure Ada makes it into that fridge. Drag her in by force if you have to."

I have to stop paying attention to Muhomor, because Williams uses the commotion to push Ethan off him, and he's again ready for action.

"Watch out," I scream for both Gogi's and Muhomor's sakes. I get a strong feeling that Williams is about to do something desperate.

Gogi and I duck behind the table, and through two camera views, I see Williams stick his gun around the badly damaged Volvo. My whole body tightens as Williams squeezes out a round of bullets in our general direction.

The table shatters into little pieces of stone, and a bullet whooshes by my ear. I guess tables aren't as good a cover as they make them out to be in Hollywood.

My breathing is racecar fast, but since I'm out in the open, I decide to take advantage of the situation and put the aiming app's line in the center of Williams's exposed hand.

Two shots go off, mine and Williams's.

My bullet goes right for his gun hand and must do damage, because his gun clinks to the ground. I see him clutching his right hand with his left and hear his pain-filled curses. To my horror, though, I also hear a scream behind me.

It's Ada.

CHAPTER TEN

Though it's intensely tempting, I don't dare look back. Instead, through the restaurant's security feed in my HUD, I see Muhomor fall down, a huge red stain on his back.

To make a horrible situation worse, Ada rushes back from inside the cover of the restaurant, her face whiter than Mr. Spock's fur.

"Run back in," I telepathically shout at her, imbuing the message with as much anxiety and fear as the Telepathy app will allow. "Now, Ada!"

She doesn't listen. With Mr. Spock in a death grip, Ada squats over Muhomor and grabs him by the back of his shirt.

"Cover her!" I scream at Gogi and mentally calculate how long it will take Ada to drag Muhomor's body far enough inside for her to be safe.

Through the camera, I spot Dylan—a thin, bug-eyed flunky who's been hiding to Williams's left—rising to his feet. I aim the gun where his head will be in a moment and squeeze the trigger. I figure if he puts his head in the bullet's path, it's manslaughter, not murder. It could even be considered suicide. Dylan yelps and clutches the top of his head, and I both hate and respect myself for my relief at knowing I didn't kill him.

Just in case the head wound is too light, and since I have a clear shot at his right shoulder, I reluctantly put my sixth bullet into it. He collapses, screaming and clutching at the injury.

I breathe easier when I see Ada disappear inside the restaurant again, though instead of going to the freezer as I ordered her to do, she crouches by the entrance, ripping Muhomor's shirt from his body.

"The bullet hit his spine." A wave of horror accompanies her telepathic message. "He might never walk again— if he doesn't bleed to death."

As Ada's words register, the utter despair I feel makes me wonder if this whole thing is one of those pre-cog moments that happen during the adjustment period of a new brain boost.

Mitya did, after all, recently give us a new boost.

"Is this really happening?" I ask myself in desperation. I'd give anything for this to be a pre-cog moment or a dream.

Unfortunately, nothing changes, so this is happening for real.

Someone's gun glints in the sunlight, and Gogi fires a shot. A rush of adrenaline takes me out of my wishful-thinking stupor. Gogi just shot and killed a guy who was aiming at me. If he hadn't done that, I'd be toast.

Doubting reality will have to take a backseat for now.

Justin, the crew's youngest member, tries to be bold, so I have no choice but to put my seventh bullet through his upper arm.

Aiden Williams—Vincent's younger brother and right-hand man—peeks out from behind the bullet-riddled, bumperless Camry that has served as his shield until now. After all this, and even knowing that these fuckers hurt Muhomor, I can't believe I'm still uncomfortable with shooting to kill—something my new shrink and I will probably need to work on. Gogi, however, doesn't share my qualms. He shoots, and through the camera view, I witness Aiden's brains turn the pavement behind him into a macabre Pollock painting.

Vincent stops clutching his bloody hand and gapes at his fallen brother with shock that seems foreign on his overly angular face. Then I can practically see something inside him snap. He yanks a gun from a leg holster, gripping it with what's left of his damaged right hand, and screams, "Everyone, charge now or I'll shoot you myself!"

In that slow-motion, bullet-mode of being, I watch as Vincent Williams and five of his remaining men—Gabriel, Nathan, Connor, Isaac, and José—struggle to their feet.

In a moment, I'll have six targets and only three bullets left. The HUD has no count for Gogi's ammo, though if my brain hasn't failed me, Gogi should have four bullets in his Makarov pistol.

"Go for the ones on the left," I shout at Gogi and shoot Gabriel in the right upper arm.

Seeing Gabriel lose both his gun and the will to keep attacking us, I focus on his blond neighbor, Isaac, determined to hit his shoulder instead of his arm on the assumption that it'll be a more painful wound.

Shots ring out, and I feel like Godzilla just bit off my left ear after spewing its fiery breath. I must not be hurt too badly, though, because I'm still standing. With a fresh blast of adrenaline, I hit Isaac's shoulder, and his fall is my reward.

Gogi fires twice. José gets a bullet in the neck, while Nathan is shot through his nose.

The adrenaline in my veins makes the world around me crawl as I watch both Connor and Williams aim at us in slow motion. I extrapolate their movements and guess that Williams is about to aim for my head while his prematurely graying ally has Gogi's center chest in sight. As soon as my mind draws this grisly conclusion, my body reacts.

In a move I learned in the dojo, I half fall, half crouch as my finger spasms around the warmed-up metal of the trigger.

The bullet Williams intended for my head whooshes harmlessly an inch above my skull, hurting only my eardrums.

My own bullet hits Connor in the elbow, destroying his chances of shooting again for a long time and, critically, causes the man to drop his gun.

This is when Gogi makes a tactical error.

He shoots the already disarmed Connor in the face. Like the prior couple of instances today, Gogi must figure the injury I inflicted wasn't damaging enough.

Connor's face explodes, but Gogi's momentary distraction was all Williams needed to swiftly aim at Gogi and pull his trigger.

"No!" Screaming both mentally through all the apps and out loud, I aim my empty gun at Williams and pull the trigger.

Unsurprisingly, nothing happens.

Desperate, I throw the gun at Williams's head—and miss by a wide margin.

Before my gun lands on the ground, I focus on Gogi. He's hit, but I can't discern whether the bullet got him in the groin or upper leg. Then, as he falls, grunting, I see him clutch his leg—which I guess is better than the groin.

Williams moves toward us.

I prepare to dive for Gogi's gun, though I suspect it's empty.

"Move another muscle, and I'll shoot you." Williams's voice is reminiscent of a dental drill. "I mean it. Freeze."

The man is halfway to us, and his gun is pointed steadily at my head.

Surprised to be alive, I raise my hands. "I'm unarmed." A bizarre calm settles over me as I simultaneously scan my environment for any advantage and find few. Almost unconsciously, I mentally order, "Einstein, give me a status report on Zapo."

"Step away from the Georgian," Williams orders and waves his gun toward himself.

I drag my feet in his general direction and try my best to put my body between Williams and Gogi, figuring if he's reluctant to shoot me for some strange reason, perhaps this will stop him from finishing off the bleeding man. Inside the restaurant, I see Ada coming toward me, and I telepathically bark, "Ada, don't move. If you spook Williams, Gogi and I are as good as dead."

What I don't tell her, since I'm trying to save her life, is that we're as good as dead anyway.

"Brake system unresponsive," Einstein reports somewhere in the periphery of my attention. "Cooling system reports it's damaged. Headlight controls unresponsive—"

I dare pay only a tiny sliver of attention to Einstein as I focus on Williams. He's now close enough that he could pistol-whip me if he so desired.

Stopping, he gives me a simian stare. "If you tell me where Cohen is," his vocal cords drill out, "your last moments will be blissfully quick."

CHAPTER ELEVEN

I spot the bloody stump that, as a result of my shooting, has replaced Williams's right middle finger and know he's lying. He'll hurt me for that, no matter his promises. I'm about to say something brave, or at least sarcastic, about his proposal, when Williams adds, "I'll even consider forgetting I saw that girl here, and the Georgian will also get a quick death—even though his name is on the list."

Adrenaline further spikes my heart rate, but I mentally note the mention of a list as I answer, "I'm Cohen, and I'm right here." As I talk, it dawns on me that the guy must've been hired to track down Gogi and Joe, with an emphasis on Joe, who must be at the top of the list. That's why Williams is asking me questions.

Williams correctly realizes I'm being a wise-ass, so he presses the barrel of his gun against my upper arm. I can see his muscles twitch, and I'm sure I'm about to get a bullet in my flesh.

In a flash of brain-boosted insight, I see Williams has made a critical mistake. He looked at me or read my bio someplace and figured he'd be safe coming within striking distance, perceiving me as a rich and spoiled venture capitalist dork.

He didn't count on me being a quick learner due to the boost, nor on the many disarming drills Gogi put me through. He also probably doesn't know that disarming one's opponent is a cornerstone of the Systema martial art—or at least Gogi's flavor of it.

With a hopefully sudden motion, I allow muscle memory to guide me as I grab the gun and twist it the way I rehearsed.

My movements are smooth as silk, and before Williams's eyes register surprise, his gun clanks onto the pavement—and that's only because I didn't have a good angle to apply the move in a way that would allow me to keep the gun.

My opponent yelps in pain; the disarming move applied pressure to his mutilated finger.

I see his eyes follow the trajectory of his gun and take advantage of that distraction by punching the larger man in the middle of the chest, hoping to hit him in the solar plexus.

Gogi would be proud: my strike is textbook perfect. Only my fist feels like I've punched concrete. Instead of doubling over in pain like a normal human, Williams doesn't even blink.

What's worse, he swings his giant fist at my face.

I block the hit with my right elbow, but unlike the training version of this block, my elbow feels like it has split into little shards, and each shard has a pulsing nerve attached to it. I try to score a kick—as I've been taught is optimal in this situation—but unlike Gogi during training, Williams sidesteps my kick and lands a fist to my jaw.

Now, it's not like I haven't learned how to take a hit. In a way, I should be an expert, since Gogi has hit me by accident a couple of times during training, and Joe has hit me on purpose more times than I can count. But I now realize they've been pulling their punches. I didn't expect that from Joe. Hell, even Anton—Mom's kidnapper who punched me months ago—was a wimp compared to my current attacker.

The impact of his punch is instant, and it's only my brain extension that allows me to think at all. The biological parts of my brain, and by extension, my body, shut down and enter knockout mode.

In a moment, I might take a nap right here in the middle of the road, and it takes everything I have to fight for lucidity. Desperate, I put all my focus on the parts of my brain that run on faraway computer servers—the impact-resistant parts.

"Back lights are undamaged," Einstein says somewhere in my head, and I recall that I instructed him to tell me the status of Zapo 2. "Nitro boost undamaged."

By the miracle of Brainocytes, I maintain enough control over my body to duck the next punch and take the punch that follows on my left forearm.

As the pain of the block scorches my brain awake, I frantically launch the Batmobile app and try to start Zapo 2 again as a plan forms in my head.

"Stop," I croak at Williams, but his fist lands in the middle of my stomach. Regrettably, unlike his, my solar plexus works the way it should, and I almost faint from the pain and loss of air.

"Joe," I try to say. "I'll tell you where Joe Cohen is."

My words come out garbled, but Williams pauses, perhaps out of curiosity. I take advantage of the reprieve by dropping to the ground and rolling to the right on the dusty pavement. My destination is the side of the road.

Through the camera views, I see Williams's face contort, as if he's debating whether to kick me or ask me more questions. The desire to kick seems to win out, and he raises his foot.

Putting Zapo 2 in reverse, I will the car to start and mentally promise it complete repairs, gold rims, and an oil change every week if it will just please, pretty please *start*.

To my shock, my desperate plea is answered.

Despite the earlier crash, Zapo's electric engine activates, and the car is ready for action.

My attacker's foot is about to connect with the side of my head when I mentally slam the gas and rip the wheel all the way to the right.

My world explodes in white stars, informing me that Williams's foot has reached my head.

The trick of relying on willpower and the distant server extensions of my brain won't work much longer.

Still, before consciousness finally abandons me, I see Williams's body grow larger and larger in Zapo's back cameras. I also notice he's turning around to see what's going on.

I do my best to make myself as small as possible and roll farther to the side of the road. Then, in the last picosecond of consciousness, I activate Zapo's nitro system to make the car zoom forward.

CHAPTER TWELVE

"You have been unconscious for twenty seconds," Einstein reports. "The current time is 3:55 p.m."

Twenty seconds isn't my usual eight hours of sleep. Something other than catching z's must be responsible for my mind outage. Fleetingly, I wonder if Joe knocked me out in the dojo again. Until now, our sparring has only resulted in me losing consciousness once, and even then, I was only out for a second.

Sirens blare somewhere in the distance. Is that an ambulance coming for me? If it is, this would be the first time Joe has damaged me this badly.

Ada will never let me hear the end of it.

Then I see all the camera feeds in the AROS interface and register the bullet-riddled cars on the street. With a jolt, I remember everything, particularly the part where I was just fighting for my life.

"Einstein," I mentally command. "I'm unable to see through Zapo's cameras."

"It's been twenty-two seconds since I was able to ping the car's computer systems," Einstein laments. "Based on my assessment, Zapo is totaled."

If Einstein were human, he would've sarcastically added, "Again."

With monumental effort, I roll over onto my side and survey Zapo's sad leftovers.

I half expect, half hope to see Williams pinned between Zapo's back bumper and the remnants of the Ford Mustang I must've inadvertently killed half a minute ago. Alas, the giant man isn't there. Williams's absence raises a critical question. Where is he? I'm pretty sure I positioned Zapo to hit him before I blacked out, but I guess he rolled off the hood or something along those lines.

Fighting the feeling that I've swallowed concrete, I scan for Williams with all the cameras.

Nothing.

As more of my mental acuity returns, I remember to look for Williams's wounded compatriots, but I can't find any. They must've escaped from the sirens with him.

Speaking of sirens, they're accompanied by flashing lights, so the authorities are on the scene.

High on relief, I try to get up, but decide it's too soon to try something so drastic.

From the comfort of the pavement, I use the restaurant's camera to assess the damage Gogi endured. Luckily, the Georgian fared better than my most optimistic hopes. Someone, probably himself, wrapped a makeshift tourniquet around his leg, and the bleeding has slowed to a trickle.

Unlike Gogi, Muhomor looks bad. He's marble white and unmoving, and telepathic messages from me don't seem to get his attention.

"Mike," Ada says out loud from the restaurant entrance. "Don't move. You might have a back injury."

"Go back inside," I insist telepathically. Seeing that she's not complying, I demonstratively wiggle my fingers and add, "I just wiggled my toes too, and it was a great success. No back injury. Go inside. Please."

Her reply is interrupted by the commotion of the emergency vehicles that consist of police and paramedics, though a fire truck is also on the scene.

Despite the migraine the sirens are inducing, I welcome the blaring sound, and when cops and EMT personnel flood the street, I allow myself to relax.

In a blink, Muhomor, Gogi, and I find ourselves on stretchers, each one loaded into a separate ambulance. Ada joins me in mine.

"I'm okay," I valiantly lie to my paramedic team when they close the ambulance doors behind Ada. "Please focus on my friends."

"Your friends have at least three responders with them," the larger paramedic reassures me. His sleep-deprived eyes look too hollow for someone so young. "We can and will focus on you. Can you tell me your name and date of birth, please?"

I carry on a conversation with the EMT guy while also talking telepathically with Ada, who seems overwhelmed in her post-adrenaline slump. Her eyes glisten with tears as she stares at me, and fine tremors wrack her slender frame.

Since my EMTs don't know how Muhomor and Gogi are faring, or are refusing to tell me, I try using Muhomor's nifty app to hack into the other ambulances to see if I can learn something—but no luck. The cars don't have complex enough computers to hack, and the EMT personnel don't write patient information into their private phones.

"No, I don't feel any pain," I lie to the EMT guy for the fifth time. "I don't want any painkillers."

"How much pain are you really in?" Ada asks, apparently recovering from her shock. Her eyes are dry again, and her telepathic message is filled with a mixture of worry and annoyance. "You're paler than I've ever seen you—too pale even for a programmer."

"I feel like someone kicked me in the head," I mentally reply. "And what do you know? I probably feel that way because I *did* get kicked in the head."

"Then why don't you tell them you're hurting? Why are you always needlessly trying to be a hero?"

"If they give me painkillers, the drugs will likely knock me out. That's what happened when I crashed the last Zapo," I explain. "I want to say conscious. I want learn what happened to our friends."

Sometimes, the brain boost allows me to perceive the world fast enough to catch so-called microexpressions—those brief, involuntary facial ticks that appear in accordance with the emotions the person is experiencing. Ada's momentary scowl is classic annoyance. The expression is instantly gone, though, and to Ada's credit, her telepathic message is patient and soothing as she suggests, "How about you at least use Relief? It won't knock you out. This is probably the exact situation that app was designed for."

I consider her suggestion, even though she's talking about an app that's among the scarier software we've developed. In fact, this app, which Mitya dubbed Relief, is at the top of my scary shortlist because it's designed to dampen pain and, along with BraveChill (the app that helps with fear and anxiety), is ripe for abuse. When I tested these apps, BraveChill reminded me of chasing a Xanax with a beer—something I did once back at MIT and liked too much to ever allow myself to do again. The Relief app is even scarier, since I felt warmth and pleasure from it. Though I've never abused that class of drugs, I'm guessing the feeling was akin to what morphine or oxycodone would feel like. Of course, using those apps when I wasn't frightened or in pain wasn't a fair test.

Out loud, to emphasize the seriousness of my words to Ada, I say, "In those experiments where rats could stimulate their pleasure centers, rats would press the lever that delivered the artificial pleasure over pressing the lever for eating, drinking, and even sex. They pressed the button to the point where they starved to death."

The EMT guys exchange confused glances but remain silent, likely ascribing my statement to my head injury.

Worried that Mr. Spock understood what I said and is horrified by the idea of such barbaric rat experiments, I pet the little guy—which causes the EMT folks to exchange yet more looks as it's not every day you see a pet rat. Mr. Spock seems to be okay, at least gauging by his EmoRat output and the visual cues I'm getting better at recognizing.

"You have better self-control than a rat, Mike," Ada counters out loud and scoots closer to me on the gurney. "No offense," she tells Mr. Spock. "Besides, the Relief app provides a precisely calculated mild stimulus to the pleasure center. It dampens pain by—"

"Fine," I mentally interrupt, worried that Ada was about to praise Mitya's genius again—a common activity that never fails to activate my greenest jealousy. "I'm turning it on."

She smiles knowingly, and I wonder why I even try resisting her wishes. When it comes to arguing with Ada, I'm learning it's easier to give in. Deep down, I know she only wants what's best for me and wouldn't convince me to use an app that could lead me into trouble—not on purpose anyway.

I explain Spock's presence to the paramedics as I turn on the Relief app. As a concession to my fears about the app, I dial the app settings all the way down, so it becomes the approximate equivalent of a couple of adult doses of Tylenol or maybe a single Tylenol with Codeine.

"Damn it," I mentally send Ada when the app's bliss makes the pain in my bloody ear and my awful headache subside. "I do feel better, but as I said, I'm worried I'll get hooked on this."

"We could always write you a rehab app." Ada touches my shoulder soothingly and winks at me. "Something that would block the Relief app from connecting to the servers."

"I'd just write something to overrule you." I put my hand on top of hers, and the warmth is better than anything an app could induce. "If you didn't want me to become addicted, you shouldn't have encouraged me to get so good at coding."

"Don't worry. If you do become an addict, I'll lock you in a room with no access to internet if I have to." Ada's tone is much too playful given the cruel and unusual scenario she described. "In all seriousness, if Muhomor can write an app to help himself quit smoking, we can write an app that would help you quit using another app if needed. But it won't be."

Her mention of Muhomor gets me worried again, and I debate running BraveChill to lessen that bout of anxiety. In the end, I decide against using the app, since *not* worrying about my friends in *this* scenario would make me a horrible friend and less of a human being.

"Speaking of apps," Ada says, picking up on my shift in mood. "You should run the Neurogenesis app in case you got brain damage from the fight."

Neurogenesis is the process of growing new brain cells, and it's arguably one of the scarier apps that I have no problems with. I actually use it on a regular basis. Besides the obvious idea of "the more brain, the better," assuming neurogenesis does give you "more brain," my rationale for using the app is that many good-for-you activities seem to cause neurogenesis. In other words, I figure if running, sex, enriching environments and experiences, and even random dietary things like fish oil, turmeric, and blueberries cause neurogenesis, then neurogenesis might be behind some of the benefits of those activities, and thus it's a good idea to get neurogenesis any way I can. Mom and the rest of the folks in the study run a heavy-duty version of the app, and even I have to admit it was a stroke of genius when Mitya thought of the idea. It's helped patients with more advanced Alzheimer's like nothing else in the treatment, leading me to believe that neurogenesis *does* give one more brain power. For me, it's hard to separate neurogenesis's impact on my intellect from the brain boost, but I still think the benefits exist. Plus, if Ada ever did lock me up in a room without internet, I would at least be left with a naturally boosted brain.

"Done," I tell Ada once the Neurogenesis app is up and running. "I think we're arriving at our destination."

Punctuating my words, the ambulance stops and the EMT guys take me to the ER.

"Stop fidgeting," Ada says out loud—a sign of annoyance— after I contemplate leaving the hospital bed for what feels like the thousandth time. "You *have* to get seen by a doctor. It's not negotiable."

"I'll stay still if you go and find out what's going on with Gogi and Muhomor," I counter, opting not to use the words "benevolent dictator."

"Deal," Ada replies telepathically and leaves, proving I must be fine, or else she wouldn't have left my sight.

Even as Ada walks away, the wait begins to feel like hours—a negative side effect of my super-fast new mode of thought. To stay sane, I try to occupy my mind. I start with my work email, going through and replying to the couple of hundred of the most urgent emails. That kills a few minutes and takes longer than it should because I read and type at a leisurely pace. Done with work, I decide to play with my phone for a bit. I only got this unit a few days ago, but I've already dubbed it Precious 3. Precious 3 is better than its predecessors in every way, and it has hardware a supercomputer would've been happy with a decade ago. Ada, Mitya, and I designed my favorite feature—a light-sensitive solar charger incorporated into the outer shell. When combined with the efficient internal battery, Precious 3 can charge itself even in room illumination. I haven't had to plug it into the wall since the first time I got it. The only problem with Precious 3, if you can even call it a problem, is that I can do just as much, if not more, with the Brainocytes in my head. Still, there are thousands more games available on the phone than the Brainocytes Club could ever hope to put together. I choose a newer strategy game and give it a spin, though playing games on my phone doesn't fully keep my attention. The games are optimized for regular people.

Recalling that Lyuba is in town, I get in touch with her and tell her Muhomor got hurt. I urge her to stop by the hospital, figuring he'd be happy to see her when he can. I assure her that no, I have no clue what his medical condition is at the moment. Then, for a few long minutes, I debate telling Mom where I am. In the end, Mitya agrees with me that it's not essential that Mom know about my mishaps, unless I have something seriously wrong with me. I don't consult Ada, as she might think Mom has the right to know. Since I have Mitya on the line, I agree to play a virtual game of Go with him and promptly lose. Then, as we agreed, we play chess, and of course I win. As usual, we have a telepathic/verbal fight about which win is more impressive, Go or chess.

"Go is an ancient Chinese strategy game that's older and arguably more complex than chess," Mitya says, regurgitating his usual argument. "Look at artificial intelligence. AIs have been able to beat the best chess player for ages now, while they've only recently mastered Go."

"That has more to do with people wishing to build the right AI," I counter. "Besides, since you mentioned AIs, I can beat the best AI at chess, while you can't beat the best AI at Go."

"That's not my point," Mitya says distractedly, and I suspect he just challenged an AI to a Go match.

With Mitya occupied, I look for more ways to keep myself busy.

"They're taking Gogi for some scans, and they're stabilizing Muhomor," Ada tells me when she comes back fifteen minutes later. "Getting information here is like pulling teeth."

The mental image of pulling teeth doesn't help my usual white-coat-generated anxiety, nor does the knowledge that Muhomor's condition is so bad that he requires stabilizing. On the subject of neuroses, if the shrink did help me with my paranoia, that progress has been undone, because some insistent part of me feels like someone at the hospital is covertly watching me. This eerie sensation makes me recall how I felt inside a recent nightmare where faceless people wearing suits were coming to get me.

After what feels like another week of anxiety-filled waiting, a doctor breaks the monotony by confirming what I've been saying to Ada all along: my condition is not a true emergency, and I can leave the hospital soon.

Of course, "soon" is a relative term in hospitals. Since I'm fine and a low priority, I have to wait a long time before I get my ear stitched and various cuts and scrapes bandaged. The nurse who helps me informs me I have to speak with a police officer. It's standard procedure for gunshot victims, and that includes people whose ear barely got grazed by a bullet.

"Ada, please check on Gogi and Muhomor again," I mentally plead as a cop enters the room. "Maybe there's more information available?"

"Of course," she replies soothingly. "Do you want to play chess and talk while I walk around? It might help you keep your cool while the cops question you."

"Sure," I reply to Ada mentally as the cop introduces himself as Officer Jackson. "Though I can keep my cool on my own."

"Maybe we can also pair code this app I've been thinking about," Ada mentally says after I skillfully take her first pawn in our chess game.

"Whatever you want, sweetie," I mentally reply, realizing all this multitasking isn't just for me, but also to ease Ada's anxiety at the prospect of seeing what happened to our friends.

"No, I never met these men before," I explain to Officer Jackson for what seems like the tenth time. "I only know their names because I used facial recognition on them."

As the incredulous cop asks me another set of follow-up questions, Ada and I play chess, and I watch her write a piece of software meant to integrate Brainocytes with a specific model of smart lights. It would allow us to mentally turn lights on and off in our place. I don't point out that we can already work the smart lights via Einstein, as diminishing the value of Ada's work will only upset her more.

"And how does Joe Cohen fit into all this?" Officer Jackson asks, and I understand his unsurprising and not-so-subtle agenda.

My cousin is always of interest to the police.

"I don't know," I reply as politely and patiently as I can. "My cousin and I aren't close."

"Well, what's your theory?" the cop persists. "Why do you think they attacked?"

"I really don't know why they attacked," I tell Officer Jackson, and it feels like I've answered a variation of this question before. "If it did have anything to do with Joe, as you're implying, you can discuss your theories with the man himself when you speak with *him*."

In actual fact, I keep wondering about the reasons behind the attack, and I plan to ask Joe some pointed questions when he gets here, so the cop will have to wait his turn.

As the officer pesters me with more questions, I make a chess move that means a checkmate for Ada and mentally text Joe, "There's a cop here asking a lot of questions about you. Take that into consideration when you arrive."

"How's Gogi?" My cousin's reply is almost as quick as from someone with Brainocytes, though, of course, he writes in English, not Zik.

"I don't know yet," I reply to my cousin as I say out loud, "Officer, I really need to go check on my friends. If you have more questions, I think I'd like to have my attorney, Mr. Kadvosky, present. Perhaps you've heard of him?"

Joe's text is clear and to the point. "I want a report on Gogi's condition ASAP." My cousin doesn't need to add niceties such as, "Or else I'll break your neck when I get there," because it's implied when conversing with him.

"I've heard of the Kadvosky law firm," says Officer Jackson, and his expression is such that you'd think we were talking about a den of vampires or an earthquake. "We're done for now. Thank you for your help."

Though it's clear he's being disingenuous, I still shake the cop's hand. As he exits the room, Ada finalizes her code and submits it to our new, Muhomor-secured source control repository.

Figuring now is as good a time as any to try walking, I swing my legs off the bed and carefully put my weight on them.

I don't fall or scream in pain, but I strongly suspect I would've at least yelped without the Relief app. I tentatively disable the app and see that I'm right. I'm still aching all over, the pain as tolerable as a root canal without anesthesia.

"Any update?" I mentally ask Ada and take a deep breath to see if it'll help with the pain.

"I finally located Gogi in this maze," Ada says. "Going to check on his condition now."

"I'll look for Muhomor then," I tell her and enable the Relief app. The deep breath made the pain worse.

For the next half hour, I stalk around the ER, asking nurses questions when I can find them. The staff aren't used to patients asking questions about other patients, so I have to turn on all my boosted intellect and attention to seem sane and charming. My work eventually pays off, and I learn that Muhomor was stabilized and taken for an X-ray and CAT scan, and that he's now inside an MRI machine.

"I'm in Gogi's ICU room," Ada says at the same time as I plead with a nurse to let me speak to the doctor who examined Muhomor in the ER. "You should hear this for yourself."

The nurse gives me the name of the doctor, and Ada enables the Share app, allowing me to see through a new virtual window into Gogi's room. I hear someone, likely Gogi's doctor, say, "He just got out of surgery, and it went well. There's laceration of muscles and some shattered bones, but I think he'll recover well in time."

As soon as I hear Gogi's diagnosis, I exhale with relief and instantly relay the information to Joe. He replies with, "I'll be over in twenty minutes. I've also sent Jean and Nick to join you. They're closer to your location."

Nick and Jean are two guys I sometimes see at the gym. As far as I can tell, they're a rare subset of people in my cousin's world who do exactly what his official business is supposed to be about. They work as high-end bodyguards and nothing else—meaning nothing shady. Even their backgrounds are more legitimate than usual. Nick almost made it into the Navy SEALs. Rumor is, he was rejected because he wasn't smart enough. And Jean almost made it onto a professional football team (that's American football, not its European namesake, soccer).

Sounds like Joe doesn't trust hospital security and wants us to have extra protection—a sobering thought.

The relief I felt upon learning of Gogi's condition dissipates, and I concentrate my remaining worry full force on Muhomor.

After a few minutes of fruitless searching, Ada joins me. Together, we ambush an MRI technician, the only person we can find who's seen Muhomor recently.

"I only take the tests. I don't interpret them," the woman says and nervously pushes her glasses a millimeter higher on her nose. "You'll have to speak with Doctor Zane once he's done with the surgery."

"You do MRIs all the time," I point out. "Can't you tell us what *you* think? We won't hold you to it."

Seeing she's going to be stubborn, I decide to try an age-old Russian persuasion technique. I mentally ask Ada to take out all the money she has on her. Ada takes out a couple of hundred dollars, and I demonstratively place it all on the tech's small desk, saying, "We just want your uneducated guess. Please."

The woman looks stunned by the bribery—something that I guess never happens in this expensive American hospital. After a second, though, she pockets the money and says in a low tone, "If he makes it, I doubt he'll ever walk again."

As we gape at her, she fiddles with her glasses, and I can see her debating if she should say something else. Something, maybe decency, wins out, and she quietly adds, "I'm sorry, but it's a complex surgery, and I think you should prepare yourselves for the worst."

CHAPTER THIRTEEN

Ada and I frantically pace the hospital corridors, trying to deal with the fact that our friend might die at any moment. In an effort to calm down, I stroke Mr. Spock's fur, but after a few minutes, he uses the EmoRat to notify me he'd rather I stop, so I do.

As I try my best to hack into the hospital computers, I can't help but dwell on the painful irony that Muhomor would be the best person to help with this. But if he were in a condition to hack, we wouldn't need to hack into the hospital computers to check on him.

"I've taken him for granted," I message Ada, adding sadness to my telepathic words. "I didn't tell him how highly I thought of his skills."

"I think we all could've been better friends." Ada stops pacing and puts a comforting hand on my forearm. "Let's treat this as a life lesson."

Ada's touch calms me enough for me to focus, and I begin mentally tasting and smelling the hospital computer networks through the Muhomor app. It takes a couple of minutes—ages for someone with my speed of thought—but I finally find a yummy loophole in the hospital security.

I notify Mitya and Ada about my finding so they can exploit the system with me.

"I can't find much beyond what the MRI technician already told us," Ada says after some time, echoing my own conclusions.

"I had a bit more luck," Mitya chimes in. "I figured out where the surgery is taking place. Sending you the info now."

Ada and I get an electronic delivery of a map of the hospital with a (typical of Mitya) giant red cross in the middle of the third floor.

When we're halfway to our destination, I get a text from Joe that states, "Nick and Jean are in the hospital. Where should I send them?"

I forward Mitya's map to Joe and ask, "What about you? When will you get here?"

"Shortly," Joe replies. "Where's Gogi's room?"

I send Joe directions on how to find Gogi and again wonder if Joe is the reason for this horrible mess. I'll risk my life by asking him, but not over the phone.

As Ada and I walk through the hospital corridors, the smells of formaldehyde and bleach compete with the much worse medicinal aromas I'd prefer to ignore. The reason I focus on smell instead of sight is my resurgent paranoia. Though my eyes see medical beds and equipment all around, and though, on the surface, we're surrounded only by people wearing gray-green scrubs, part of my brain is aware of unseen people watching me, and that same part of me insists these people are wearing suits—like in my nightmare.

Nick and Jean are waiting for us in the surgical waiting room, and they're the only people there. The big men are occupying two of the cheap, uncomfortable-looking chairs and flipping through yellowing magazines with last year's headlines. This windowless room must be a low priority for the hospital staff in charge of restocking magazines.

Nick's greeting is more monosyllabic than Jean's, but only by a narrow margin. I wonder if they're trying to live up to some kind of bodyguard stereotype. So far, they're succeeding.

We sit down, and I grab a magazine from the pile on the decrepit-looking end table and pretend to read while I take another stab at navigating the labyrinth that is the hospital Wi-Fi. In the meantime, Ada uses her entire mental capacity to engage the two brutes in a semblance of conversation.

"Jackpot," I mentally shout at Ada and Mitya. "I found two security cameras in the operating room."

I access the first one, and my blood pressure spikes as I take in the room with its masked surgeon and slew of faceless helpers. Muhomor is barely recognizable with the mask over his face, and the hospital cap covering his signature hairdo is extra depressing. A green sheet covers his poor body, somehow making him look thinner than usual—almost frail. The second camera shows a gaping red hole in the back of his getup, with bright light streaming down at it from the special surgical lamps. I can see the grisly details of the surgery, and I let my eyes wander around the room, focusing on anything but the gore to avoid fainting. My chest aches even more, and guilt gnaws at me as I think of all the recent jokes I made at Muhomor's expense, not to mention the stuff I told the shrink. "This is so bad," I mumble to myself in Russian.

"Hey, he's alive," Mitya says from somewhere. I guess I accidentally transmitted my thoughts, or Mitya overheard me through Ada's Share app. "Don't mourn him yet. It's bad luck."

I shake my head in an effort to clear it. Though I didn't think Mitya had a superstitious bone in his body, he has a point. In the Russian culture, it's a bad sign to cry on the behalf of someone who's sick; it's believed that those who do might contribute to a fatal outcome. Though I'm even less superstitious than Mitya, for Muhomor's sake, I decide not to tempt fate and calm down.

"He's a fighter," I say, trying to believe my own words. "I'm sure he'll make it."

"Are you hungry?" Ada asks, whispering out loud in my ear, and I could kiss her for the change in topic. It refocuses me, and though I can still see the operating room in my peripheral vision, my stomach shocks me by rumbling so loudly that Nick chuckles.

"I'll take that as a yes." Ada looks from my belly to Jean and his partner and says more loudly, "What about you, gentlemen? I'm about to go get some food. Would you like me to get you anything?"

To Ada's chagrin, Nick and Jean ask for two meals that are the antithesis of veganism—not a surprise, given their meaty builds.

"An oatmeal for me," I say out loud before Ada can start debating nutrition with the two muscle-bound bodyguards. "With lots of nuts if they have it."

Mr. Spock's vocabulary is still severely limited, but he knows the word "nuts." Through EmoRat, he expresses his excitement about the possibility of nuts. Incidentally, he also knows the words for a bunch of other treats, his name, both with the Mr. honorific and without, and the phrase, "Fresh air?" He loves that question, because it means he can jump into my pocket and hitch a ride outside.

"Ada, get some extra nuts on the side and some raisins too," I mentally add, knowing full well that the word "raisins" was understood and appreciated by the little schemer too. "Mr. Spock wants a snack."

As I suspected, at the mention of raisins, his second favorite word of the day, Mr. Spock exudes excitement and begins bruxing in anticipation.

"Okay." Ada looks pacified by my choice. "I'll be back soon."

I watch Ada walk through the room and into the hallway. When she enters the elevator, I put down my magazine and turn my attention to Nick and Jean. "I haven't seen you guys at the gym lately," I say.

My mention of the gym brings warmth to Jean's eyes, and in a booming voice, he says, "Been busy. I've seen you practice with Gogi, though. You're not bad, for a civilian."

"Thanks," I reply while writing a mental message to Ada and Mitya that says, "I need more distraction than this glacial conversation."

"What?" Ada replies instantly. "You don't find talking to Tweedledee and Tweedledum intellectually stimulating enough?"

"Sorry to interrupt." Mitya's Zik message is full of anxiety. "I've been looking through the hospital cameras, and there's something you *need* to see."

Mitya sends a link, and when I click it, every part of me, tips of hair included, freezes in fear.

CHAPTER FOURTEEN

The view through the camera is familiar. It's the elevator we used to get to this floor.

A group of three men walk out of the elevator and look around furtively. One walks up to the nurses' station near the corridor entrance and says something to the nurse. I can imagine what he said since it probably wasn't all that different from what Ada and I recently told the nurse: "We're here to wait for a patient."

"Sketchy person alert," Einstein says loudly three times—once for each man on the screen.

"I knew that this time," I mentally reply to the AI as my adrenaline levels skyrocket. "Pull up their profiles so I can read them." To Nick and Jean, I say sharply, "Someone is coming for me. Be ready."

In the moment it takes me to load the screens into my AROS interface, I compose a Zik message and send it.

"Ada, leave the hospital if you haven't already. When you're outside, get as far away as you can."

"I'll give Ada the rundown and make sure she gets to safety," Mitya says. "Don't waste any brain bandwidth worrying about anything but the men coming your way."

"Okay," I reply. "Just get her out. If you have to, tell hospital security she's a dangerous psycho and they need to throw her out ASAP."

"I'll make sure she gets out," Mitya promises grimly. "Don't worry about it."

I wish it was so easy not to worry about Ada, but I have no choice. Screens with faces and words show up in front of me as Einstein provides me with the profiles I requested.

I have to hand it to Jean and Nick. They don't waste time asking needless questions. In the brief time it takes me to read the bios, the two bodyguards are already up and reaching for their guns.

I reach for the place where *my* gun should be, but I remember I ran out of bullets and lost it earlier today—probably a good thing, since an unlicensed gun would've been hard to explain to the emergency responders. Still, I wish I had it now, as the profiles tell me a crucial piece of information.

These men work for Vincent Williams.

Aside from that, the profiles tell me what I could've guessed. These are dangerous people. One, Keyon, did time for murder, and another, Broderick, also served time, but for racketeering. The third man, Cristiano, isn't a criminal, but that doesn't make him any less dangerous. He served in the Exército Brasileiro—a branch of the Brazilian army.

For now, I shelve questions such as "How did they find me?" and "What's Vincent's beef with me in the first place?" Given how my last meeting with Vincent Williams's men went, I hiss out loud, "Nick. Jean. The men you're about to face work with the fucks who put Gogi in the hospital."

At the reminder that his comrade's hurt and that he's about to get a chance to even the score, Nick's eyes glint with Joe-like homicidal glee. Jean's face is harder to read, but both men take the safeties off their guns and launch into motion, performing maneuvers that remind me of police procedurals. Nick slides against the wall adjacent to the corridor and aims his gun at the entrance, while Jean herds me behind him and as far away from the entrance as possible. Once Jean is satisfied with our position, he points his gun at the entrance too.

My pulse hammering, I watch the AROS view and whisper the bad guys' movements to Jean until the three attackers get out of the camera's range. Then I search the Wi-Fi network for another viewpoint, but the closest one I can locate is the security camera right above my head, showing me an extra few inches of the corridor compared to my eyes.

"Have the rat peek into the corridor," Mitya tells me after I share the reconnaissance problem with him. "You have an app that shows you what he can see."

"This isn't the time for cruel jokes." I imbue my Zik retort with as much righteous anger as the interface will allow. "He could get squished."

"Wow. Ada has you whipped," Mitya grumbles. "You're treating a lab rat like a person."

"If you want to be useful, tell Joe what's happening," I reply tersely. "Maybe notify hospital security and the cops of what's going on."

"I already notified hospital security and the cops. Now, regarding Joe." Mitya's reply is slower than his usual telepathic messages. "Ada and I were debating if we should distract you with that part."

"With what?" I didn't think my adrenaline level could go any higher, but I was clearly wrong. It's so bad that my hands are shaking and Einstein pops up an alert about my stress levels on my AROS screen.

"A picture is worth more than words." Another link accompanies Mitya's message. "This is a camera view into Gogi's room."

When the screen pops up, I recognize the outside of Gogi's room. Only there are two large men there fighting Joe. Their movements are so fast they appear blurry through the cheap security camera.

From the broken-looking wrist of the larger of the two attackers, I can guess Joe recently disarmed him. A gun is on the floor. The slightly smaller attacker is bending over to grab it, but he meets Joe's knee instead.

"Why doesn't Joe have his gun out?" I message Mitya. "Did he not get a chance to take it out, or did they snatch it from his hands somehow?"

"Focus on your own problems," Mitya retorts. "According to my calculations, *your* trouble is about to start."

Mitya is right. I enable the Recorder app to capture everything so I can review it later and prepare to focus on my own attackers.

This is when an object flies into the room from the corridor.

Since my thinking is fast, I'm probably the first, if not the only, person in the room who has time to process what the object is and what's about to happen.

It's a grenade about to explode.

CHAPTER FIFTEEN

"Grenade!" I try to scream, but the word doesn't come out because the explosion goes off.

Jean's body slams into mine with the force of a baseball bat hitting an ant.

Despite Jean's body blocking me, my retinas get blasted with a supernova-bright light that's about as pleasant as seeing a million camera flashes go off at once.

With my vision gone, my ears get assaulted next. The grenade's boom feels like Thor banged his Mjolnir hammer against my exposed eardrums.

It's as if someone dropped me on my head and then drove over me with a pickup truck.

"Judging by what I saw through the camera, it was a stun grenade," Mitya comments telepathically. "That means that, in a moment, the attackers will barge in."

"I'm going back to the hospital," Ada intrudes. "Mike might need my help."

"Don't—" I start, but Mitya beats me to it.

"You will do no such thing, Ada," he snaps. "You need to get *farther* away. Stop this. You're distracting him, and he's already concussed."

With colossal effort, in less than a nanosecond, I mentally look through the camera above my head.

Jean looks as stunned as I feel, but Nick seems to have fared much better. Must have something to do with his SEAL training.

One of the attackers becomes visible in the corridor. My brain is jumbled, but I believe this is Keyon, the murderer of the bunch.

Before I can warn Nick somehow, the big bodyguard realizes we have company and aims his gun at approximately where Keyon should be in a moment.

Even through the ringing deafness in my ears, I hear the gunshot. I hope that means my ears aren't permanently damaged.

Keyon grabs his chest and falls to the ground. Before I can allow myself to whoop in joy, Keyon's partner, Broderick the racketeer, comes into view. A warning is about to leave my lips when Broderick shoots Nick in the face.

Nick falls, but the shooting has brought Jean out of his confusion—at least enough for him to unload his gun in the direction of the corridor. Since I still can't see anything with my eyes, I'm pretty sure Jean can't either and he's just shooting blindly. Still, Jean must be lucky or well trained, because a bullet hits Broderick in the neck. The man clutches the wound in what I hope is his death throes.

"One left," I scream, though I doubt Jean's ears have recovered enough to hear me.

Jean begins to reload.

I really hope Cristiano, as a guy who served in the army, will be careful after seeing his comrades killed. If he moves slowly, his hesitation might give Jean the few precious seconds he needs to load his gun.

Without much will on my part, my attention goes to the camera overlooking the elevator, and I watch the elevator doors open.

People dressed in hospital garb run out pushing a gurney—which sort of makes sense. They might be here to rescue any survivors of the explosion. I wish these were hospital security guards or cops instead. Didn't Mitya summon them?

What I see next doesn't make any sense, though. The remaining people in the elevator are wearing suits.

"Is this a dream?" I ask Einstein in panic.

"No. You're conscious." Einstein's reply holds no trace of humor.

In case this is a pre-cog moment, I ask myself, "Is this really happening?"

However, I'm still where I am, and the suits are still there. I briefly wonder if a dream might include Einstein saying I'm conscious, but I decide it's unlikely and focus on the camera input.

I count at least four suited men, but when I try using facial recognition on their angular faces, nothing happens. In two cases, I get an excellent look at their features— enough that I'll remember them in the future—so I know the lack of recognition isn't some issue with the camera's angle. These men must not be in any of the facial recognition databases—a feat that seems close to impossible, as that means, among other things, that they have no social media or DMV records.

Moving on from the mystery of their identities, I take a closer look at the strange weapons in their hands. They're reminiscent of Nerf guns.

As though they rehearsed the most efficient way to storm out of the elevator, the group of Suits heads toward the corridor leading to my waiting room.

I mentally blink, but the camera view doesn't change, and people in suits are still rushing down the corridor, out of view.

Jean is done reloading and points his gun at the wall. He must think it's the room's entrance, but he's about twenty-five degrees off.

"Jean!" I scream in his ear.

The big man doesn't flinch, so I grab his arm to redirect his aim.

My world explodes again, but I fight to stay conscious, understanding what just happened. Blind and confused, Jean must have mistaken me for a bad guy and elbowed me in the face.

I slide down the wall and cradle my poor head in my hands, unable to peel my secondary gaze from the two camera views.

The last attacker, Cristiano, runs into the room and fires at Jean. Jeans shoots where he was aiming, at the wall, and misses Cristiano.

Cristiano fires another shot, and Jean falls on top of me.

Cristiano approaches. I think he intends to push Jean off me and put a few bullets in my head.

Even if I had the strength to grab for Jean's gun, it's way out of my reach.

I realize this is a situation when the brain boost can play a cruel trick on me and make my last moments feel subjectively longer. I debate saying goodbye to Mitya and Ada, but decide against it. Ada might do something crazy, like rush back in. Instead, I take a moment to check on Mr. Spock and find him still alive, though deaf and blind like me. He's managing something I thought was impossible.

He's even more frightened than I am.

"Slide into my pants and hide behind my leg," I order Mr. Spock through the EmoRat app. "If he shoots me in the chest, he might hit *you*."

Cristiano is in the middle of the room when I see the first suited figure walk in. The suited man raises the weird weapon—a Taser.

Unaware of the people behind him, Cristiano takes careful aim at me, his features impassive, like he's about to snap a picture of me with his phone. His finger twitches on the trigger—and the tallest Suit shoots.

Cristiano convulses and collapses to the ground. One of the medical personnel runs up to the fallen Cristiano and injects him.

A square-shouldered Suit approaches the pile that is Jean and me and aims his Taser at my exposed leg.

"No—" I try to scream, but the weapon's sharp prongs reach me and my whole body convulses. Every muscle gets jolted and paralyzed at the same time.

I barely register the guy with the syringe come up to me and prick my flesh in the same careless fashion as he did with Cristiano a moment ago. For some reason, my biggest concern is whether he used a different syringe and needle.

"Did you see all this?" I frantically write to Mitya. "What the hell is going on?"

"No idea." Mitya's reply is equally panicked. "But the Tasers imply they want you alive."

I glance at the camera view where Joe is fighting for his life. No people in suits have interfered on my cousin's behalf. It's hard to tell whether that's good news, but at least he's still alive and fighting.

"Hide from them," I order Mr. Spock, who's managed to crawl down my right pant leg as I instructed. "If you can—"

I don't finish my mental command to Mr. Spock. Whatever the injection was, its effects reach my brain, and the cloud extensions can't help me stay awake any longer.

My world fades to black.

CHAPTER SIXTEEN

"You have been unconscious for twenty-six minutes," Einstein reports somewhere in my bleary mind. "Current time is 6:48 p.m."

My whole body aches and pulses. I feel like a banana after it's been frozen and pulverized into one of Ada's smoothies. I seem to have regained my hearing, but what I hear—booming, whirling sounds like in the loudest circle of hell—makes no sense.

I open my eyes, and I'm glad to learn that, like my ears, they work again. Taking in my surroundings, I realize where I am.

I'm in a large helicopter, the source of that noise.

"He's awake," I hear someone say from behind me.

"Then what are you waiting for?" says a square-shouldered Suit and waves his vein-crossed hand in my general direction. "Put him back under."

"Wait—" I attempt to say, but burning warmth spreads into my arm, and I descend back into the abyss of unconsciousness.

I wake up, but since opening my eyes caused me to get knocked out the last time, I decide to get my bearings before I show anyone I'm awake.

It takes me less than a heartbeat to realize something is terribly wrong.

Actually, many things are wrong, but the biggest issue is my state of mind. I can barely form a coherent thought.

At first, I think my mental handicap is from the concussion the stun grenade gave me and the drugs the Suits pumped me with, but I soon determine that the truth is more horrifying.

I have no access to the internet.

Frantically, I launch one AROS app after another, and all of the network-reliant ones, a large majority, report connectivity errors.

Eyes still closed and determined not to panic, I launch the Muhomor app to jump onto a Wi-Fi network or, failing that, a cell network.

The app shows me the visual representations of two Wi-Fi networks and a number of faint Bluetooth connections from unknown devices (likely smartphones). When I try smelling for a tasty connection, I find that both Wi-Fi networks have the sulfur stench of high security that the app can't hope to penetrate.

One of the Wi-Fi networks has the option of entering a password, and I take a few guesses before giving up. Guessing would take a million years, and my failed login attempts might get detected after a couple more tries.

Panic sets in.

Concussed, drugged, and without the brain boost, I feel like I've smoked a few pounds of pot, drank a gallon of vodka, and then received a botched lobotomy. If I could magically inhabit my four-year-old brain, this is probably what it would feel like.

Cringing mentally, I try to hack the foul Wi-Fi connections, knowing full well it won't work. Muhomor's app makes the experience extra disgusting before informing me of "penetration failure"—an error text that would usually make me chuckle but isn't even remotely funny now.

Desperate, I tackle the Bluetooth connections one by one. Failure follows another failure until I discover the faint smell of a familiar phone connection.

Its taste confirms my suspicions.

It's my phone, Precious 3, but it's almost out of range. Being a Class 1 Bluetooth device (a rarity for smartphones), Precious 3 has a transmit power of 100 mW, giving it a rather impressive range of 328 feet—a lesson I recall from Muhomor's diatribe into the often overlooked topic of Bluetooth security. As he put it, most people think Bluetooth is safe because of its short range. It's often true, but not always, and it looks like whoever is holding me prisoner underestimated my phone's capabilities, or more likely, they don't know I can connect with my phone.

With my connection to Precious 3 established, I enable the phone's hotspot feature and brace for the cellular internet connection. It's less than ideal, but better than nothing.

The boost doesn't happen.

I check the phone stats and see it's also outside cell-tower range. Perhaps whoever has me isn't so stupid after all.

After I triple and quadruple check that there's no way to get online with the phone, I try to use it to gather intelligence and create an AROS screen that gives me a view through my phone's front camera. The screen is black, so I try the back camera in case the phone is lying face down. The back camera works better, and I see a boring cement wall. The only interesting detail is an air duct, adding to my growing impression that I'm somewhere underground. I see the battery on the phone is full and realize I got lucky that it's lying face down, with the solar charger on the back facing the industrial halogen lamp.

"You're awake," a man says. His tone reminds me of a jaded customer service representative who's trying to sound friendly but would rather stab his ears with a pencil than talk to yet another person on the phone. "No need to pretend."

I open my eyes and see that the voice belongs to that square-shouldered Suit I saw earlier. Only now, for whatever reason, he's wearing aviator sunglasses in this poorly lit, windowless room.

Stifling a fresh jolt of panic, I examine my surroundings and find blank concrete on all sides, further corroborating my underground bunker idea. That could explain the lack of cell service.

"Where am I?" I attempt to ask, but something unintelligible and hoarse comes out. It feels like my throat is filled with cheap kitty litter sand. "Who are you?"

"He might be too weak for a conversation," says a man whose face is covered by a surgical mask.

"You're done here, Doc," says the Suit. "Someone will come get you when it's time."

Doc's eyes glint with mild disapproval, but he listens to the Suit and leaves.

I try to lift my hands to scratch the tip of my nose but find that my wrists are restrained by leather straps attached to the sides of the hospital gurney. I also note that I'm wearing a drab hospital gown. There's an IV in my arm, explaining the painful gnawing in the back of my hand. In general, I feel a symphony of pain and discomforts. Some are strange—like the really weird feeling in one of my most private parts.

"I'm glad you're awake, Mr. Cohen," the Suit says in that same falsely cordial tone. "I'm Special Agent Lancaster."

He takes out his ID and shows it to me—but so briefly that I don't get a chance to see what agency he's with, if any. Not that it matters whether I get a good look at the ID, since those things can be falsified. I do weigh his claim that he's with the government against what I know so far. I was inside a helicopter, and the fact that he isn't in any facial recognition databases does suggest this is something government-related and clandestine. Who else would have the resources to remove people from every facial recognition database?

"Okay, why did you kidnap me, Mr. Lancaster?" I ask, fighting to sound calm while my sluggish brain tries to figure out the answer to my own question. It comes up with a vague list of conspiracy theories that includes my adventures in Russia at the top and Brainocyte technology in general at the bottom. I long for the brain boost like never before. I bet if I had it, I'd know what these people want from me.

If neurogenesis made my biological brain any nimbler, I don't feel that at all.

"We didn't kidnap you. We saved your life." Lancaster's fake niceness springs a small crack. "And it's Agent Lancaster."

A surge of anger chases away my anxiety, clearing some of the fog from my brain. Since I'm connected to my phone, I begin recording our conversation to Precious's local disk. This way, I can replay this exchange and look for extra clues at my leisure when I have my brain boost enabled.

"Okay, *Agent* Lancaster," I say, emphasizing his title. "Let's review the facts, shall we? I'm tied to a bed." I demonstratively yank on the straps. "I wasn't read my rights. I have no clue where I am. Given our interaction so far, I choose to call this a kidnapping."

"This is a place where you can be safe," the agent says and cracks his knuckles with a disgusting pop—a gesture I find vaguely threatening. "As you no doubt noticed in that hospital, dangerous people tried to kill you. If we hadn't intervened, you would be dead. I thought you'd be more appreciative of *these* facts."

"Well, thank you for saving me," I begin and realize what the odd sensation in my private parts is. They stuck a catheter into my bladder. It's one of my worst nightmares, nearly as dreadful as being in a room without internet. Gritting my teeth, I finish with, "Now I'd like to be seen by my own doctor, in a hospital of my choosing."

I'm about to mention my lack of clothes, when I realize I've been the most selfish rat owner ever. While worrying about myself, I completely forgot about Mr. Spock. I last recall him hiding inside my pants. Now he's missing—as are my pants. I bring up the EmoRat app, and it gives me an error code that states, "Unable to establish contact with sweetums." If I wasn't terrified for Mr. Spock's life and my own, I'd probably chuckle at Ada's error message, but as is, I fall into deeper despair, my stomach knotting with anxiety once more.

"I'm afraid that leaving isn't safe," Agent Lancaster says without a hint of genuine regret in his tone. "This is the only way we can make sure you're not attacked again. Also, the doctors tell me you're in no condition to go anywhere."

My molars grind together again. "I don't feel too safe. But I am feeling well enough to go, so please let me go."

"You're on pain medication," the agent says. "Otherwise, you wouldn't be so eager to get on your feet."

The mention of medication prompts me to mentally ask Einstein for a report on the contents of my blood. He's the way I interface with the "lab on the chip" imbedded under my skin. Of course, Einstein requires connectivity, so I instantly get an error message.

"I walked out of a hospital after a car accident," I tell Lancaster, trying not to cringe at the memory. A sign of weakness wouldn't help my case, so I make my face expressionless as I say, "For that matter, even after getting into a car accident, the hospital didn't find the need to take the draconian measures you've taken. Why the catheter? Why can't I pee on my own?"

The agent's lack of expression matches mine. "If you leave, you'll die. I'm sure you're aware that Vincent Williams will never forget the death of his brother."

"You're well informed." My eyes narrow. "Maybe too well informed. How do I know you didn't hire Vincent Williams to attack me in the first place?"

"Come now, Mr. Cohen." Agent Lancaster pushes his shades higher on his nose with his middle finger in a flip-off gesture that may or may not be inadvertent. "According to your dossier, you're supposed to be a smart man."

A dossier? My hands tighten into fists. "Right. I'm smart enough to know you got me here for a reason that has nothing to do with my health or safety. Smart enough to have noticed your surveillance a while ago. We both know you've been following me for months before the attack."

The words burst out of me before I even realize the truth of them. Once I say it, though, I know I'm right. These guys must've been following me around. They grabbed me when they thought I was about to get killed before they could learn whatever it is they want to learn from me. Or, more likely, they grabbed me after Vincent Williams, a goon they hired, scared me enough to cooperate with my "saviors." Because if they aren't behind Williams, why didn't they assist me during the attack at the restaurant? Were they having a change in surveillance shifts or something?

My headache intensifies as my world paradigm realigns, and I fully consider the reality of being spied upon. All the paranoia I thought was irrational wasn't. To paraphrase the popular saying, you're not paranoid if some shady government organization really *is* out to get you. Thanks to the brain boost, on some level, I must've known these guys were surveilling me. Gogi didn't believe me because he isn't enhanced, and they must not have been following Ada. That might be a clue. Then again, maybe they did follow Ada, and she might be less observant than I am, even with a boost. Or perhaps I noticed my surveillance because I *am* more prone to paranoia. I decide to later look up if paranoia correlates with being more observant.

Agent Lancaster takes off his aviator glasses and looks at me with gray eyes that eerily match the naked slabs of concrete behind him. "Since you brought it up, why don't we start with that? How did you know about our surveillance?"

I can see this bothers him more than he's letting on. I guess he has a high opinion of his organization's tradecraft, and my claim that I spotted them doesn't fit neatly with his ego.

"What do *you* think? What's the likeliest answer to that question?" I'm hoping he comes up with some kind of theory, because truthfully, I have no idea. Besides my vague paranoia, all I had were bad dreams featuring people in suits.

"None of the likely scenarios are possible." For the first time, anger openly appears on his face, and I wonder if it's a good idea to get him angry while I'm in such a vulnerable position. "I handpicked every person on this task force."

Now I understand why he's so pissed. His worst nightmare is probably having a double agent working for him. At the risk of making him angrier, I decide to pursue this idea, seeing a chance to probe him for critical information. "You picked them, yet it looks like you have a rat in your midst."

I choose my words carefully, figuring if they have Mr. Spock, he might reveal that upon hearing the word "rat."

I know the actual expression features a mole rather than a rat, but the agent understood me fine, as evidenced by the tension in his jaw. After a moment, however, the anger leaves Agent Lancaster's face. He's either a good poker player, or he considered the idea of a double agent and decided it couldn't be the case. Or he figured if there is a traitor on his team, someone I know about, I wouldn't tell him about it so openly. I think about pointing out that I could be double bluffing, but I opt instead to watch him quietly and not think about the uncomfortable tube inside my penis.

"You're just a paranoid guy who got lucky," the agent says, reaching the correct conclusion. "That's all that was."

I breathe a small sigh of relief that he didn't mention any actual rats and focus back on the issue at hand.

"I notice you didn't deny the surveillance," I say, attempting to stare him down. I can only hold his gaze for a few moments before I get the urge to look away. "Was it legal for you to follow me around all this time? Did you have a court order? For that matter, why on Earth were you following me?"

His eyes narrow to icy slits. "You don't want to have an adversarial relationship with me, trust me."

"So now you're threatening me," I say, wishing I felt as brave as I sounded. "I'd like to go on record. I want my lawyer present. I want to make a phone call. I don't want to be here, and you have no right to keep me." My voice rises as righteous anger grips me again. "If I'm guilty of a crime, then tell me what it is. I want—"

"I need you to calm down." Lancaster's words are clipped. I spot his fists clenching and unclenching at his sides and realize again I'm yelling at a guy who has me at his complete mercy.

I hear beeping from the device that's monitoring my heartbeat, which means I'm not imagining the pounding pulse in my ears. Losing my cool is a bad idea, so I activate the BraveChill app—which doesn't work for the same reason as most of the others. Forcing myself to take deep breaths, I mentally curse the server client architecture design we chose. It makes logical sense to do the heavy-duty computations on remote servers, but I'd give anything to be able to do this stuff in my head.

"Look," I say when my breathing steadies a bit. "It's hard to calm down when someone ties you to a bed and shoves needles and tubes into your orifices."

"I understand, but your best course of action is to cooperate." Lancaster's tone goes back to fake friendliness and concern.

"Answer my questions, untie me, and get me a lawyer, and I'll think about cooperating."

His friendly mask slips. "You're in no position to make demands."

"A US citizen is always in a position to ask for a lawyer. And I'm asking."

"Cooperate, and then we'll talk about lawyers."

I stare at him, and he stares back at me.

"I want a phone call and a lawyer," I say again. "I'm not cooperating until I get that."

"No? We'll see." He turns and walks to the door.

"Wait," I yell, and though I know he can hear me, he shows no sign of it as he strides toward the exit. "Don't leave. I really need to go to the bathroom."

He ignores me, and I find myself alone in the room.

If Lancaster's goal was to rattle me, he succeeded spectacularly. Though I knew I was in an awful situation, being left alone like this is infinitely worse.

It makes me realize just how screwed I am.

CHAPTER SEVENTEEN

In case there's a microphone in the room, I proceed to yell obscenities at Agent Lancaster until my throat gets scratchy and I feel overwhelming thirst.

Then I yank at the restraints, but all that does is give my wrists a nasty rope burn.

Ignoring the pain, I try talking politely this time, emphasizing the whole bathroom issue as a priority, but to no avail.

What's really annoying is that, unlike movie heroes who lie about their bathroom needs to aid in their escape, I genuinely have to go. Though nauseatingly unpleasant, the catheter takes care of me needing to do number one, but it does nothing for the more and more urgent call of number two.

My panic builds, and under my breath, I curse Ada's high-fiber diet for leading to this situation. Then I channel the negativity where it belongs and curse Agent Lancaster some more—but mentally this time.

For a few minutes, I distract myself with violent revenge fantasies of what I'd do to Agent Lancaster if I got the chance. It makes me wonder if I could wind up as bloodthirsty as Joe if pushed too far.

My stomach cramps, and I strongly consider yelling about cooperation, but I can't bring myself to do it. My anger at being put in this situation feeds something stubborn in me, something I didn't even know I had.

I also realize the aches I was feeling have evolved into pains. I recall Agent Lancaster mentioning pain medicine. Could I be due for another dose?

To distract myself, I decide to check on my blood contents via the lab on the chip in my body. When Mitya originally made Einstein work with this technology, I pair coded with him and saw how he used the special API that gives direct access to the chip's outputs.

Loading the AROS IDE, I begin coding.

Coding without a brain boost is *much* harder than I ever imagined, especially with the distraction of pain, my growing hunger, and the overwhelming need to use the bathroom. The app I want to put together is completely no frills—just a little screen that will show the findings of the micro-laboratory in plain text. Given all my handicaps, what would have been a ten-minute project takes me what feels like two hours.

The good news is that the coding effort somewhat distracts me from my troubles. The bad news is what I learn upon completing the project. There are indeed small traces of oxycodone and acetaminophen in my blood. That means they gave me some Percocet—a drug consisting of that combo. The last time I used this pain medicine, it worked on me for about four hours before I needed another dose, but that was when I was dealing with a toothache. Assuming they gave me the dose in the helicopter when Einstein told me it was 6:48 p.m., and since it's now 11:20 p.m. according to Precious 3, I need another dose. Otherwise, I'll be in worse pain soon. I guess the pain might be part of the point Agent Lancaster is trying to make.

What's even worse is that I also have bisacodyl in my blood. Bisacodyl is a laxative that the doctors gave my mom after her accident, and its presence in my blood means one of two things. Option one, my captors are genuinely worried about me having constipation as a side effect from Percocet. When I took Percocet for that toothache, I *did* experience constipation. Option two, the likelier one, is that they're using the pretext of option one to engineer a deeply humiliating situation for me.

Determined not to give the bastards the satisfaction of seeing me squirm, I try to think of some solutions. One simple idea arrives right away. It's nighttime, so I could try sleeping. Hopefully, the bisacodyl can't do its job while I'm unconscious, but even if it does, at least I won't be aware of it happening.

I close my eyes and do my best to even out my breathing.

My eyelids grow heavy, and I'm gladly slipping into oblivion when a brain-shattering noise jolts me awake.

I cringe and curse the bindings for preventing me from cupping my ears. The hellish noise sounds like a giant is drilling through a mountain. To my concussed brain, this experience is similar to having a chainsaw buzzing inside my head.

"Stop," I yell with my exhausted vocal cords. "I won't sleep if you don't want me to."

The noise doesn't stop.

They're purposely torturing me. I realize that now. This drilling is to stop me from sleeping—not so different from the infamous "enhanced interrogation techniques" used on terrorists. Lancaster claims he's a government agent, and he let slip that he's part of a task force. Is the government allowed to torture civilians? Or is this treatment a sign that forces more sinister than Uncle Sam are holding me captive? For all I know, Russian KGB/SVR might have me because they want the Brainocyte technology—or as payback for what happened in Russia a few months ago. If that's true, I might never want to cooperate, since the SVR wouldn't keep me around after I told them whatever it is they need to know. Alternatively, could these people be a part of some private organization? Could my half-brother be doing this to me because he learned of my role in our deceased father's fate?

On second thought, a Russian connection is kind of a long shot. They had that helicopter—something too high-profile for an intelligence organization from another nation. Lancaster's English is flawless, and he's either an award-winning actor or really a government agent. It's possible that torture is allowed under certain anti-terrorism laws, or else they have plausible deniability for everything. They could say, "Well, he was hurt, so we had to provide medical help, and we had to use the catheter and everything else. He was in danger, so we hid him from his foes. Cell phone signals are crappy in our hideout, so we couldn't let him call his lawyer—or anyone. Oh, and we had to do some last-minute construction work around our secret lair, hence the drilling from hell."

Remembering the drilling brings me violently back into the present, and before I recall how bad of an idea it is, I throw up. Lucky for me, I just dry-heave. Having no food in my stomach is at least good for something.

Acting almost on instinct, I start the Music app in my head and bless the day I decided it should have a feature to play music from my phone on top of playing music from my cloud collection. Unfortunately, my phone's music library is all workout music. I set it up this way so I could hook my phone up to the dojo's speaker system on the days Gogi felt like fighting to music. The shuffle feature gives me a song called "One" by Metallica, and the guitar riffs completely mask the drilling noise, as Brainocytes deliver sound directly to my brain, overruling input from my ears. Though this song is infinitely preferable to the drilling, the irony is that this kind of music was used as an enhanced interrogation technique that involved loud bursts of metal music, including songs by Metallica. The key difference is that I like this music and I feel more in control, given that I can change the song if I feel like it or return to the drilling sounds if I start to feel masochistic. The effect is the same as what my captors intended, though.

I can forget about sleep.

After an hour, the lab on the chip informs me all traces of pain meds are out of my system—something I already knew based on how much the pain has worsened. The bisacodyl is still there and working, though, and out of all the hurts, my stomach is the worst. It feels like a creature from *Alien* is slowly growing inside me, preparing to burst out.

I kill some time by figuring out if I can write something that will work like the Relief app. Though Brainocytes don't have the computing power to run an app so complex, maybe I can use Precious 3's hardware to do the heavy lifting? Thinking about it more, I see two insurmountable issues. First, without the brain boost, I'm less capable as a programmer, and this kind of app will require finesse. Second, and this is more critical, I lack the resources to guide me when it comes to affecting the right parts of the brain in the correct way. I could easily end up stimulating the pain center of my brain, or give myself seizures.

Oh well, at least thinking about the app distracted me for a few minutes and briefly gave me the illusion that I had some control over my fate.

After another half hour of stomach agony, I wonder how bad it would be if I relieved myself right here in the bed. I mean, yes, it would be disgusting beyond belief and humiliating, but it should make the cramps from hell go away and hopefully make it unpleasant for Lancaster to be in the room with me when he comes back.

I remain strong for another hour before my body takes the decision out of my hands and the inevitable happens.

Babies cry when they do this to themselves, and I totally understand why. It's an extremely unpleasant set of sensations, both physically and emotionally. I'm on the verge of shedding a few tears fueled by self-pity, but I don't want to give Agent Lancaster the satisfaction of thinking this treatment broke me. In fact, if Lancaster's idea was to damage my will so I would start babbling information at his whim, I feel like he accomplished the reverse. I find solace in my anger, and it makes me resolved to not utter a single word when the asshole inevitably returns to speak to me again.

To stay semi-sane, I replicate my phone's screen in a big AROS window and launch the Chess app. With the brain boost, beating the in-game AI was so easy I gave this app a low rating in the app store after I first installed it. In my current state, the game gets its revenge as it defeats me twice in a row. My only excuse for losing is that thinking while in pain and trying not to breathe air is as difficult as it sounds.

I'm halfway through another match when the door opens and Agent Lancaster strides in.

I turn off the music blazing in my mind and find that the drilling sound is gone. The quietude envelops my ears with pure pleasure—until Agent Lancaster steps up to me and ruins it by speaking.

"Hello again, Mr. Cohen," the object of my hatred says. "I hope we can have an adult conversation this time."

CHAPTER EIGHTEEN

Though I'm thirsty and my mouth is dry, I somehow gather enough saliva to spit at Agent Lancaster. The spittle flies across the distance between us and hits him square in the eye—a lucky shot.

The agent leaps forward and slaps me across the face. The sting is sharp, and my eyes water.

However, having him hit me is inspiring. It makes my boiling anger turn into a plan that might allow me to get even. Before I fully formulate the plan or get a chance to put it into motion, I see Agent Lancaster's face contort from anger to confusion to disgust. He must've registered the smell, and maybe he thinks he smells my reaction to his bitch slap. Does he think I'm such a weak coward? I sure hope so, because that would aid my half-formed plan.

Before I can blink, Lancaster storms out of the room and slams the heavy door shut with enough force to break a weaker doorframe. I wonder if he's upset with himself for reacting so strongly to my provocation or if he's that pissed at me. The second option would be bad for my newly hatched plan.

The plan is simple. I'll pretend to cooperate enough to get them to take off the restraints, and then, when I get the chance, I'll attack Lancaster and attempt to damage him using the skills Gogi taught me. Yes, it won't allow me to escape this place, and it'll probably lead to worse treatment, but it'll give me the satisfaction of revenge that I desperately crave. Of course, part of me knows I'll be much more comfortable in the interim as I go through the pretense, and an even more skeptical part of me worries that I've rationalized genuine cooperation under the guise of fake one.

I'm dead tired, but I don't dare close my eyes for fear that they'll turn the buzzing on again. I'm enjoying the silence too much for that. I'm convinced Lancaster will retaliate against me for the spitting incident, and I hope I'll get the chance to convince him I'm ready to cooperate before that happens.

After what feels like many hours—though according to my phone, only twenty minutes have passed—the door opens again.

Two people wearing scrubs come inside. They're carrying a tray of objects I have trouble making out. Just like earlier, the medical people hide their faces behind surgical masks, and when I try to look them in the eye, they avoid my gaze.

The larger of the two holds a huge syringe to my neck and says in a deep male voice, "We're just here to wash you and make sure you don't starve. If you move a muscle, I'll be forced to use this." Matching actions to words, he pricks my skin with the giant needle.

The smaller person, probably a woman, undoes my right wrist restraint.

I clear my throat. "I won't fight, but can you please get me out of here? I'm being held against my will."

The people in scrubs ignore me, and the smaller one turns me over to clean me up.

I debate fighting them despite my promise, figuring if he knocks me out, it might make the washing less embarrassing. However, I decide to tough it out so it'll be more believable when I claim I'm ready to cooperate as part of my new plan.

When the humiliation is complete, the smaller person ties my hand back down and reaches for something on the tray.

"Don't move." The male's eyes dart from me to his partner as he gives a little nod. "We have one more thing we need to do."

The smaller one is holding a long tube in his or her hand and brings it closer to my face. I recall the guy saying something about making sure I don't starve and realize what it must be.

"Wait." My voice rises. "I'd rather starve."

"It's just a nasogastric tube," says the smaller one, her soft voice confirming that she's a woman. "You need food, and all other methods for getting it into you are more invasive."

"I can eat the fucking food with my mouth," I snap. This device, the NG tube, was installed in Mom's nose after her horrible accident, and I was horrified just seeing it done to someone else. When my words don't seem to have an effect, I yell, "I refuse this treatment! There's no medical necessity for it. None at all. You hear me? I don't want this thing!"

My raised voice is half for them and half for the benefit of a hypothetical listening device. The tube moves closer to my nose, and I squirm in place. The restraints leave burns on my wrists as I struggle. Blinding anger returns in full force, and without realizing what I'm saying, I scream, "I don't care how much you hide your faces! It won't help. I'll find out who you are, and I'll end your careers!"

That seems to discomfit the woman, but I realize I made a mistake if my plan was to maintain the pretense of cooperation.

"I think you should give him that shot," the woman says, though I see a glimmer of doubt and perhaps even sympathy in her eyes.

"Well, *I* think you should do your job," the man tells her sternly. To me, he says, "If you move around, the tube could go into your lungs, and that would cause a number of problems, not to mention you'll make the whole process more uncomfortable."

"Exhale," the woman says and sticks the tip of the tube into my left nostril.

Panicking, I loudly exhale as my heartbeat accelerates so fast the nearby monitoring equipment rings in alarm.

"Try to relax," she says and slowly inserts the tube into my nose.

At first, the feeling reminds me of getting water in my nose while also getting a giant brain freeze from a Slurpee, but multiplied a thousand-fold. Then a burning that feels like I'm snorting a pepper-spray-covered porcupine sears my sinuses.

"Don't move," she says, but it's too late. I pull my head away and rip the tube out of my nose, but even with it out, the burning is still there.

"Please, don't do that again," I croak. "Just tell Agent Lancaster I'm ready to tell him anything he wants."

The woman looks at the man, but he shakes his head.

"I'll try the other nostril," she says without looking at me. "Please, try not to pull it out this time."

Since I know what's about to happen, the dread of having it happen to my other nostril is impossibly worse than my original fear. She begins the insertion, and the process hurts worse than the first time. It takes all my willpower not to pull my head away.

The tube clears the back of my nose and spreads the burning downward into my throat. My gag reflex kicks in, and I can't take it anymore. In a swift motion, I pull my head away and rip the tube out of my nose—an action that hurts nearly as much as the insertion.

I know I can't handle another attempt. Like a cornered animal, I feel myself getting desperately dangerous. The woman must not realize my state, because her hands are still close to my face.

In a blur of motion, I crane my neck, jut my head forward, and sink my teeth into the woman's left pinky as hard as I can. The woman screams like a pig family during slaughter, but instead of letting go of her flesh, I clench my teeth so hard that my jaw spasms in pain.

At some point in the past, I heard an urban myth that a finger is as easy to bite through as a carrot. I now know that story is false. I can tell I won't be able to snap the finger in half as I originally intended, but at least I did a lot of damage to it.

I consider doing a zombie-like ripping motion with my head to further hurt the finger, but then I feel the needle go into my skin. The oblivion comes almost instantly, allowing one last thought—a hope that they'll insert the NG tube while I'm unconscious.

CHAPTER NINETEEN

I wake up but don't open my eyes, figuring I should get my bearings first.

According to Precious 3, it's 9:01 a.m. on November 16. I was out for eight hours. Despite getting the rest I was craving, I feel sleep deprived for some reason. Maybe the drug that induced my unconsciousness didn't provide any real sleep benefits?

I also feel new pains. My left eye is swollen. Someone, probably the woman I hurt, must've punched me in the face. Additionally, there's the most horrid sensation in my throat—the cursed tube. I try to swallow and instantly gag. Despite my conscious wishes, I try to swallow again, and it's just as unpleasant.

On the plus side—if it's even a plus—I don't feel any signs of hunger, so the tube has fulfilled that part of its purpose. It was used to deliver food into my stomach.

To relax, I try breathing slowly and evenly, hoping to forget about the obstacle in my throat, but I might as well be trying to forget my name.

"Are you awake, Mr. Cohen?" asks a new voice. "My name is Agent Pugh."

I open my eyes, and once they've adjusted to the light, I see a woman standing in front of me. She's wearing a pantsuit and holding one hand behind her back. Her face is extremely symmetrical, except her green eyes are much too big in proportion to her features. There's sympathy in her eyes as she says, "I work with Agent Lancaster, but he doesn't know I'm here."

Bullshit, I think to myself, but out loud, I croak, "Help me." The tube in my throat makes my attempt to talk extremely uncomfortable, and my eyes water to the point where she might think I'm crying.

"That's why I'm here." She takes out a napkin and wipes my face. "I'm here to help you."

I stare at her. It doesn't take a brain boost to understand what's happening. It's the oldest trick in the book—the good cop/bad cop routine.

"I'm uncomfortable with the way things have escalated," Agent Pugh says. If there were Oscars for government agents who could say rehearsed lines with proper regret, she'd at least get a nomination. "Please, work with me, and I'll get you more comfortable."

"What can I do?" I choke out, but I'm not sure she understood me with the gagging sounds coming out of my mouth.

"Just nod if you agree with me and shake your head if you don't," she says.

I nod to show I understand.

"I want to tell Agent Lancaster you're ready to cooperate," she says. "Would you like that?"

I nod vigorously.

"I also have news about your medical condition," she says. "When you were unconscious, we did some X-rays, and it appears you're intact."

"The tube," I gurgle out. What I mean is, "How do you expect me to talk with the tube?" as well as, "Why the hell is this tube in my nose if I'm intact?"

"Now that we got nutrients into your system, the tube will be removed," she says, her nose crinkling. "We'll also give you something for the pain, if that's okay with you."

I nod even more vigorously this time.

She moves her hand out from behind her back, and I see she's holding a syringe. Instead of sticking the needle into my skin, like the asshole in the mask did, she uses the IV that's already in my arm to deliver the medicine.

Warmth slowly spreads throughout my body, and I watch her leave the room as my vision blurs and I fall under.

———

I wake up feeling amazing. All the earlier pains and aches are gone, and when I try to swallow, I confirm that the tube is blissfully missing from my nose and throat.

My phone states that it's 11:05 a.m. on the 16th, so I was out for three hours this time.

Opening my eyes, I see I'm no longer in the window-less cement room. Someone sat me on a chair in a new location—a room that seems to have been modeled after the most stereotypical interrogation room you'd see in a police procedural show. I spot three gray walls and one mirrored wall, a chair, and a table. Instead of leather straps as before, standard-issue police handcuffs bind my hands. I guess someone did this out of a need to stay consistent with the new decor. There's even a glass of water on the table—out of my reach, as per the *Interrogation 101* handbook.

Hopeful, I search for a Wi-Fi network but find none.

"Hello, Mr. Cohen," says Agent Lancaster in his signature fake-friendly voice. His eyes are hidden behind his aviator sunglasses again, and his posture exudes calm confidence. "I'm glad you decided to cooperate."

"Hello," I say. Even with the pain meds, my throat is still sore from my earlier ordeal. Raising my handcuffed hands, I ask, "Is this really necessary?"

Instead of answering, Agent Lancaster slams a giant paper-filled folder on the desk in front of me and says, "Before we begin, I wanted to show you this." He opens the folder to a random page and pushes the whole mess toward me.

I look at the page in question and feel the hairs on the back of my neck rise. I remember this email. It's an email an investor sent me a couple of months ago—the one where he was thanking me for an outstanding quarter.

When he notices my reaction, Agent Lancaster flips the page, and I see a number of my emails. Some are from my personal account, including a very private email where

Ada asked me to get us more condoms for a romantic evening we had planned (Muhomor was testing Tema for us at that time and our Brainocyte traffic was not private).

Thankfully, I don't see any private texts or emails sent via Brainocytes. That would've meant that Agent Lancaster and his minions literally had access to our private thoughts. I wonder if our Brainocytes communications are somewhere else in that folder, but I doubt it. Before Tema was ready, Muhomor insisted we all get email and text accounts that couldn't be traced back to us, and he had us all get new accounts on an annoyingly regular basis. With Tema in place, he agreed to be more lax in the future.

"As you can see"—Lancaster's voice takes me out of my paranoid reverie—"we know a lot about you, Mr. Cohen." He closes the folder and moves it out of reach. "I'm only showing you this so you know a large majority of my questions will be about things I already have answers to. That means if you lie, I'll know it, and if I catch you in a single lie, no matter how small, our polite conversation will end." He leans across the desk and looks me in the eye. "Am I making myself clear?"

"Yes," I say, and it comes out too meekly for my liking. My earlier plan of pretending to cooperate might've suffered a major setback. I was, of course, planning to lie about everything just to spite the bastard, but now I have to be careful since I don't know what he knows.

"Good." Agent Lancaster sits back and steeples his fingers. "Let's start with an easy question first. How long have you been an agent for the Russian Federation?"

The question catches me so far off guard that for a few moments, I sit there, blinking at a rate of a hundred eyelid flops per second. I'd be less shocked if he'd slapped me in the face again.

"I'm not a Russian spy," I finally say, feeling dumb at having to say these words. The whole thing reminds me of having to deny something extremely obvious, like not being an invisible pink unicorn. "So, zero time."

Even as I say this, I realize how much trouble I might be in if he believes the accusation he made. I know very little about due process when it comes to captured spies. In movies, it doesn't look like habeas corpus. Do suspected spies get phone calls or lawyers? I imagine it would be dangerous to let them have those things since they could code a message to their handler through the phone, or the lawyer they use can help them kill themselves to prevent giving away state secrets.

"Come now, Mr. Cohen." Lancaster demonstratively massages his temples. "We know."

"If you indeed know, then you *know* I'm not a spy for any country, least of all Russia. Doesn't it say somewhere in there"—I point at the folder—"that I came to the US as a refugee? Or that I arrived at an age much too young to be recruited into the spy business?"

"I thought we agreed you'd cooperate." Agent Lancaster flips through the pages in his folder and stops on something he must like, because he pushes the image toward me.

I'm stunned. The image is blurry because someone took it with their phone inside a poorly lit nightclub, but I can tell it's a picture of me standing on a DJ's stage. It looks like I'm aiming a gun at the crowd, though in reality I was aiming at the goons who'd come to attack us.

"That was taken at the Dazdraperma club," Agent Lancaster says triumphantly. "In Moscow."

"That's me protecting myself *from* the KGB—err, I mean, SVR," I say, then realize I might have admitted to something my lawyer would've advised against. Weakly, I add, "That's the opposite of working for them."

"Sure." Agent Lancaster's tone is dripping with sarcasm. "All venture capitalists are known to take little trips to participate in shootouts in Moscow."

"I was saving my mother," I retort. "Her kidnapping was in the newspapers. She wasn't the only person I saved. There are a dozen American citizens you can interview."

"You mean those handicapped Americans whose brains are being manipulated by the technology you created?" He rubs his temples again. "I can see this isn't going anywhere."

There's a small silver lining to what he said. He didn't refer to the Brainocytes by their proper name—something I'd expect him to do if he was interested in the technology. Then again, if he doesn't want the Brainocytes, I can't think of what else he might want.

If he truly believes I'm a spy, that would be really bad.

"Look." I fight the temptation to get up and start pacing the room. "How can I prove I'm not a spy?"

"You can't prove you're not a spy because you are one," Lancaster says. "But if you're useful enough, we could overlook your other indiscretions."

I already miss the brain boost with a passion, and right now, I'd pay a million dollars for a few seconds on the internet. Though thinking is difficult without the boost, I'm beginning to feel like I'm being skillfully manipulated. Agent Lancaster might be accusing me of being a spy as an interrogation technique. I've seen it used in shows. The detectives will often mention a murder or something big to get suspects to admit to a smaller crime. At least I hope that's what's going on. Unfortunately, if the purpose of this technique is to make me scared enough to tell them whatever they want, it's working spectacularly well.

"I'm as much of a spy as I am a ballerina," I reply, though my bravado sounds hollow, even to my own ears. "You want something. I get that. Just come out and say what it is."

"Fine." He removes his aviator sunglasses and looks at me with his colorless eyes. "In that case, let's talk about Viktor Tsoi."

I repeat the bit where I blink at him repeatedly and then vow to perfect my poker-face reaction to strange questions and behaviors in the future. Viktor Tsoi is the name of a famous Russian rock singer who tragically died in a car crash at twenty-eight. True, I love his songs even to this day, but I fail to see why Agent Lancaster would be interested in him, so I ask, "And why are we discussing Russian music?" He looks confused for a moment, so I add, "Viktor Tsoi was a songwriter and singer. He's dead."

"In case you don't know," Lancaster says in the tone of someone who's sure I'm just messing with him, "Viktor Tsoi is the name of a man who is very much alive." He opens his folder to a new page and hands me a picture of Muhomor and me sitting in a downtown café. The picture was clearly taken during last month's Brainocytes Club meeting. "Viktor Tsoi goes under the hacker alias 'Muhomor.'"

CHAPTER TWENTY

Things become instantly clearer, to the point where I'd smack my forehead if my hands were free. Of course this misadventure is connected to Muhomor. If I weren't so worried about Muhomor's life, I'd want to kill him. As is, I channel my anger at the agent in front of me instead. But seriously, how many times have I told Muhomor to cool it with the hacking? Now something he did got me into this situation. I really hope we both survive our ordeals so I can properly express my displeasure toward the skinny hacker.

Since the agent is still waiting for an answer, I say, "I genuinely didn't know that was Muhomor's real name. Now that I know Viktor Tsoi is his name, I'm not surprised he goes by a nickname. Muhomor loves his individuality, and his celebrity namesake was as famous as Elvis Presley." The agent doesn't look impressed by my disclosures, so I add hastily, "I'd be glad to talk to you about Muhomor.

Why don't we start with his current medical condition? Is he alive? How did his surgery go?"

I expect Agent Lancaster to answer with the cliché, "I'm the one asking questions," or something along those lines, but he surprises me by saying, "Muhomor is alive but in a coma." There's a dose of genuine regret in his voice, though I can't tell if he's upset that Muhomor is alive or that they can't question him because he's in a coma. "His spinal injury was severe."

The ache in my chest returns in full force, and I instinctively try pinging Muhomor with the Telepathy app. The error message is a painful reminder that I can't get in touch with him or anyone else.

"Look." I take a deep breath and let it out. "Agent Lancaster, if Muhomor is in a coma, he isn't a threat. Why all this?" I raise my handcuffed hands, and the chains clink against the table.

"The situation is more complicated than that." Lancaster rubs the stubble on his dimpled chin. "As you well know."

"I honestly don't," I say in confusion.

"All this"—he waves his hand around the interrogation room—"had to be escalated because you all nearly got yourselves killed."

"Or you nearly got us killed as a way to pressure me to speak," I reply, though I now wonder if it would be logical for Lancaster and his minions to hire Vincent Williams to come after us. After all, if they're interested in Muhomor, killing him or putting him in a coma is a really bad plan— assuming he *is* in a coma, as Lancaster claimed.

"I thought we had an understanding." The agent's jaw tenses, and he puts his glasses back on—but not before I gleam the anger in his eyes. "If you need more time to think…"

I know that "time to think" is a euphemism for more torture, and the threat sends a wave of anxiety through me. However, my pent-up anger swiftly overrides it.

"We do have an understanding," I say and do my best to look scared rather than pissed off. Perversely, I'm annoyed at how well I manage to sound meek, but I continue my performance by having my voice crack as I add, "I'll tell you what you want to know. I really don't want any more time to think."

"Tell me about Muhomor's recent hacks." Agent Lancaster's tone is patronizingly soothing. "In as much detail as possible."

"He penetrated the IARPA systems," I say. Though it feels shitty betraying my friend's confidence, I'm sure I'm telling Lancaster something he already knows, so I look at this revelation as a necessary evil to earn the agent's trust. "IARPA was working on a project to reverse engineer the algorithms that run the human brain. Muhomor was interested in the research."

Agent Lancaster must be an excellent poker player, because he betrays no clues as to what he thinks of my statement. Since he's waiting for me to continue, I say, "Prior to that, he hacked into the Verizon servers to gain free cell phone service."

What actually happened is that Muhomor hacked into Sprint's servers, but I added that small discrepancy on purpose to see how detailed Agent Lancaster's knowledge is.

The man slightly turns toward the mirror to his left, and his hand almost goes to his ear before he stops himself. Did someone feed him information on Sprint versus Verizon? Was it someone behind that mirror?

"Are you sure it was Verizon?" Agent Lancaster interlaces his fingers in front of his face and stretches his arms out. "Details are important."

"I'm sorry," I lie. "It was one of the major ones. I thought it was Verizon, but it could have been AT&T or perhaps Sprint?"

The fact we're being watched limits my new plan to attack him when I can.

"What are the Qecho servers?" he asks.

If he wanted to catch me off guard, he failed.

"A 100-qubit quantum computer," I reply right away. "Muhomor likes to use it."

"What does he use it for?" This question comes out faster and more forcefully.

"Encryption and decryption. But I bet you already knew that."

"What's Tema?" The intensity in Agent Lancaster's voice is now set to eleven out of ten. "How does it work?"

I'm not at all surprised at the direction this conversation has taken. The moment the agent brought up Muhomor, I suspected he would ask about Tema—Muhomor's unbreakable cryptosystem. Out of everything the Russian hacker has done, Tema is the epitome of what would get on a government's radar. Muhomor said so himself many times, but I always thought there was a dose of self-aggrandizement in my friend's rhetoric. He claimed that governments rely on reading everyone's communications at will and that his unbreakable cryptosystem would revolutionize the world, because Tema is impervious to attacks by quantum computers, unlike most "legacy" cryptosystems that rely on multiplying large primes. Looks like Muhomor was right on every count.

When the government can't crack your messages, they do indeed get upset.

The biggest problem with this is that I can't help Lancaster even if I wanted to. I barely understand the basic principles behind Tema with the aid of the brain boost, and right now, it might as well involve magic as far as my understanding goes. Worse, Agent Lancaster probably wants to know how to break Tema and won't believe me if I tell him that the most powerful minds in the world haven't been able to break Muhomor's new baby, leading us all to believe that the thing is unbreakable.

"Tema is short for the Russian word 'kryptosystema,'" I begin. "It's a cryptosystem Muhomor invented. He thinks it's unbreakable." I'm tempted to add, "Given my presence here, I take it he was right."

"How does it work?" If Agent Lancaster wanted to hide the importance of this question, he certainly failed. His whole body tenses, making him look like a jaguar preparing to leap at a deer.

"It's complicated," I say as earnestly as possible since the next part of my plan depends on this. "Do you have paper and something to write with? I'll do my best to break it down for you."

Without hesitation, Lancaster takes out a fancy pen from his inner jacket pocket and hands it to me. He then takes a couple of pages out of the thick folder and says, "You can write on the back of those."

I take the pencil in my right hand and write as clumsily as I can. As I hoped, even without the pretense, the handcuffs make writing difficult.

"I think this would go a lot better if I didn't have these on." I jiggle the handcuffs and try not to look too eager.

Agent Lancaster betrays his excitement again by getting up and walking over to my side of the table. Heart drumming, I watch him take out a key and undo the cuffs.

As soon as my hands are free, everything around me comes into focus to the point where I momentarily feel as though I've regained internet access and my brain boost. In less than a blink, I relive the moment Agent Lancaster slapped me in the face and the indignity and pain I suffered while strapped down in that cement room. The awful recollections culminate in the memory of that feeding tube going into my nose, and my slow-boiling anger explodes with the force of Vesuvius.

My left hand forms into a fist, and I punch Agent Lancaster in the crotch—a move made easy by his current stance. Something soft crunches under my knuckles, and I almost feel male sympathy for my enemy.

Almost, but not quite.

A grunt escapes Lancaster's lips, and he begins to double over.

Then again, maybe he isn't doubling over. His hand is balled into a fist, and I suspect he's planning to hit me back.

I turn my head, and his fist whooshes past my right ear. I grip the pen in my right hand and randomly stab the source of my angst in his quickly approaching face.

The aviator glasses fly into the mirrored glass on the right wall, and the pen tip enters his eye with a stomach-twisting squishy noise.

Agent Lancaster's scream is inhuman, and I gape in horrified trance at the damage I just wreaked. Again, more thoughts than normal swoosh through my mind, the main one being a conviction that my usual PTSD nightmares will expand to include this scene—assuming I ever get to sleep again.

To his credit, despite the agony he must be in, my enemy uses my hesitation to reach into his jacket for what I assume is his weapon.

If I survive the next moment, I'll have to build Gogi a statue for all the disarming drills he had me do. I leap to my feet, and my hands move with practiced confidence. As soon as I see the gun gleam in the halogen light, I twist Lancaster's right wrist, and the gun clanks against the table before falling onto the chair and then hitting the floor with a metallic, tile-cracking sound. Continuing almost on autopilot, I put my foot behind my opponent and push him.

As Agent Lancaster's body flies into the mirror, I hear the door behind me crack open.

I leap for the gun.

In the mirror, I catch a glimpse of someone wearing SWAT gear, but I still hold a glimmer of hope. Maybe I can get the gun and somehow shoot my way out of this mess.

Unfortunately, the harsh reality of this universe doesn't comply with my hopes. Something bites painfully at my right shoulder. The impact is too mild to be a bullet, though. The prongs of a Taser, perhaps?

I grab the Glock's handle and begin to pivot, ready to aim. But before I'm even halfway facing my opponent, fifty thousand volts spread through every muscle in my body.

I drop the gun as my body jerks uncontrollably. My vision blurs as pain spears through my body, but I make out a shadow looming over me.

A needle pricks my skin, and a hard boot connects with my head in a violent kick.

My world fades to black.

CHAPTER TWENTY-ONE

I slowly become self-aware, but my mind is hazy to the point where I can't tell if I'm awake or dreaming.

Figuring the solution is simple, I open my eyes.

Though it takes great effort to think, I still have enough wits to note that if the last room they kept me in was cliché, then this room outdoes it in strides. I've never seen a closer representation of an insane asylum with padded walls. Everything around me seems to be made out of cheap pillows in gray pillowcases, including the floor.

There are no cameras that I can see, but I feel someone's unfriendly eyes watching me.

As I could've predicted, when I look down, I see a straitjacket binding my upper body, with my arms forcefully crossed in front and secured in the back. Now that I think about it, I also feel something on my face, and there's a pulling sensation at the back of my head, as if I'm wearing that signature Hannibal Lector mask.

My sense of being watched gets stronger, and I feel like bacterium under a microscope as I try to puzzle out my strange surroundings.

Once I start looking around, I find that the action of thought is getting harder with every second. My senses seem to blur, and I swear I see the restraints holding my arms sprout tentacles of warm light. They paint a pretty mosaic across the room, making it momentarily less gray and unhealthily cheery. The nice colors make my paranoia subside, and I feel good for a moment.

Unfortunately, the warm light soon turns on itself, and it looks as though the room is surrounded by a herd of miniature black holes—places in space determined to suck in all the light and warmth in the universe. Worse, eyes of dark intelligence stare at me from the event horizons, and I get the urge to crawl under the floor pillows.

"Einstein, am I sleeping right now?" I ask out loud and realize that to someone who doesn't know about Brainocytes, this question might seem as crazy as everything else in this room.

Neither the AI nor the real scientist named Einstein reply. From some remnants of critical thinking, I recall this was a way I could tell if I was dreaming or not. Then again, wouldn't the realization of being inside a dream wake me up? And if not, wouldn't my current level of panic accomplish the same trick?

"Is this really happening?" I ask myself, but nothing happens—nor did I expect anything to happen since I can't have a pre-cog moment without a brain boost.

In grim wonder, I watch the black holes turn into smaller black dots. The dots stream toward me to cover my skin like insects.

I wish I hadn't thought of insects, because as soon as I do, my skin feels like an army of spiders decided to battle centipedes on the outer and inner surfaces of my dermis.

If I hadn't been restrained, I'd be clawing at my skin to get rid of the creepy crawlers.

As my breathing speeds up in panic, I tell myself there's nothing on my skin and certainly nothing under it. I tell myself I'm sleeping, but the experience feels more visceral by the second.

I begin screaming, and the bugs fly back into the air and merge into an amorphous malevolent presence in the room. The presence oozes gray colors that spread everywhere, including into my nose and ears. I inhale the gray colors and feel like I'm being polluted and turned into something less human. I try to cough out the poison, but only suck in more grayness into my lungs.

"If you bite off a bolt from a choo-choo train, how does it affect the price of a kilo of hotdogs?" a loud male voice booms all around me. "Keeping in mind that a brick is floating on the glass river, of course."

I'm attempting to compute the question or statement I just heard, when an even louder female voice demands, "What are you *not* thinking about right now?"

I feel like my head is about to literally explode as I ponder the second question, but the burst is prevented by a chorus of new voices that boom, "This sentence is false."

I contemplate screaming again, but it seems impossible to drown out these voices, especially a moment later, when they all begin speaking out of sync with each other, each voice louder than the next, each statement like a knife stabbing into the remains of my fragile sanity.

I no longer feel paranoia. Paranoia is what I am, and she feels me.

I try to ignore the visual and auditory onslaught and meditate, but it's a disastrous idea because it allows me to pay attention to the bodily sensations that, like everything else, are out of control. I'm a beehive of aches that swiftly turn into pains in my right shoulder, which morph into a vaguely pleasurable sensation in my left toe and finally circle back into the pain spreading evenly throughout all my extremities. The rest of me feels like it's made out of clay that someone cured into a solid state and shattered against the wall.

I then try using pure willpower to ignore the sensations and voices, but it's hard. The walls in the room breathe in and out, as though they're the stomach lining of a giant squid that has swallowed me whole and is about to digest me. However, when I close my eyes, sunspots form images on the insides of my eyelids. They remind me of fairies having a rave, followed by an orgy, followed by a laser lightshow. The visuals assault my eyes even through the closed eyelids.

"Have my Brainocytes gone awry?" I ask someone mentally, though I only half recall what Brainocytes are and have no idea who I'm talking to. Realizing questions have a higher chance of getting answered if I ask them out loud, I add, "Have I gone insane?"

"No," I mentally reply to myself. "Can't even think about insanity right now, because if I think it, I might summon it."

The feeling of being watched intensifies, and because I have nothing better to try, I roll on the floor. The movement instantly triggers the feeling of dropping through a soft surface and free-falling like during the HALO jump. Until this moment, that was the worst experience of my life.

As I fall, the air around me takes on the putrid, sulfuric stench of the color gray, and I can taste the pungent sourness of the number twenty. In the next moment, my thinking clears enough for me to recall that colors don't smell and numbers have no taste—but Wi-Fi networks do. Piggybacking on this moment of clarity, I wonder if the voices and tricks of light are somehow being introduced from outside my brain? Are projectors and speakers surrounding me? Or is all this stuff being fed directly into my noggin? Something tells me nothing good can come from theorizing about thoughts being put into my brain, as that road leads to tinfoil hats. Then again, something also tells me that a properly insulated tinfoil hat made out of something suitable, like lead, could cause my brain to experience connectivity problems.

Realizing my eyes are open, I close them again, and it eases the feeling of my mind melting into a puddle. The free fall turns into a feeling of forward movement, and I swear I'm about to drive into a tunnel made of a kaleido-scope of bright symbols.

With my eyes closed, I wish I could close my ears too, because voices are still assaulting me. In fact, I'd give any-thing to simply put my hands over my ears, and it's mad-dening that I can't. I can't even recall the reason my arms are stuck in place, refusing to move. I just know it has nothing to do with aliens.

Actually, the reason is on the tip of my tongue, but I can't quite remember it. Maybe my arms belong to some-one else for the moment?

The cursed voices are now speaking as though from underwater, giving me the conviction that time is slowing around me, a feeling I'm familiar with, though I can't recall why.

"I'd like to wake up now," I yell the next time I feel a moment of clarity, but nothing changes and my journey into hell continues unabated.

What feels like a month later, I develop deep revela-tions about the ultimate nature of reality and wish I had a pen, paper, and hands to write them down with. I feel con-nected to a web of conscious beings that create the fabric of what we all know as existence. I realize that my world, such as it is, might only be a glorified videogame meant to amuse godlike intelligences that exist outside this play-thing universe.

Soon, I understand that these metaphysical musings are there to mask a fear I've been unsuccessfully ignor-ing. It's a rather familiar fear—the fear of losing my mind. In fact, I recall that this is something I've been worrying about since I learned I had a half-sister with schizophrenia. What really bothers me, though, is that I have trouble remembering what my half-sister's name is or what her symptoms are, for that matter. Part of me even doubts I have a half-sister. I'm certainly not used to the idea of having one.

As soon as I allow myself to consider the possibility of insanity again, panic grows like a parasitic worm in my chest. For a moment, my rapid heartbeat silences the voices, and all I feel is the need to throw up.

A couple of dry heaves later, the sense that I've completely lost my mind grows stronger until it's a conviction deep in my bones. My biggest worry seems to be how my mom will react when they tell her I'm genuinely crazy. What will she say?

"Make it stop," I yell and roll on the cushioned floor. "Please. Someone. Make it stop."

As though in reply, the voices get louder, and the lights in the room flicker from blindingly bright to nearly pitch black with increasing speed. I soon realize that the lights are speaking to me in Morse code, revealing important secrets only the chosen few are supposed to know. They tell me that the experiences in this current life can have a deep impact on the person you might become in the next life.

After what feels like another few years, the lights stop, and the voices speak at a lower volume.

I realize my eyes are open and I'm staring at the door to my room—though I could also be staring at a supernova that's about to explode.

A figure is standing in the doorway. The bright light behind her makes me think of saints or angels, though there's something more reminiscent of an alien visitor about the figure.

The being or person gets nearer. Though her edges are blurred against the gray backdrop of the room, I discern with some disappointment that this is merely a human woman plodding toward me.

A spotlight falls upon the woman's face, and it takes me a only few moments to recognize her gently smiling face. She looks exactly like the therapist I visited a lifetime ago, though it could've been yesterday.

"Hello, Mike," she says calmly. "I'm Dr. Golovasi, your psychiatrist."

CHAPTER TWENTY-TWO

Memories flood my consciousness.

As I recall Ada, a galaxy of warmth dances through my heart. I float in happy feelings related to Ada until I remind myself what I'm seeking in my memory. Ada made me see someone named Dr. Golovasi. It had something to do with me having problems sleeping. Ironically, there's a high probability I'm inside a bad dream at this moment.

"Hello, ma'am," I mumble through sandpaper lips. "Are you really here?"

Dr. Golovasi smiles sadly at me. The problem is that her large white teeth seem to come alive and grin at me, though *their* smiles are more sinister for some unfathomable reason.

"Do you know where you are?" Dr. Golovasi asks.

As though scared of her presence, the cursed voices stop screaming in my head long enough for me to consider her question.

"I'm in a government facility," I reply, almost on autopilot. I don't know how I arrived at the answer, but I feel a conviction that it's true. My convictions might not be worth much, though, because I'm convinced the doctor's forehead just sprouted a third eye that can see inside my deepest inner thoughts. The rest of her face looks confused, so I clarify my earlier statement by adding, "I think I might just be inside my head."

Instead of saying anything, she walks over to where I'm lying and helps me sit up. Her hands are soft, and I feel their psychiatric healing warmth spread into the shoulder. I end up sitting in a crouch on the floor. The position is more comfortable and could come in handy if I decide to do some sit-ups later, though I guess it might look crazy if I suddenly started exercising while wearing a straightjacket.

"How would you feel if I told you this is a private mental health institution?" Dr. Golovasi asks, all her eyes, even the third one, radiating caring warmth. "Do you recall getting committed? Do you remember our sessions? What's the last thing you recall?"

"It's difficult for me to think," I say, and the effort required to give her this answer makes me want to rest for a while. Since she just stands there, patiently looming over me, I do my best to recall more. "I remember how I was sitting on a comfortable couch in your office, and we were talking about Russia."

"Yes." She crouches and sits in a lotus pose on the soft floor. Her face is closer to mine, and this makes her third eye dissipate. "That's excellent. Anything else?"

"I recall vague flashes of violence," I say and realize that talking like this seems to make the world around me more solid—proof that talk therapy works miracles, I suppose. "Did that violence really happen?"

"Some of the violence was real." She fiddles with her glasses, her face the epitome of concern. "That's how you ended up in this room. Most of the violence you recall, however, is part of a persistent delusion."

"I hurt someone," I whisper, half to myself, half to her. Images of bitten fingers and stabbed eyes flit through my mind, jacking up my heartrate, and I dry-heave again before gasping out, "Is Ada okay?"

"Ada is taken care of." Dr. Golovasi's posture and serene face make her look like a saint again. "Ada misses you and wants you to get better. We all do."

"What's wrong with me?" I take a breath in an effort to calm my racing pulse. "Actually, wait, I'm not sure I want to know."

"You had an episode," the doctor explains. "You got some ideas in your head that made you distraught. You attacked one of the nurses at this facility and badly injured one of the guards. Do you remember any of this?"

Something about what she says rings at least partially true. I do recall biting someone's finger and stabbing someone with a pen—classic mental patient behaviors. Part of me rejects something about her explanation, though. On some level, I feel like the people I hurt deserved it. They were after me—but could this be my paranoia talking?

"You've been having persistent, intrusive thoughts," Dr. Golovasi says when I don't answer. "Thoughts about being followed, thoughts about a big conspiracy where the government wants something from you. You made progress on some of these issues before the last episode. Does this ring any bells?"

I consider her words, then shake my head. My heart is still thudding against my ribcage in a mad rhythm. "It's all muddy in my mind. It's like what you say sounds familiar, but I don't think it's the full story."

"That's normal," she says. "The fact that you can recognize me again is a big step in the right direction. Yesterday, you thought I was an evil librarian."

"How can I get out of here?" I ask and take another calming breath in an effort not to tell her she does indeed look like a librarian. "I don't like this room."

"You can make progress," she says soothingly. "You can show you're not a danger to yourself or others. I recommend we have a session. Would you like that?"

"I guess." I shift from foot to foot, my bent knees beginning to ache.

"Great," she says. "We can develop tools and practices that will clear your thoughts and center you in the present moment."

"I see," I say and wonder if I should mention that us talking is clearing my thoughts. What's even more impressive is that the voices I was hearing before are completely gone now. "What should we try?"

"Hmm," Dr. Golovasi says, and I realize she has her trusty notepad and pen out and is looking through her notes. "How about free association?" When I look at her blankly, she adds, "I'll say a word, and you blurt out the first thing that comes to you, so long as it's inspired by the word I say."

"Okay," I say hesitantly. "I can try." What I don't add is that she's already made me think of umbrellas and class-rooms just by being here.

"Russia," she says.

"Darkness. Trouble."

"Good." She gives me a smile. "Next word. Sister."

"Madness," I say instantly. "Heredity."

"Ada." She points her index finger at me, indicating I should speed up my answers.

"Fluffy puppies, and, err, thongs." I chuckle nervously.

"Joe." She clearly doesn't want me to get a chance to regroup my thoughts.

"Alligator tears." When she doesn't say a new word, I add, "Icebergs?"

"You're doing really well," she says and rewards me with another smile. This time, her teeth merely look like chunks of porcelain. "Now, I'll give you a topic, and I want you to free-associate a true story from your life. I'll start with something safe, something not too personal to you. How does that sound?"

"Sure," I say. "Shoot."

"Open source."

"Hobby."

"No." She gives me an intent look. "This time, I want you to form a story."

"Oh." I try to banish the pretty colors swirling through the doctor's gray hair and do my best to come up with a story about open source.

"I assume you know what open source generally means," I begin. "It's a computer program in which the source code is available to the general public. Of course, the term spread from the software world, and now there are open-source colas and beer, not to mention open source in medicine in the form of pharmaceuticals and genetic therapies, as well as open-source science and engineering." She nods sagely, so I continue. "The reason I said hobby is because I've been helping write open-source software on a number of projects. It started because I wanted to sharpen my C++ skills, and, to a smaller degree, I wanted to give something back. My friends and I use a ton of open-source software as starting points for our apps."

She's still listening, so I go on.

"Once I was part of the open-source community, I learned more about the spirit and purpose of open source, and the more I discovered, the more I liked what I learned. It was a shock because I thought that, as a venture capitalist who invests in software companies, I would be driven by self-interest to find faults with open source." I note that her eyes are glazing over, but my spiel is clearing my mind, so I keep talking. "Open source is a great development model. It's decentralized, and—this is key—it encourages collaboration. Many companies found that, despite intuition stating the opposite, they can and do make money supporting open-source software—"

"This is great," Dr. Golovasi interrupts. "Now here is a new topic. Morality."

Since this therapy is clearing my mind, I share my personal moral philosophy with Dr. Golovasi. As I speak, her hair takes on the appearance of the snakes in Medusa's hairdo but rapidly returns to normal—another sign of my improvement. Her reading glasses try to grow eyes, but the eyes soon dissipate. The story (if you could give my ramblings such a lofty title) takes me something like forty minutes to get out, but then I realize I could've just said two words—the Golden Rule (or is it three words? English can be confusing sometimes). "So basically," I say in conclusion, "I treat people the way I want to be treated."

"Keep it up," Dr. Golovasi says encouragingly. "Next topic—cryptography."

"It's something my friend Muhomor can talk about for hours," I say, then falter as I notice the good doctor's countenance change. She's looking at me with more intensity than ever before.

Something about this topic really bothers me.

I struggle to clear my mind and succeed enough for me to recall something dire about Muhomor.

He's badly hurt.

He was shot.

Remembering Muhomor getting shot triggers a cascade of other memories. I recall the shootout at the Georgian restaurant and the hospital visit that led to me being taken by people claiming to be part of a government task force. I recall the tube up my nose and Agent Lancaster and his questions about Tema—Muhomor's cryptosystem.

Suspicions and revelations mushroom in my brain, then spread through my synapses like a nuclear explosion.

My hands turn into fists as I realize the full depth of the grievances committed against me.

Something must show on my face, because Dr. Golovasi asks, "Is everything okay?"

"You fucking bitch," I grit out through my teeth. "Everything is far from okay."

CHAPTER TWENTY-THREE

Part of me knows that, despite my suspicions, I might still be crazy. This could be a *Total Recall* type moment that's part of my delusions. Maybe what I think is happening is really the problem, and the truth is what Dr. Golovasi wants me to believe. My counterargument is that if my insanity were that far gone, saving me would require strong medication, not therapy. And if that's the case, being rude to my shrink is the least of my worries.

I have to hand it to Dr. Golovasi. The look of shock on her face is genuine. If her goal was to make me doubt reality, I'd give her at least an eight out of ten. But before I can get lost in my muddy thoughts again, I decide to verify my suspicions by doing something concrete and summoning the AROS interface.

Icons show up across my vision.

Good.

The icons look exactly as I remember—meaning they either work as I recall, via Brainocytes, or they're as real as those snakes that were part of Dr. Golovasi's hair not long ago.

Almost on autopilot, I seek out Wi-Fi connectivity, but alas, I find none. Actually, the lack of internet is a clue. Why make your networks Muhomor-proof in a mental hospital?

Next, I connect with my phone and see if Precious 3 can get onto any new Wi-Fi networks, but again, all is for naught. Seeing the cement room my phone is in tells me I'm either sane or so crazy I might as well give up and wait for electroshock therapy.

I check the video files on my phone and verify that I have my session with Dr. Golovasi in her New York office recorded on there. So I didn't dream that up—unless I'm dreaming now. I also have recordings of some of the things they did to me in this facility, another bit of proof.

Encouraged, I begin recording our new conversation just in case and finally get around to the main reason I opened up AROS in the first place. I run the AROS app I recently wrote—the one that gives me access to the lab on the chip imbedded in my body (assuming that's real too).

The earlier output from the chip was bisacodyl, oxycodone, and acetaminophen. I run the app again, and the output is replaced with a long list of new chemicals. I scan the list and recognize a few entries. Lysergic acid diethylamide is LSD, also known as acid—the famous psychedelic drug. Tetrahydrocannabinol is better known as THC, one of the fun ingredients in cannabis. 5-trimethoxyphenethylamine is the scientific name for mescaline, a drug made from the famous peyote cactus. Also on the list is psilocybin, the active ingredient in "magic mushrooms"—a factoid I happen to know because Muhomor's nickname is Russian for amanita mushrooms. He likes to correct people who think that amanita shrooms (his namesake) contain psilocybin, because they don't. Consequently, the two hallucinogenic chemicals amanita mushrooms do contain, muscimol and ibotenic acid, are also present in my bloodstream. Finally, I also recognize sodium thiopental—a substance I came across in that TV show about spies, where it was used as truth serum.

They gave me a cocktail of drugs designed to make me think I was crazy.

The visions, the bodily sensations, the memory problems, the paranoia, and even my eagerness to chat with the shrink were all chemically induced.

"You wanted me to think I'm a paranoid schizophrenic?" I'm so angry I barely get the words out. "After I told you about my half-sister?" Her eyes bulge, but I'm not even close to done. "You injected me with LSD?" I yell. "And THC?"

I rapidly read off the list of junk in my bloodstream, and with every substance I rattle out, Dr. Golovasi looks more and more like I punched her in the stomach.

"How can you know this?" she finally whispers. "How can you know about the medicine?"

I can't believe she just pretty much admitted to this atrocity—but I'm glad I'm recording it. If I get out of here, her career is over.

Then another wave of revelations hits me.

She isn't a real doctor. She's not worried about her career. She's just surprised I know something I shouldn't, or perhaps she's worried about her organization getting into trouble over drugging a detainee.

Things fall into place, and the universe all of a sudden makes sense—though it's feasible my epiphany is the result of the drugs in my system.

Agent Lancaster mentioned he was part of a task force. They must be a cybersecurity task force with a mission to learn as much as they can about Muhomor in general and his genius invention, Tema, specifically. They had everyone Muhomor knows followed, including me. Thanks to either my brain boost or my innate paranoia, I spotted the surveillance and told the people closest to me that I was being followed—except no one believed me. When the task force got an opportunity, or became extra desperate, they imbedded a secret agent into my life in the form of Dr. Golovasi. Who better to learn secrets than a therapist? Their job is to ask questions. Hell, I recall how interested she was in my friendship with Muhomor during that first session. That should've stood out as an odd interest for a doctor to have, but I was too focused on my problems to notice.

The task force must've hacked our computers, or at least Ada's. Maybe they managed to control Ada's Google searches too. When Ada Googled "best psychologist in Manhattan," the task force made sure she saw a fictional site for Dr. Golovasi at the top of the results. Muhomor has bragged about doing similar hacks, so I know it can be done, no matter how paranoid it sounds.

If all my theories are correct, the woman in front me might not even have a psychology degree, or if she does, she might be an expert in criminal profiling. More likely, though, she's just a CIA agent or something similar.

When I was being uncooperative, I bet it was Golovasi, or whatever her real name is, who suggested they make me think I'm crazy. I told her about my private fears during our therapy session, and she thought she could leverage that against me—and it almost worked.

As my angry haze lifts a little, I realize she's been frantically talking to me all this time, saying something about me falling back into psychosis and delusions again. Her story sounds like the plot for that film where the staff at an insane asylum playacts the hero's delusions as a form of therapy. "You agreed to participate in an experimental treatment," she says. "The medications—"

I tune her out and focus on my legs instead. If I leap fast enough, I can smack her in the face with the mask I think I'm wearing. Though if there isn't a mask on my face, the impact will hurt me as much as it'll hurt her.

Decision made in a blink, I leap forward as quickly as I can.

I brace for impact, but to my shock, Golovasi counterattacks. Her movements remind me of Aikido or another martial art where you use your opponent's momentum against him. More specifically, while still sitting in the lotus pose, she manages to tilt her body left, grab my shoulder with both hands, and direct my motion away from her.

I plop face down onto the soft floor and do my best to regain my breath. The cocktail of drugs they gave me must dampen my pain perception, because I don't feel much. My pride is probably more hurt than my body, since I was thwarted by an old lady in a meditation pose. Granted, she might've gotten CIA training, and I'm a living pharmacy of hallucinogens, which probably isn't helping with my coordination. Still, I thought I had her, and she kicked my ass.

A needle pricks my left shoulder, and I forget about my wounded pride. I'm not sure if it's Golovasi or someone else who injected me with whatever I just got injected with, but I know it won't matter soon.

"You should've talked," Golovasi says, not bothering to disguise the venom in her voice. "I was the good cop."

As the drug takes away my awareness, I reflect on her words. She might actually be telling the truth. She might be the good cop to Agent Lancaster's bad cop. And if so, I shudder to think what I'm going to face when I wake up.

CHAPTER TWENTY-FOUR

I come to, and the first thing I feel is pain all over my body. Did they beat me while I was unconscious?

Actually, there are other possibilities. They could've beaten me after I half-blinded Agent Lancaster, but before I was tripping on every drug known to man. The drugs could've been masking the pain. This last scenario is likely, because I vaguely recall some bodily sensations that must've been echoes of pain.

The good news is my mind is clear, or as close to clear as possible without Brainocytes. Sadly, that isn't all that clear.

I check for Wi-Fi, but it's still as unbreakable as before. My phone is available to me, so I check if it has internet access—maybe someone moved it to a room with cell reception—but the answer is no. I look through the phone camera and see the same room with the same air vent—the only non-concrete object I can see.

The lab on the chip confirms all the drugs have been flushed out of my system. I don't have any painkillers left in my blood either. No wonder I feel so many aches and pains.

According to my phone, it's November 17, 12:30 p.m. Last time I checked the clock was yesterday, when I had that conversation with Agent Lancaster right before noon. The bad trip must've happened later that day, though I don't know when.

Carefully, I open my eyes.

I'm back in that original cement room—though it could easily be another one just like it. It wouldn't be hard to mass-produce a legion of underground bunker-style rooms like this.

I'm tied to a bed again, but it doesn't look like I have any medical equipment hooked up to me, not even an IV. My throat is sore, and I wonder if I was tube-fed again, maybe even recently.

My other bodily functions are blissfully calm. If that implies I used the bathroom while unconscious and got washed again, I don't want to know about it.

Despite the seeming lack of threats, my mind goes into overdrive with angst. My biggest worry has to do with Muhomor. If Agent Lancaster is to be believed, my friend is in a coma.

My second worry is Ada. She was supposed to leave the hospital, but I recall Golovasi (if that's her name) saying, "Ada is taken care of." What did she mean?

My third worry is a vague one about Mr. Spock. Where is he?

Last but not least, I have no idea if Joe survived that attack. And if he didn't, was Gogi killed with Joe?

As I lie there ruminating about it all, my worry priorities change. I realize my primary concern should be about me. Given how badly I antagonized and hurt my captors, what will the consequences be?

Logically, when they resume their questioning, it'll be worse than what preceded it, but it's hard to imagine the situation getting worse. Though I'm doing my best not to think about torture, I can't help but imagine getting waterboarded. As someone who once choked on soda, I have some idea of what the feeling of drowning is like. I'm guessing the real thing—or its approximation via waterboarding—is a million times worse. Will I talk if they do that to me? And even if I'm able to resist waterboarding right now, could I resist it after not sleeping (or eating or drinking) for a long time?

I'm not going to kid myself. Some things would make me talk for sure. Any of the more brute-force approaches would do the trick, like breaking a bone, blowtorching any body part, drilling a tooth, or cutting off a finger.

The worst part is that even if I decide to talk, I can't tell them anything that would make the torture stop, not if they want the Tema cryptosystem cracked or thoroughly explained. I barely understood Muhomor's baby while on Brainocytes, and even then, only on the same level as a layman comprehends the workings of a TV. We all know there aren't little people sitting in that magical box, but only some of us know that LCD screens work by switching liquid crystals electronically to rotate polarized light.

Something I see through my phone's camera distracts me from my musings.

No, not some*thing*.

Some*one*.

I zoom the camera to make sure I'm not having a residual hallucination, and my heart rate jumps as one of my worries resolves itself.

It's Mr. Spock.

He's sitting behind the ventilation grill, munching on something.

When I puzzle out what he's eating, I nearly scream at him to stop.

The little guy is eating a giant cockroach.

Frantically, I launch the EmoRat app, route the connectivity through my phone, and pray Ada didn't recently do something clever, like routing all the EmoRat app's traffic through a fancy server I can't access without internet.

Mr. Spock stops munching and perks up—and I feel us connect.

I get flooded with rat happiness that proves Mr. Spock was as worried about me as I was about him.

"Where have you been?" I send him through the app. "What happened?"

Mr. Spock reacts to my words with more warmth, but also with confusion. It takes me a few moments to understand why he's being a bit dense. Like me, Mr. Spock isn't as smart as he used to be because his brain boost also requires internet connectivity.

"Why are you eating such disgusting food?" I ask, hoping he can understand something as simple as that.

Even more confused, he replies with the same emotions he typically does when I give him peanuts—his favorite treat. I think he's trying to say, "Dude, this cockroach is yummy."

I project my relief that he's okay and my love for him in general, and he shines with a deep violet aura—his happiest state of being.

He then crunches on his snack and tries to send me the resulting emotions, as though he's trying to say, "See, I told you it's yummy."

I do my best not to gag and wish I had access to Google so I could check if it's safe for rats to eat cockroaches. Common sense tells me it should be, or else New York would be littered with rats that died from cockroach poisoning. I bet that in the wild, rats eat a ton of insects for protein, so why not cockroaches? They're nonpoisonous bugs, after all.

An idea forms, and I ask, "Mr. Spock, can you get outside?"

He doesn't seem to understand, so I try a command I typically use when I'm leaving the house. It tells him to jump in my pocket if he wishes. "Mr. Spock," I send. "Fresh air?"

I see that he recognizes what I said, because I'm hit with a wave of ratty excitement that typically accompanies the idea of riding in my pocket.

I wait to see if he extrapolates the command to be as I meant it, which has nothing to do with going in my pocket.

Gulping down the last of his gross meal, Mr. Spock scurries away, telling me he's probably looking for fresh air, or, just as likely, for me and my pocket.

The app that allows me to see what he sees doesn't work due to lack of connectivity, unfortunately, but I do get an idea of his progress based on the emotions I gleam from the EmoRat app.

After a few minutes, the EmoRat app disconnects, informing me Mr. Spock is out of range from the phone—a sign he went somewhere far, though not necessarily proof that he went outside.

My theory is that Mr. Spock hid somewhere in that helicopter. That means his journey brought him to the ventilation shaft of a garage or hangar or roof—places that are likelier to have exposure to the outside and cellular connectivity, assuming we're near cell towers right now and not somewhere like Antarctica.

What's key is that after Mr. Spock finds fresh air and enjoys it, he must then get back into the app's range. If he doesn't, my idea won't work. I'm hopeful he'll do the right thing, because once he does find cell connectivity, he should get his rat version of the brain boost back, and that will increase the chances of him coming back. Or he might just come back in any case when he wants my company again.

Deciding to work on the assumption that I'll see Mr. Spock again soon, I rush to fully implement my idea and launch the AROS IDE.

Luckily, the required code is something I should be able to handle without the boost, though all the pains in my body and worries about my immediate future are distracting.

The premise of the app is simple. I plan to use Mr. Spock as a high-tech carrier pigeon of sorts. Each Brainocyte is a tiny computer with a basic processing unit and memory. The Brainocytes' resources are limited. This is why we use the server/client architecture that puts most processing and memory requirements in the cloud. But, in a pinch, Mr. Spock's Brainocytes have more than enough memory to store a short email and another app. The new software will run in Mr. Spock's version of the AROS system and scan for internet connectivity. Once the app gets online, it will send the pre-prepared email to a predetermined list of people.

I code away, and the work makes time fly, which is great, especially since my captors are probably leaving me be so I can ruminate in my tied-up boredom. What would usually take me minutes in my enhanced state takes two hours—and by the time I finish, I'm really worried about Mr. Spock not getting back, thus making this whole programming exercise pointless.

I review the code I wrote about a hundred times and test parts of the code that can be independently tested. It would suck if I missed my chance to get in touch with my friends due to a mundane software bug. When I feel like I'd rather have another tube up my nose than review the same lines of code again, I stop coding the email-sending part of the app and write a module to receive emails, in case my friends reply.

When all the coding is complete, I consider what to include in the actual email.

"Hi, all," I begin. "People who claim to be part of a government task force have taken me." I go on to explain my predicament, what they did to me, and take care in describing the people I've encountered. "Ada, the shrink you booked for me is with the CIA or something similar. I know how crazy that sounds, but I assure you it's true. I bet you could confirm it if you dug deeper into her cover as a psychologist. Joe, the pseudo shrink's receptionist might know something. She didn't seem like a government agent to me. Her name is Monika."

I pause and check if Mr. Spock has returned, but the EmoRat app is silent.

To kill more time and stop myself from going crazy, I review my recording of the session with Golovasi to see if I can include anything else in my email that might assist my friends in helping me. I come across something useful, but I'm not sure if I'm upset enough with Golovasi to include this tidbit. Then I decide I am, and end the email with, "Joe, Golovasi mentioned she has a son. It could be part of her cover, but by the way she said it, I don't think so."

Since Mr. Spock isn't back, I work on expanding the email app to support image attachments, figuring I could include a snapshot from the Golovasi videos, as well as one of Agent Lancaster's face. Once the task is complete, I attach a couple of images of my captors.

When I can't think of any more improvements to the app, or anything to add to my message, I begin to fret about Mr. Spock's return in earnest.

Suddenly, the door to my room opens, and two masked people walk in, dragging some sort of wheeled table.

A green piece of cloth covers the table, but despite the obstruction, the setup makes my bare feet grow colder as blood leaves my extremities.

"What is that?" I demand, trying to sound brave. "And do you realize you're keeping me here illegally?"

Instead of responding, one of the men pulls the cloth off with a flourish. Dumbfounded, I stare at the objects on the table as the two people leisurely exit the room.

Nausea curls in my stomach as I catalog each item. There are mallets, scalpels, saws, drills, a car battery with sinister-looking clamps, and a vast number of sharp and painful-looking things I can't even name.

My worst fears are manifesting.

They plan to torture me for real now.

CHAPTER TWENTY-FIVE

No.

These are government employees, and the government doesn't torture people. Okay, maybe they do, or did, but not officially and certainly not like this—with equipment a Bond villain would cringe at. At least I don't believe they do, even in the case of spies and terrorists. Then again, they shouldn't have pumped me full of drugs either, but they did.

There's a small chance this is a psychological tactic meant to scare me into cooperating. If that's the case, it's working really well.

Battling my nausea, I examine each tool for signs of prior use, but that doesn't lead anywhere. If anything was used before, it's probably been sterilized, and that makes a dark sort of sense. You wouldn't want to give your captives HIV or hepatitis while torturing them, since that would go beyond breaking the Geneva Convention. It's a bit like the alcohol swipe used on prisoners before a lethal injection.

I begin to scream obscenities at my captors and continue until my throat hurts. Then I plead for them not to use this stuff on me and to let me go. I get no results, aside from bringing myself to the edge of a panic attack.

I'm about to burst with worry, when a wave of positive rat emotions interrupts my tribulations.

"Mr. Spock, buddy, you made it back." I cram my message with all the relief I'm feeling. "Please, stay where you are. I need to do something."

I have no idea if he listens to me or runs toward the room with the phone, thus staying in range of the hotspot, but I stay connected to Mr. Spock long enough to load the new app that will turn the rat into a high-tech carrier pigeon.

Now for the trickiest part of all.

"Now, Mr. Spock," I send. "I need a huge favor. I want you to go outside again."

A dose of confusion mars the happy feelings coming from the EmoRat app. Without his boost, the little guy has trouble understanding human language.

"Who's a good little rat?" I reassure him as soothingly as I can. "Don't get scared."

When he's content again, I mentally cross my fingers and try the whole "go outside" thing again, though I fear he might reply with something like, "Hey, fool a rat once, shame on human. Fool a rat twice, shame on rat."

"Mr. Spock," I send casually, as though I'm about to head out for a stroll in Central Park. "Fresh air?"

I guess his lack of brain boost can work in my favor.

Mr. Spock gets excited, and I can tell he's going for it. I just hope he *was* outside when I lost contact with him—a big assumption.

After ten nerve-racking minutes of hoping to lose connectivity with my rat, the EmoRat app throws a connectivity error.

Having nothing new to do, I resume looking at the cursed table and wonder if it's considered a form of torture to make someone wait to get tortured. Eventually, I force myself to close my eyes to stop staring at the damn table.

A couple of seconds after I close my eyes, the horrific drilling sound resumes.

"Hey, I wasn't trying to sleep," I yell, knowing full well that my complaints are pointless. "I'll keep my eyes open. Just shut that down."

The sound remains, so I override the noise with music again. This time, a song by Evanescence comes on.

Since it's 10:12 p.m. and I know it'll take Mr. Spock hours to complete his task, I start playing games on my phone to kill time.

After more anxiety-inducing hours, I decide that, by all rights, Mr. Spock should be back by now. It's almost six in the morning on the eighteenth, meaning it's been an hour longer than the last time I waited for him, assuming that, with all this lack of sleep, my math is correct. Also, is it safe to assume it would take Mr. Spock the same amount of time to go outside and come back as the last time?

In another hour, I start to wonder if I should develop a Plan B.

When no Plan B occurs to me, even after another hour of concentration, I realize I'm starving and thirsty and, paradoxically, need to go to the bathroom. I guess my circadian rhythms know it's morning, and my body is demanding breakfast and a bathroom trip as per usual.

I stop playing with my phone, open my eyes, and resume making myself crazy by imagining the horrid equipment on that table being used on me.

After another half hour that feels like it spans half my life, the door to the room opens.

I turn off the music and find the drilling sound is gone.

Tensing all over, I watch Agent Lancaster slowly amble into the room.

If I thought about it, I would've expected him to be wearing a black patch over his eye, like a pirate. Instead, the entire right side of his face is covered in bandages. He looks more like an unfinished mummy.

"My superiors doubt my objectivity," he says, his voice colder than Siberian winters. "They're sending a replacement interrogator to this facility, which means we only have twenty-four hours to enjoy each other's company." He brushes his fingertips over the torture instruments with a lover's caress and adds, "I intend to make the best of what little time we have left."

I open my mouth to plead for mercy, though nothing I say will give this guy his eye back. Before I can get a word out, his cell phone goes off, the heroic ringtone sounding like the theme from a show like *24*. How the hell does *he* have reception in this place? I guess his phone must use Wi-Fi for calls, like some of the more recent phone services allow, or maybe this wasn't a call at all, but an email message or text.

Agent Lancaster looks at his phone, his remaining eye narrows to a slit, and he storms out of the room.

I frantically check the EmoRat app to see if Mr. Spock is in range, but he's not. Did Mr. Spock even get outside? Do my friends know what's going on with me already? Could that message Agent Lancaster received have something to do with it?

Could they somehow save me before he gets around to his grisly task?

For another two hours and forty minutes, nothing happens, and the wait is driving me insane. Suddenly, the door opens again, but instead of Agent Lancaster—and to my slight relief—Golovasi walks in.

"We need to talk," she says, her face wearing a mask of motherly concern. "Steven—I mean Agent Lancaster— might have lost it." She scrunches her nose at the torture devices. "I couldn't—"

I don't catch what she says next because, to my huge relief, I'm hit with Mr. Spock's emotions.

"You're the best rat ever," I send him and check for any emails he might've brought me. "I'll get you a whole pound bag of peanuts once we get out of this."

There's an email from almost everyone I know. I'm about to read the email from Ada when I catch Golovasi looking at me quizzically. I guess she didn't expect me to not pay attention to her.

"Look, Jane, or whatever your name is," I reply, my tone clipped. "I understand the game you're playing. Your colleague, Agent Pugh, already tried a similar technique. You're the good cop right now. Lancaster is the crazed bad cop. I watch a lot of Netflix and know the drill."

She looks thoughtful, probably considering how best to handle me. Finally, she says, "He really will hurt you. I can promise you that."

I believe her. Though she's a liar, I'm convinced she's telling the truth right now, and despite my renewed hope, that knowledge floods me with dread.

"It's not like we're asking you to betray your friends or your country," she says earnestly. "We just want—"

I don't listen to her sophistry about the government's need to be able to crack any crypto security that its "enemies" might deploy. Before this debacle, during a recent Brainocytes Club meeting, I argued with Muhomor about this very topic, and my views at the time were sympathetic with what she's saying. Things are different now. I won't lift a finger to stop Muhomor from unleashing Tema into the world, open-source style. Hell, I'll help him, or do it instead of him, just to spite these people.

Holding eye contact and nodding at Golovasi like I'm listening, I read Ada's email.

"Sweetie," it begins. "I hope it's okay, but I had to delay Mr. Spock from going back to you to give us time to do some research into your situation. Look on the bright side. We can now pass some useful information your way. You're going to get messages from the others, but just know I got out of the hospital and no one bothered me, so you don't need to worry about me. Muhomor is indeed in a coma. Your situation made your cousin crazier than usual, and I didn't think that was possible. He thinks he has a way to get you the help you need, but he said we don't want to know the details. You should read his email—"

I stop reading Ada's message, ignore the email from Mitya, and open Joe's, noting there's an attachment to his email, which is odd.

"Her real name is Jean Berger, and she indeed has a son," Joe's email begins, and I feel a chill run down my spine as I look at the person Joe is talking about. "The son's name is Mark. His wife's name is Evelin. Her granddaughter's name is Mary. I'm in their home in Queens. See attached." My mental finger shakes as I double-click on the attachment icon. I see an image of a man my age. His eye is black and swollen, his face looks scared, and Joe's gun is to his temple. "Tell that bitch that if I don't hear back from you in a few hours, I'll kill them, one by one, starting with the kid."

I nearly choke on a mix of horror and relief, but push the emotions aside.

Joe just gave me the little bit of leverage I need.

"Your name is Jean Berger, and your son, Mark, is in deep trouble," I say in a hushed whisper, interrupting Golovasi-Berger's tirade.

She pales and looks over her shoulder, confirming my suspicion that this place has a camera and microphone embedded somewhere. "What? How can you—"

"Come closer," I hiss. "I'll whisper the rest."

She eyes the table, and I can see she's tempted to grab something sharp and stab me. Her motherly instincts win out, however, and she approaches close enough that I could bite her ear if I wanted to.

"Do you know what kind of monster my cousin is?" I ask her as softly as I can, hoping the microphone behind her isn't sensitive enough to pick up my words.

She nods, her chin trembling.

"Then you understand the severity of the situation." I realize I sound inhumanly cruel, but it can't be helped. I don't have much sympathy for this manipulative woman. "Joe is in your son's home. Besides Mark, he also has Evelin and Mary. He says he'll kill them if he doesn't hear from me. He says he'll start with Mary." I describe what Mark looks like in the picture.

"Tell that psycho if he so much as touches a hair on their heads, I'll skin you alive," she hisses vehemently, forgetting to whisper.

"You're wasting valuable time," I whisper. "I don't want *innocent* people to get hurt."

Something inside the woman seems to break. Her shoulders droop, and tears flood her eyes. "Look, I don't know how you're communicating with him, but I can't get you out, even if I wanted to. I'm not—"

"Let's make sure Joe doesn't do anything crazy," I interrupt. "I'll tell him to stand down, but you have to get me onto your Wi-Fi so I can make that connection. Quickly."

She looks confused but says, "The Wi-Fi password is in my phone." She reaches down, plays with her phone, and shows me a long string of digits. "How do you plan to reach your cousin? Do you want me to bring you your phone? It might be faster if you call him with mine."

"Jean." Agent Lancaster's voice manages the impossible feat of sounding colder than ever before. "I can't believe you're falling for his social engineering hacker tricks."

CHAPTER TWENTY-SIX

C*rap.* He must've heard me call her by her real name through the surveillance in the room and came to make sure she didn't let me out.

What he might not realize, though, is that I already got something extremely valuable. I recorded the Wi-Fi passcode she showed me, and I'm getting onto their network while they argue.

"How can he know the names of my son and his family?" I hear her ask as though in the distance. "Or that they live in Queens, or what my son looks like?"

"He saw you for that therapy session in Manhattan," Lancaster replies. "He must've hacked—"

I don't hear what the agent says next, because I get online and my brain boost hits me like a ton of pleasurable bricks.

"You've been offline or unconscious for three days," Einstein says. "Current time—"

I ignore Einstein because I'm overwhelmed with the sensation of becoming whole again. It's like regaining sight after being blind for ten years, waking up from a coma, and coming home after a military tour, all rolled into one package and multiplied a millionfold. The time dilation effect kicks in instantly, and I feel like I could write a philosophical treatise in the moment it takes Agent Lancaster to say a single angry word to Jean-Jane.

I form a plan to get out of this place almost seamlessly. Then I realize I can come up with a dozen more, though none will get me out of here as fast as I'd like.

In the span of a breath, I sweep through my captors' computer network and verify this is indeed a government task force, as Lancaster said. Their specialty is cybersecurity, and they recently formed due to some bullshit political pressures. I also see clues that explain past events. For example, when my pseudo-shrink told them about my paranoia, they stopped spying on me for the rest of the day, which explains why I felt relieved after therapy. They genuinely weren't following me anymore. And when they found out Muhomor and I were admitted into the hospital, they freaked out, in part because of some interesting information I discover about Muhomor in the task force's files.

As it turns out, despite all the frequent bragging, Muhomor never told us about his most dubious accomplishments. For example, under other aliases, he's participated in the creation of cyberweapons for the US, UK, and Israel—software that makes the Stuxnet worm, a weapon designed to sabotage Iran's nuclear program, look like child's play. The agents also think he has a whole database of *kompromat*—the Russian word that stands for blackmail materials.

I soon see that this is why the task force didn't go after Muhomor directly, no matter how much they wanted Tema for homeland security purposes. They had good reason to believe he has a sophisticated version of dead man's switches/insurance in place that would get triggered if something happened to him—like being locked in a room with no access to the internet. The task force believes that much of his kompromat will go public if he's in a jam, and they even worry that automated cyber attacks might hit American and/or Russian targets. These attacks would create a major scandal, because the weapons used would be of state design. What's really telling is that they fear a scandal more than the cyber threats.

When they learned about Muhomor's condition, they risked hacking some of his servers to prevent his countermeasures from getting released, but it was all encoded using Tema, giving them an extra reason to need to crack the system as soon as possible. Though I get the sense they would've done what they did to me even without the rush.

It's ironic that they feared a scandal from Muhomor, because now, they're going to get one anyway, courtesy of *me*. I upload all the videos from my phone's disk onto Mitya's most secure server in case someone figures out I'm in their network and shuts the whole thing down. Once the videos are safe, I create a nice montage of the most shocking violations of my human rights, shown in the grisliest details. That done, I email the footage to Mitya and start a Teleconference app connection with him and

Ada, frantically saying in Zik, "Hey, Mitya. I'm back online. Sorry, but I didn't read your email. What can you do with this video?"

"Mike," Ada responds instantly, her message full of so many turbulent emotions that I can't tell them apart. A torrent of Zik messages follows so fast I wonder if Ada got an extra boost while I was away and can now talk faster than I can register.

"Slow down, please," I interrupt her. "I have a ton of favors to ask of you too, but let me talk to Mitya first. He has connections who can help me."

"Start Share," she demands and appears in the air in front of me as her normal self, only smaller. Her worried face is a balm to my overactive nerves.

I start the Share app so my friends can see what I see. I also locate the camera in my room and send them the video feed. This way, they'll have two vantage points.

"Dude," Mitya butts in, his telepathic message a discernable mixture of concern and relief. "As I mentioned in the email that you didn't read, I know who has you and I started the ball rolling on getting you out." Mimicking Ada, he appears in the room as a small, floating figure near Agent Lancaster's shoulder, and like Ada, he's wearing his usual clothes. "Your task force was formed by agents from the CIA, FBI, NSA, and a slew of other acronyms. A certain Congressman Chandler is the driving force behind it."

I multitask as Mitya talks, doing a quick mental internet search that reveals Congressman Chandler was a victim of a major hack by Russia. Somehow, he turned that embarrassment into a political crusade. It's not surprising that he's behind this task force.

"I'll be meeting with the congressman shortly," Mitya continues. "I'll inform him of what kind of shit his name is about to be associated with, not to mention the fact that I'll spend a few hundred million dollars on negative ad campaigns against him if you're not released in the next hour."

I put a large red circle around the torture table in Mitya's view of my room and say, "You best cut that hour down to minutes."

"Of course," Mitya says, this time out loud. "I'm watching the video you edited, and I can't believe these people."

"Me neither," Ada chimes in, her face full of horrified sympathy. She turns her gaze from me to my arguing captors, and her sympathy morphs into wrath. "I can't believe what they've put you through."

"Let's post that montage on YouTube," I tell them. "Plus the live feed into this room."

"Great ideas," Mitya replies and looks thoughtful for a moment. Then he nods and says, "Video's already on YouTube, and I'm messaging James, my marketing guru. He'll make it his top priority to push that video until it goes viral. The live feed will also go online, and I'll send it to the congressman."

"Speak with Kadvosky as well," Ada suggests vindictively. "Once we're done with these people's credibility and careers, we'll need to destroy them in court."

"And have my cousin visit a few." I nod at the slow-speaking Agent Lancaster.

"That one-eyed asshole will probably end up in jail after all of this is over. For a cop, that can be a fate worse than a visit from Joe," Mitya says. "I'll also look around their network. If I find something embarrassing, I'll distribute it as publicly as possible."

"Thanks, guys." I switch from Zik to English for emphasis. "I owe you big."

"Don't mention it," Mitya says.

"It'll take a *lot* of sexual favors for us to be even," Ada mentally replies.

"TMI." Mitya's face reddens. Ada must've said her joke in the shared conversation instead of privately.

"Okay, here, look around." I send Mitya the task force's Wi-Fi credentials.

"So," I say to Ada as Mitya starts his work. "I have something I want to ask you to do, something less urgent."

"Of course. What is it?"

"I want to fulfill Muhomor's dream," I say. "I want to make Tema open source."

"I see," Ada says with obvious enthusiasm. She always took Muhomor's side when we argued about Tema's fate. "Once the whole world has access to Tema, this task force will no longer need you."

"Exactly," I say. "But it's also meant as a big fuck-you to them."

"And," Mitya chimes in, "once it's wide, the world will see that Tema is uncrackable, and no one will ever want to kidnap any of us to get some kind of edge on it."

"That's what I thought too," I say. "Which leads me to another, even less urgent idea. I think we should share the Brainocyte design and software with the world—open source it all like I've been suggesting for months. Had these people known about Brainocytes, I'd be in worse shape. The next bunch of idiots might want Brainocytes, and they might kidnap one of us to get it. Plus, of course, my usual argument about openness leading to faster development of more features and apps and cheaper production of nanos, etcetera, ad infinitum."

"You're just distraught and want to disrupt the established world order." Mitya whistles as he considers a world where millions of people become members of the Brainocytes Club. "You know I was never against this idea. Muhomor was."

"I wasn't against it either," Ada says. "And I suspect Muhomor will forgive us once he learns we released Tema."

"Then it's settled," I say, relieved they're going along with my idea. "Mitya, did you talk to your congressman yet?"

"Dude," Mitya says sarcastically. "Congressman Chandler is working on regular-people time, so he obviously hasn't even opened the email yet. But I'll text him and urge him to check his damn email."

"Okay, thanks." I then look at Ada's image and say, "Babe, can you lead Mr. Spock out of the building?"

Since the little guy is still not connected to the internet, I connect him, and he instantly showers me with positive emotions. I guess he likes his brain boost as much as I do.

"I'll get him out," Ada says, and her forehead crinkles in determination. "What do I tell your mom? I've been covering for you, but she's getting suspicious. It's been a few days since you last spoke. Also, Lyuba and Gogi want to know where you are."

"Stall Mom a bit longer," I say. "But you can tell Lyuba and Gogi where I am. How's Gogi, by the way?"

"Healing well," Ada says. "He and Lyuba are keeping Muhomor company."

"I'm sending a car to your location," Mitya says. "Oh, and you'll be happy to learn these morons kept records of the drugs they gave you, as well as the surveillance video of some of the atrocities they did to you—including stuff you missed because you were unconscious. Kadvosky and his gang will have these people's firstborns."

"And speaking of atrocities," Ada says. "Are you listening to that conversation?"

As soon as she directs my attention back to it, I realize I indeed wasn't paying attention to what Agent Lancaster was saying, but I am now, and I hear him say, "I want you out of this room. Now."

Less than a few seconds of real-world time have passed since my friends and I started our hyper-quick Zik chat, so I know I didn't miss much of Lancaster's monologue. I can extrapolate that he said something like, "He lied to you about your son."

The old woman looks scared and for good reason. Lancaster looks like he might choke her if she disobeys his demand for her to leave.

"Joe," I text my cousin. "I'm almost out of this. Don't kill anyone. Talk to Mitya or Ada. We're in touch."

"Where are you?" Joe's reply is again impressively quick for a Brainocyteless human.

"Talk to Mitya about that also," I text Joe. "And I repeat, leave her family alone."

"Fine," Joe answers. "We'll meet shortly."

I gleam a lot of sinister subtext in Joe's words, but since it's directed at people who deserve it, I don't care. Besides, he's not suicidal enough to take on the government.

"Your family is safe," I tell Golovasi-Berger as she shuffles toward the door. Unsure why I'm being nice to her, I decide to get something for myself out of this setup and add, "After you leave, please tell whoever's in charge to call Congressman Chandler. Also, tell him or her to check YouTube for a viral video that'll surely make all of you infamous."

At the mention of the congressman's name, the eyes of the fake shrink and the only eye of the agent look like they want to jump out of their sockets.

"What did you tell him?" Agent Lancaster looks ready to grab a scalpel and slice open his colleague. "What did you do?"

"Nothing." Golovasi-Berger sounds panicked.

"Out," he shouts. Before she even exits the room, he grabs an icepick-like object from the table and leaps at me. "He's going to tell me everything in a couple of minutes. I guarantee it."

"Oh shit," Mitya says in Russian. "That doesn't look good."

"Activate the Relief app," Ada orders me, and I instantly obey.

I enjoy a couple of breaths free from the million aches and pains plaguing me. I also enjoy how the app dilutes the calls of my body's functions.

Unfortunately, my respite is brief.

Agent Lancaster crosses the distance between us and grabs my left hand in a death grip.

"Oh shit," I say, echoing Mitya's earlier assessment, only I say it in Zik. I cringe and turn away, though I can still see what he does through the video feed from the wall camera. "I don't think the Relief app was designed for something like this—"

I don't finish my thought because I begin screaming.

Lancaster sticks the icepick under the nail of my right pinky finger and slides it into my flesh.

CHAPTER TWENTY-SEVEN

I keep screaming, out loud in Russian and English, but also telepathically in Zik.

My body convulses, and I fear I'm about to lose the contents of both my bladder and bowels.

If the Relief app is lessening this pain, I don't want to imagine what this would feel like without it.

My friends telepathically scream with me.

"I'm ready to talk," I yell at Agent Lancaster as loudly as I can.

"I just found his phone number in their directory," Mitya says. "I'm sending the full Tema algorithm to it."

"Check your phone," I shout. "You got your fucking Tema!"

Instantly, Lancaster's heroic ringtone goes off.

"It might not be my email." Mitya looks at the culprit phone suspiciously. "Maybe it's the congressman. If he's watching the live feed I sent him, I bet he's beyond pissed."

The problem with the brain boost is it makes the agony last longer. After an intolerable millisecond of pain, Agent Lancaster rips the icepick from my poor finger and glares at his phone.

The Relief app masks the pain in my wounded finger, allowing me to finally inhale.

The door to the room creaks open, and Golovasi-Berger storms in with a couple of Suits whose faces I remember from the hospital, plus Agent Pugh.

Just like at the hospital, the Suits are holding Tasers. Unlike at the hospital, it's Agent Lancaster, and not me, they're pointing their weapons at.

"You should speak with Congressman Chandler," one of them says in a hard tone. "Mr. Cohen is to be released, immediately. You are relieved of your duties."

Lancaster looks like a trapped animal, and in a pre-cog-like moment, I can almost see him raising the icepick and jamming it into my eye.

I guess the Suits also see his intent, because without another word, they shoot him with their Tasers.

Lancaster collapses onto the floor, and a person in a surgical mask shows up, seemingly out of nowhere. He injects the twitching agent with a syringe, and Lancaster's body slumps on the floor.

"I think I'll need to run the BraveChill app for a few weeks after this," Ada says. She sounds as shaken as I feel. "Is it just me, or did this agent totally lose his mind?"

"I guess he was attached to that eye," Mitya deadpans. "He must've wanted to literally have an eye for an eye transaction with Mike."

Ada groans, but I focus on the medical person, because he pulls out another syringe and approaches me next.

"Wait," I say. "What are you—"

The needle goes into my arm, and warmth spreads throughout my body.

"This is a good sign." Ada reassures me, though it's unclear if she believes what she's saying. "I bet they're letting you go but don't want you to know where the black site is."

"I would have preferred one of those black bags over my head," I reply, my thoughts already blurring. "And I know where I am."

"I guess it's too late to tell them we already know where their station is." Mitya sounds like he's far away.

"I can't believe I'm getting knocked out again," I send in Zik, and the drug finally does its job, making everything go black.

I wake up to the smell of coconut shampoo and the feel of petite hands stroking my back.

"You have been unconscious for five hours and sixteen minutes," Einstein says. "Current time is 5:47 p.m."

Still confused, I assess the situation and realize I must be in a car that's in motion—or sitting on a vibrating mattress, though this seems less likely.

An avalanche of excitement hits me from the EmoRat app, and I feel Mr. Spock cuddle up to my face, his whiskers tickling my cheek.

"What's that, baby?" says a voice that sounds like Ada's baby/rat talk. Since the voice is not coming from an app, I must assume Ada is the owner of the small hands working the kinks out of my back, and the source of the nice scent filling my nostrils. "He's finally awake?"

"I'm awake," I say out loud and open my eyes—only to be met by the pink gaze of my favorite pet.

"Where am I?" I turn over.

Ada's amber eyes are puffy, like she was crying, and the sight makes me want to rip someone's head off, though I'm too groggy to decide whose. As I look, I see fresh tears in her eyes, but I think they're happy tears. Honestly, I didn't let myself fully register how much I missed Ada until now. If, as the old adage goes, distance makes the heart grow fonder, then getting kidnapped and abused by the government makes the heart nearly burst with emotion.

I sit up and find it surprisingly easy to move. A quick check of the lab on the chip reveals why. I'm pumped to the brim with painkillers.

Unbidden, my arm goes around Ada's waist, my palm landing on my favorite spot—the two dimples in the small of her back. She leans into me, and I pull her in for a kiss. Her lips quiver as they explore mine, and her breathing quickens as her tongue begins to—

Someone loudly clears his throat, and I pull away from Ada to look around the car—something I probably should've done first.

We're inside a massive limousine, surrounded by a bunch of people who I assume work for Joe, because he's also here. When Joe spots me looking at him, his somber expression twists, and he does something I didn't think I'd ever—and I mean *ever*—see him do.

He winks at me.

Maybe he developed a nervous tick that I mistook for something playful?

"It's official," says a familiar voice from my right, and I realize this is the person who cleared his throat a second ago—Gogi. "You'd sleep through Armageddon."

I turn and see that Gogi is sitting between a couple of extra-large dudes, and there's a pair of crutches at his feet. He looks much better than I expected him to after four days of recovery.

"How are you feeling?" I ask and can't help but grin at the Georgian's good humor. Telepathically, I ask Ada, "So, what happened?"

In the time it takes Gogi to tell me he's healing okay, Ada gives me the rundown of what happened while I was out in swift mental Zik messages. She starts with a quick update on some of the technological advancements these guys have come up with in a deceptively short time. The most interesting development is Mitya's new algorithm that allows Einstein to pilot a drone—something that will severely cut costs for Mitya's drone delivery system that services New York and New Jersey (since the current system uses human pilots). I then learn that both Tema and the Brainocytes got released as soon as I was knocked out, and the releases are exploding the brains of everyone in the cryptography and tech fields. Amazingly, in a few hours, at least fifty articles were published on the subject of how the Brainocytes could be used. Some of the ideas proposed are things we, the arrogant Brainocytes Club members, never imagined. Ada sends me her favorite ten ideas so I can review them later, and then she moves on to a less pleasant topic that she would clearly rather avoid.

Thanks to Mitya's marketing people, my videos, especially the one where the tube is going up my nose, have gone viral. JC has been working hard at making sure my mom doesn't see the videos, but I'll have to tell her what happened at some point, or risk her hearing it from the news. Human rights organizations are on the warpath over the videos, which is good, but I'm forever cursed to be a celebrity of sorts, which is bad. A popular senator, who had experienced torture as a war prisoner, tweeted a condemnation of the things done against me, as did leaders of many countries around the world. The president hasn't commented yet, but several US government officials, both elected and appointed, already held a record number of press conferences. Some claimed that at least part of the torture was medical assistance provided to a suspect detained after sustaining severe injuries—baloney, in other words. Some also said my capture was based on faulty intelligence, and later conferences suggested the actions committed against me were the result of an agent gone rogue. Both Ada and I know this is just a case of scapegoating.

"All the medical people at that facility lost their licenses, even the woman whose finger you damaged. Everyone else behind the task force will regret their actions," Ada concludes, her real-world eyes getting that dangerous gleam I've learned to be wary of. "After the news cycles complete their witch hunt for whoever the media deems responsible, we'll unleash Kadvosky and his lawyers on any survivors and make them wish they never heard your name."

"I think you should take it easy," I tell Gogi. At the same time, I mentally tell Ada, "Thanks, but you never explained how I ended up here, in this limo, with this entourage."

"That's simple," Ada says out loud, and no one in the car so much as blinks at the sudden reply to an unasked question. "The government people dropped you off at the Hackensack University Medical Center in New Jersey. As soon as I learned your location, I wanted you transported to the NYU Langone Medical Center. Your cousin demanded the security detail tag along—"

"And she insisted on joining," Joe intrudes, and I can tell he and Ada must've argued about this issue. Somehow, he lost. "Nor did I want this invalid here." Joe points his index finger at Gogi accusingly, but the Georgian doesn't look chastised.

I look through the tinted window. The sight of greenery crisscrossed by electrical towers, as well as the warehouses and factories in the distance, suggests we're still in New Jersey. Einstein confirms this via GPS.

Still looking at the road, I start the Teleconference app and invite Mitya and Ada into the session.

Mitya says, "I'm still in the air, but I should be in New York soon." He must see my avatar show up in the room in front of him, because he smiles and adds, "Oh, if it isn't Sleeping Ugly."

"I'll let that slide, given how much you've helped me in the last few hours," I say. "Do you guys have an update on Muhomor?"

"You didn't tell him?" Mitya asks Ada.

"I didn't get the chance," Ada counters. "Here, Mike, watch this video. It was taken from the hospital security camera."

I see a hospital room that looks a lot like the luxury accommodations they have at the NYU Langone Medical Center—our destination. There's a bed in the middle of the room, and Muhomor is set up with medical equipment that gives me an unpleasant flashback.

A bunch of people are there, including a blond woman with classic good looks whom I recognize as Lyuba—Muhomor's ally, but not girlfriend. She's visiting from Russia. Ada is among the crowd, telling me I'm looking at a recording rather than a live feed.

Seeing Muhomor like this is sad. It's probably the longest I've seen him not say something snarky.

Suddenly, the monitoring equipment beeps, and medical people begin to murmur. Even without a medical degree, I can see what happened.

Muhomor's eyes are open, and he's trying to say something.

"How are you feeling?" a doctor asks him in the video.

"Viktor, can you hear us?" Lyuba asks in Russian, her hand on his wrist.

Muhomor keeps mouthing the same phrase over and over, and when I eventually hear it, I can't help but chuckle. "This hospital's cybersecurity is atrocious," he's saying. "I want all my personal data expunged from this sorry excuse of a database. I want—"

I stop the video. I suspect Muhomor's rant might be long, and I just wanted to know how he's doing.

"How is he now?" I ask Mitya and Ada and notice they're each waiting for the other person to answer the question—not a good sign.

"He's paralyzed from the waist down." In the real world, Ada puts her hand on mine reassuringly. "The doctors say this was the best-case scenario."

I grasp her hand and sever my emotional link to Mr. Spock, lest he experience too much of my sadness.

"How are his spirits?" I ask, unsure what to say in the midst of such a horrific revelation. "Is there anything I can do?"

"Why don't you ask him?" Mitya says. "I just invited him to this conversation."

"Misha." Muhomor's telepathic message is filled with way too much excitement. "I was just talking about you with Mitya."

"Yeah," Mitya echoes sarcastically. "Why don't you tell *him* what you just told me?"

"Sure," Muhomor states in Zik and manifests his usual anime-inspired avatar into the limo. "I was saying how glad I am that Mike was tortured."

I'm distracted for a second by the depressing knowledge that while Muhomor's avatar is standing on cartoon legs, real-world Muhomor will never be able to stand like that again. Then his words hit me. "What? You're happy I was tortured?"

"I'm happy about the consequences of it," Muhomor clarifies. "Not the actual pain you suffered per se, but that's irrelevant to my point."

"That's nice," Ada chimes in. Her sarcasm has a dangerous edge. "Very empathetic."

"All I'm saying," Muhomor continues, unfazed, "is that it was genius of you to release Tema and the Braincytes on the tail of this torture business, even if I wish you'd asked my opinion on releasing the latter."

"How so?" I ask. "I mean, I'm glad I got myself tortured for the greater good, but it would be nice to know what that greater good is or was."

"When contemplating the release of Tema, one of my big concerns was that the government might want to regulate or suppress it." Muhomor's avatar sprouts a cartoony pipe and puffs out a cloud of cartoon smoke. "But now, with you as the figurehead behind these technologies, things might go differently. Think about it from a politician's point of view. After all the wrongs the government has committed against you, no one wants to be known as the guy who picked on you again by attacking your intellectual achievements. In other words, whoever decides to suppress your technologies will look like they're trying to pick on you—and no one should, since they'd get tainted by this torture business."

"That makes a warped kind of sense," Mitya says. "Especially if politicians thought like you, Muhomor. Thankfully, they do not. I think this is a moot point anyway. There's little chance of suppressing either technology, given the way I distributed them—worldwide. The power these will bring will cause a paradigm shift. Suppressing it in the US would just mean the US would technologically fall behind more forward-thinking countries. Like China, for example."

We sit quietly for a moment, each imagining what the world will be like once the Brainocytes are ubiquitous.

I know I'll regret this, but I say, "Muhomor, at some point, you've got to tell us about your kompromat and cyberweapons. The task force feared you had dead man's switches prepared in case you got into trouble. Is that true?"

"To quote Machiavelli, it's better to be feared than loved," Muhomor replies cryptically. "I will only tell you about these things when I feel like I have enough kompromat on all of *you*, and I don't feel that way—yet."

"On that nice, friendly note, Mike and I are going to disconnect," Ada says. "Glad to hear about your improving health, *Viktor*."

"We're going to disconnect?" I ask in the real world.

"Yes," she replies telepathically. "I've been meaning to talk to you about something important for what feels like a year, and I don't think it can wait."

"All right, guys," I send into the group conversation. "We'll be back in a bit."

"Someone's in trouble," I hear Muhomor tell Mitya as Ada and I disconnect.

"Am I in trouble?" I ask Ada, my pulse accelerating.

She looks at me with uncertainty for a real-world second—a long time telepathically.

A sick feeling curls in my stomach as I remember my suspicions about Ada's strange behavior in recent weeks. My paranoia about being followed turned out to be warranted, so could my worry about Ada's behavior be as well?

Desperate, I blurt out, "Would you really break up with me so soon after I was tortured? Have you no heart?"

Ada looks taken aback. "What? No, you're not in trouble," she mentally replies. "At least not *that* kind of trouble."

I exhale in relief. "Okay, then what *is* this big talk about?" Before Ada can answer, my brain-boosted mind runs through different possibilities, each scarier than the next, and my stomach plunges again. "You're not sick, are you?"

"No. Not sick. Not exactly, anyway. It's more of a big news sort of deal." She chews on her lower lip. "A big surprise. Because of how unexpected it is, I wasn't sure how to tell you."

"Tell me what?" If I wasn't communicating telepathically, my voice would've probably betrayed my panic. An improbable suspicion flits through my mind, but I dismiss it, because what are the odds?

"I'm pregnant," Ada blurts out in emotionless Zik. "Or is it more appropriate to say *we* are pregnant?"

"We're pregnant?" I yell out loud, switching to Russian—something I've never done under stress before. My improbable suspicion was spot on—another score for my boosted intelligence. Not that having had that glimmer helps; I still feel utterly shell-shocked.

Ada looks around us, her cheeks reddening. "I meant for this to be a private, telepathic conversation," she says, also out loud, and I realize Gogi and my cousin are staring at me. Gogi wears a shocked expression, but Joe looks like he's in thoughtful contemplation.

Kiril, one of Joe's Russian-speaking goons, gives me a thumbs-up and starts to say something, but Joe gives him a quelling look. I interpret it as, "Don't fuck with my cousin right now. He just made me an uncle, and I always wanted to be someone's uncle."

Even Mr. Spock, who isn't linked to me via the EmoRat app, picks up on the tumult of emotions in the air and peeks out of my pocket, glancing at Ada and then me, his nose twitching nervously.

I tear my eyes away from the rat and stare unblinkingly at Ada for a couple of breaths.

Ada doesn't blink either, her gaze expectant. She's probably waiting for some sort of reaction from me.

"I don't know what to say," I finally say, still out loud. "This is huge." Then, telepathically, I add, "I'm not calling *you* huge. I can't actually tell you're pregnant—"

Figuring now is a good time to shut up, verbally and mentally, I reach out and give Ada a tight hug. With her warm body firmly pressed against mine, I process what she told me and feel like I'm riding a roller-coaster, though I'm not sure if I'm spiraling up or down.

Ada relaxes in my arms, and I realize I must've done the right thing.

It takes all my willpower not to say something idiotic like, "How could this happen?" Instead, I use my mind to quickly search the internet for answers. We always use condoms when we have sex, but I quickly learn that condoms *can* break, and the tear in the latex is invisible to the naked eye. Considering how much sex we have and with how much vigor, I can see how that could happen. As it turns out, when looking at it statistically, condoms are eighty-five-percent effective in actual use, so Ada and I are among the lucky fifteen percent. A few other things also make sense. Ada felt pretty nauseous a few days back. She didn't drink any vodka or wine, even the Georgian wine that's organic and vegan without egg whites or gelatin. Also, and this was the big clue, her period is usually at the beginning of the month, yet we never stopped having sex this month, meaning her period never happened. And—

"We never got a chance to talk about kids," Ada mentally interrupts my chain of thought. "I now wish we had."

"That's not entirely true. We had that one conversation," I remind her. "When you said one day you wanted to use CRISPR and other genetic modification tools to make a super baby with biological super intelligence, extreme longevity, enhanced empathy, and I forget what else."

"Right." She pulls away from the hug, and I see that she's smiling. "You mean that day when you said you'd prefer to make a virtual baby, 'a merger of our minds, not our genetics,' one we'd only experience via Virtual and Augmented Reality interfaces—so no diapers and other unpleasantness?"

"I guess we're both going to experience something far more mundane." I lay my right hand on her knee and run my left hand through her spiked hair. "I'm sure it'll be very interesting. Just think about it. Building an artificial general intelligence is such a difficult problem, even with the Brainocytes, yet a baby basically starts off as a dumb bundle of cells that grows to gain general intelligence out of the box. Just provide some coloring books, some food, some love, and some toys and other entertainment. Maybe we can learn how to—"

"I want to give the baby Brainocytes," Ada mentally interrupts and gives me a worried look in the real world. "As soon as it's safe to do so."

"That sounds like a cool idea," I reply without hesitation. "Some people might see it as experimenting on the baby, but to me, it's no different from those people who play Mozart to their baby or get them fancy tutors and toys. We'll be able to communicate with our kid before he or she can speak. We can probably modify the EmoRat app to—"

I stop talking, confused by the sheer amount of adoration in Ada's beautiful eyes.

"What? Is it something I said? I mean, thought?"

She shakes her head. "I'm just happy. You're going to be a great—"

Ada doesn't finish her thought because, in that moment, a gunshot rings out, and the tinted limousine back window shatters into small pieces.

CHAPTER TWENTY-EIGHT

My pulse jumps, and adrenaline floods my veins. Through the shattered window, I see a red truck on our tail. It must be the source of the gunfire. There's not much traffic on the freeway otherwise, with more cars ahead of us than immediately behind. Still, there's a small chance the shot came from a car hiding behind the truck.

I squint and confirm my suspicions about the truck. There are two people in the front seats. A black motorcycle helmet obscures the driver's face, something that's suspicious on its own, and not just because it thwarts the facial recognition app. However, it's the second person, the one with the assault rifle pointed at our limo, who seals my conviction that the truck is up to no good.

I don't need an app to recognize that I'm staring at the killer chimpanzee mug of Vincent Williams.

Just when I think the truck is the only vehicle we need to worry about, I hear the roar of two-stroke internal combustion engines revving, and four motorcycles appear from behind the truck. They must've been hiding there. The bikers are wearing helmets like that of Williams's driver, only one of them drew a fierce scowling skull over his or her helmet.

The rush of adrenaline puts my boosted mind into that slowed-down battle mode, a sensation that's unfortunately beginning to feel familiar.

My first thought is about Ada's safety, and I wonder if it's the pregnancy variable making me feel so savagely angry at the attackers. I feel myself becoming wrath. I wouldn't be surprised if I burst into green skin and rippling muscles. If I had the chance, I'd beat every one of our pursuers to death with a small hammer and then do something equally awful to their corpses.

Ada and I are still sitting within hugging distance in the back, meaning she's much too close to danger. I grab Ada by the shoulders and pull her toward the middle of the limo while telepathically saying, "Stay here, baby."

She's in so much shock that she complies—or she's just smart enough to comply. My logic for putting her in the center is that, with all these men around the car, the middle is the safest place. To reach Ada, the bullet will have to go through me or one of these men—a sacrifice I'm willing to make.

While I'm taking care of Ada, my brain boost allows me to pay attention to the world around me. I'm aware that Joe and his people sprang into action at the same time I did. Gogi gets up too, but it's clear that moving hurts him. Two men—Luke and Carter, according to the face recognition app—already have their guns out and are leaping for the broken window, probably moments away from shooting back. Everyone else, including Joe, is reaching for the seat they were sitting on—though I can't fathom why.

A number of facts surface and congeal into a partial explanation of what's happening. Agent Lancaster was adamant about not having anything to do with Vincent Williams's attacks. There was a point when I wasn't sure if he was telling the truth, but I later believed him, mostly because his words were supported by the fact that Muhomor nearly got killed during the attack at the restaurant, and the task force wanted Muhomor alive—in part due to his insurance policy, and in part because they wanted Tema. I also suddenly recall something that slipped my mind while they were holding me prisoner.

Williams mentioned a list when we faced each other. That list doesn't make sense in the context of the task force, but it does if someone has a bone to pick with Joe and me. So, if Vincent Williams attacked us for reasons unrelated to the task force, it stands to reason he would still be after us, even though the task force is done with me. Then again, whatever his original mission, Williams is likely after us now to avenge his brother's death.

Thanks to the boost, I think all these thoughts while Luke and Carter only make a millimeter of progress toward the window, moving as though underwater.

Joe and the rest are also still reaching for their seats.

Since I have no gun and no plan, I decide to do something that won't take much real-world time and jump back into the virtual conference with Mitya and Muhomor. As soon as I connect, my friends' images show up in the already crammed interior of the limo. Grateful for the speed with which we can communicate in Zik, I do my best not to sound too hysterical as I summarize the situation, concluding with, "It's Williams again. Oh, and Ada has to survive at all cost. She's pregnant."

In this moment, Ada also joins the conversation. She must've recovered from her initial shock.

"We need to work together to get us out of this." Ada's Zik is again quicker than normal. "Mike, you take the lead, like during the gunfight at the restaurant."

"Got it," I reply, careful not to point out that she's taking a lead by assigning me a role, since I'm grateful she did.

I have to give Muhomor and Mitya credit. They don't say a peep about Ada's pregnancy or complain about her bossing everyone around. Instead, in unison, they ask, "What can I do?"

"Muhomor, you're on reconnaissance and, if possible, sabotage duty," I rattle out. "Mitya, I want you to come up with a plan. Get police on the phone and find us a good place to go and maybe supplies we can use—"

"I'm already in the process of hacking into some satellites." Muhomor's anime avatar rubs his cartoony hands together in anticipation. "Also, I'll see if I can get into your pursuers' phones or their vehicles' computers."

"I don't have a plan yet," Mitya chimes in, "but let me enumerate some useful information. First, you're driving in my limo, which—"

"Please tell me it's one of the Zapo rip-offs," I interrupt. "The ones you asked Sven to mod? That would be awesome news."

"And please tell us that unlike the window, the rest of the limo is bulletproof," Ada adds. "Because in my opinion, *that* would be awesome news."

"I don't own any bulletproof vehicles," Mitya replies defensively. "Unlike some people, I don't have any enemies. Also, I wouldn't say it's a rip-off per se. An argument can be made that Zapo was a rip-off—"

"No time to argue about originality," I cut in. "Is it a limo that can be remotely driven with the Batmobile app? The one with a bunch of sensors all around it, a nitro boost, and so on?"

In the real world, Luke and Carter finally reach the window and shoot. The sound reverberates through the confined space, and Ada mentally curses. The motorcyclists or the people in the truck shoot back. I hear Luke grunt and see him clutch his shoulder. Carter is fine and returns fire.

The gunshots scare Mr. Spock to the point where his mental aura is a nervous gray. I do my best to reassure him through the app. Mr. Spock's mood turns amber, and I feel a pang of jealousy. I wish someone could do for me what I just did for him, because if I were a rat, my aura would be the darkest black.

Meanwhile, my cousin and his people open the limo seats, and I finally understand why. Under the seats is storage, and it contains an arsenal that would make a warlord squeal in glee. At a glance, I see guns, bulletproof vests, and even something that looks like a rocket launcher.

"Yes, it's one of those limos, and yes, it's Sven's work. Before you ask, I told your cousin about that storage space, though I didn't think he'd turn it into an armory." Mitya's reply is only slightly grumpy. "The limo is currently being driven by Einstein. The driver is just there to open doors for you guys, so you can have your cousin hand him a gun. Eli is a Gulf War vet, so he can probably assist you."

"Joe," I say out loud. "Toss me a gun and pass one to the driver."

Joe doesn't just throw me a gun; he also pulls out a stack of bulletproof vests and tosses three my way. He then scoots up to the small window, where the driver's hand is already sticking out, and gives the man a gun. I put on one vest and hand both the smaller and the larger ones to Ada, figuring two vests are better than one. To emphasize the importance of my request, I address Ada out loud. "Put those on, please."

I then hand Mr. Spock to Ada, figuring she's bound to stay safer if she's protecting him as well as herself.

Then I recall she's already protecting something small—our unborn baby—and this thought brings back the blinding anger. It threatens to overtake me, but I push it back for now.

I need a clear head to deal with this.

"Protect her," I tell Mr. Spock through our mental connection. "Do your best to keep her calm."

I could swear Mr. Spock gives me a small nod before letting Ada stuff him into her bra under the bulletproof vest. I bet he's already bruxing in the warm comfort of her bosom.

While I examine my new gun and put on the vest in the physical world, I also keep the hyper-fast virtual conversation going with my faraway friends. "Mitya, take over driving the limo. You have a brain boost, so your response time should be better than any normal human driver and, in this case, better than the safety-obsessed Einstein."

"Done," Mitya says. "I'll take you to my LAR facility. It's only fifteen minutes away."

Again, I multitask by doing more than two things at once. I enter the information of the gun my cousin gave me into the aim-assist app while also researching what Mitya meant by LAR. A millisecond later, I find out he's talking about Levin Aero Robotics, the facility that produces and stores his delivery drones. While I do all that, I tell Joe out loud, "Can you spare two men to protect Ada with their bodies? I want her inside a human pyramid."

I expect my cousin to protest or say I should be either at the front or back of the pyramid I proposed, but he nods decisively at Gogi and Luke. "You heard him. Gogi, bind Luke's shoulder while you're at it."

His choices make sense. Both men are wounded and can't help in the fight anyway. Gogi grunts in pain as he gets to the floor, and Luke follows him. This is the only situation I can imagine when it would be okay for other men to be so close to my Ada. Once she's in that protective formation, I feel like I can exhale the breath I've been holding since the shooting began.

"Why are you taking us to LAR?" I ask Mitya. "It's just a glorified factory."

The gun information—Beretta 92—registers with the app, and when I enable the HUD overview, a bullet count of fifteen shows up in the corner of my vision. This gun feels a bit bigger in my hand than the Glock I've been practicing with, and I hope that doesn't affect my aim.

"There are four security guards on LAR's premises," Mitya explains. "And it's not just a factory. It's also a storage facility where we do some research and development—"

"Just take us to the damn LAR." Ada looks unhappy about her passive position. "It'll give the police a specific location to go to and—"

"This isn't the best plan." Muhomor imbues his message with worry, though he's watching the events from far away in a hospital bed. "I just checked the satellites. Four more cars and five more motorcycles will join you at the next exit, and I don't think you can get to LAR without passing by that exit. I'll send everyone the link to my view."

In a fraction of a second, I see what Muhomor is talking about. Vehicles are turning onto the exit in question. The black helmets leave no doubt that these people are in league with the bikers behind us.

"Well, the limo can't get anywhere without passing that exit anyway," Mitya says, and I have to agree with him. We already passed the ramp leading off the freeway, and the tall walls on either side of the road prevent us from going off-road, either intentionally or by accident.

"How many drones do you have parked at LAR?" Ada asks Mitya. "I think I have an idea."

"A hundred percent of the ones that deliver in New Jersey," Mitya says. "And forty percent of the ones that service NYC."

As Ada and Mitya talk telepathically, I say out loud during a pause in the gunfire, "Joe, we're about to have more company."

"Mitya, does this screen work?" I ask, nodding toward the gigantic TV located next to the little window on a wall that separates the driver's section from the passenger side.

"Yes, it does," my friend replies. "I'll put up a regular Skype window there so Muhomor and I can speak with your cousin and the rest of the Brainocyteless."

"I also want you to put feeds from various cameras around the car," I say. Realizing I haven't taken the time to put the feeds from those cameras onto my AROS overview, I do so.

"Mitya, I'm taking over control of all the available drones." Ada's telepathic message is a fury of determination. "These fuckers pissed me off."

"Shit," Muhomor messages me privately. "If pregnant women are anything like bears with cubs, Ada might be a sight to behold right now."

Before I can reply to Muhomor, another bout of automatic gunfire rings out, and the side windows shatter into little pieces, raining onto the carpeted limo floor.

The cameras show that the gunfire came from the motorcyclists who were hiding behind the truck. There are four of them, and they sped up to flank us on both sides.

Two motorcyclists are level with the front doors, while the other two are level with the middle. What's worse is they're all aiming their Uzis at us, ready to shoot again.

I brace for the blast of noise and deadly danger.

"I got this," Mitya says from the screen. "It's going to get a little bumpy."

"Dude, wait," I mentally send, but it's too late.

Tires screeching, the limo veers toward the left side of the road.

CHAPTER TWENTY-NINE

Gogi curses as he nearly falls onto Ada. Joe and most of his guys grab on to the tops of the seats, and I follow their example, my wrist feeling like it might come out of its socket.

"I know this isn't a good time to complain about someone's BO," Ada shares in a telepathic chat, "but if we survive this, I'm getting Gogi a case of deodorant."

The driver's door of the limo crashes against the middle of the front-most bike, resulting in another unpleasant bump for us. The bike flips in the air, tossing the rider off like a mad bull at a rodeo. The motorcyclist's black helmet slams against the asphalt, and he rolls under the limo's back wheels. It feels like we hit a speed bump as we run the guy over.

I hope the downed bike trips up the second motorcyclist driving right behind it, creating a nice chain reaction of death for our pursuers, but the second guy must've worked as a stunt driver. In a brain-boost-worthy display of quick reactions, he lets go of his Uzi, grabs the hand grips until his knuckles turn white, and pulls in a jerky motion. His front tire lifts at just the right moment, and he runs his bike up the obstacle in the most impressive way possible. After the guy successfully finishes his maneuver (and probably feels a rush from that accomplishment), Joe shoots him in the head. The motorcyclist falls sideways with his bike without letting go.

He has a literal death grip on it now.

The motorcyclists on our right must be upset with the fates of their leftmost brethren, because they frantically shoot at us again, as do the two assholes in the truck behind us.

"What happens if they hit our tires?" Ada asks inside the virtual conference. Her wide-eyed avatar looks as panicked as I feel.

"The limo's tires are airless," Mitya says. "Didn't Sven put the same ones on Zapo?"

"You know he didn't," I reply, glad that transmitting jealousy is optional when using the Telepathy app. "What else can this car do that Zapo couldn't?"

"I'll give you the full specs when we have a free moment," Mitya promises. "For the time being, let me focus on my driving."

As though to illustrate Mitya's request, the limo wobbles, and I can tell my friend is trying to regain control of the vehicle. This means he can't repeat the maneuver he performed against the rightmost thugs. I decide to deal with them myself, or at least the front-most one since my window is closest to him. Knowing these people are shooting at pregnant Ada leaves me with few qualms about their fate. Yet, out of morality or hypocrisy, I don't shoot my target in the head. Instead, I place the line from the aim-assist app on the guy's right wrist and pull the trigger.

Since my target was effectively driving one-handed, he loses control of the bike and somersaults through the air. His bike skids across the asphalt, sparks flying everywhere, and in the satellite view, I see some bystander's Toyota Camry hit the bike and swerve into the freeway wall.

"Okay," I say into the virtual conference. "Now we only have to deal with the one remaining biker asshole on the right."

"And the truck behind us," Ada reminds me telepathically.

"And the people ahead of you," Muhomor adds.

They're both right, of course. The truck is still on our tail, and according to the satellite view, we're going to pass the ramp leading onto the freeway in a couple of seconds.

Another shot rings out from the truck behind us. I use the camera inside the limo to see that Carter got hit, and his neck wound looks bad.

Joe and Caleb, the guy on his left, both dive for the unprotected back window. This is when I notice that Joe is shouldering the portable missile launcher.

"I think that's Russian," Muhomor says. "RPG-7."

"What are you talking about?" Mitya asks telepathically. "Don't distract me with video-game talk. Now that I've evened out the car, I'm going to do that maneuver again."

In a flash of insight, I realize Mitya isn't seeing what's happening inside the limo at the moment, and he thinks Muhomor is talking about Role Playing Games instead of the Ruchnoy Protivotankovyy Granatomyot. In that same flash of insight, I see a big problem with what's about to happen and mentally yell, "Wait—"

Mitya either doesn't hear me or my message arrives in his brain a moment too late, because the car swerves right—exactly as Joe shoots his rocket/grenade.

The last motorcycle guy, the one with the skull painted on his helmet, slams into the back of the limo and cartwheels backward in a mess of metal and meat.

Unfortunately, Joe's missile doesn't even scratch the truck as it flies by and explodes against the freeway wall. The bang is so loud it blows out the remnants of glass from the window in front of me and turns Mr. Spock's aura black.

Through the ringing in my ears, I become aware that Muhomor is chastising Mitya for ruining Joe's shot while Ada's telling them to focus on the task at hand.

Shaking off the stunned feeling, I look at the cavalcade of enemies that just got on the freeway up ahead. They're slowing, which means we'll have to deal with them soon.

"Do you see that Jeep Cherokee?" Muhomor's question jerks me out of my thoughts, and I realize I was just looking at the car he named.

"Yes," Mitya says. This must've been part of an argument they're having.

"This is how it's done." Muhomor's avatar waves his hand in a gesture worthy of a crappy magician, and the Jeep Cherokee's tires suddenly stop spinning, causing the driver to lose control. As the Jeep careens into the freeway wall, it takes out one of the bikers.

"Great job," I chime in. "Now do that to the rest."

"The rest aren't as hackable as the Cherokee was." Muhomor's avatar suddenly appears less smug. "I'll keep trying, though." More defensively, he adds, "I've been distracting your opponents by having their phones text each other nonsense and vibrating at random. It beats messing up someone's RPG." Muhomor gives Mitya's hoodie-clad avatar a derisive stare.

I ignore Mitya's reply and my own racing heartbeat as I assess the remaining enemy forces ahead. There's a yellow Hummer driving in the rightmost lane, a silver 4Runner in the leftmost lane, and a blue Honda Ridgeline truck ahead of the others, riding in the middle. Plus, there are four more bikes riding between civilian cars ahead of the 4Runner. Of course, there's still the red truck behind us, the one Joe is still shooting at—a truck I finally recognize as a Toyota Hilux. This is odd, because I don't think this model is sold in the US.

"They're slowing," I tell my friends in the conference. "I think they're planning a TPAC."

When I get asked, I explain what I read online. TPAC stands for Tactical Pursuit and Containment formation. The maneuver is used in England. Specifically, it involves boxing in a car between four other cars, one in the front, one in the back, and one on each side.

"Screw that." Mitya's avatar angrily pushes his glasses higher on his nose. "I'll take their British pursuit tactic and raise them a good-old American one called the PIT."

Mitya must activate the nitro—that, or someone shot the limo with a rocket—and we torpedo forward at 250 per hour.

We whoosh between the Hummer and the 4Runner so fast no one gets a chance to shoot at each other. In a blink, we're on the tail of the Ridgeline—the car that must've planned to position itself at the front of the makeshift box these people wanted to build around the limo.

I research the PIT, and as soon as I do, I want to object to Mitya's idea, but it's too late. The limo is already passing the Ridgeline on the right, nitro boost gone.

The PIT, or Precision Immobilization Technique, is something American cops do, and it involves ramming the offending car behind the back tire.

And that's exactly what Mitya does.

The limo shudders with a disgusting crunch, but it's worth it. The Ridgeline loses control and swerves onto the median strip that separates us from oncoming traffic, sparks and plastic flying in every direction.

As a bonus, the yellow Hummer is forced to slow down to avoid crashing into the remnants of the blue truck.

"That's a lot like the maneuver you did to those bikers," Muhomor points out. "Just with a fancy name."

"Cops aren't allowed to do a PIT on motorcyclists," Mitya responds pedantically.

I don't shut either of them up since their competition to get rid of our problems is a win-win fight.

Unfortunately, the impact makes us lose speed, and the 4Runner gains on us. The bikers in front of us slow down as well.

"Boys," Ada intervenes. "Can you focus on keeping us alive until the next exit? It's a measly minute away at this speed."

Mitya replies to Ada, but I don't listen because my attention is on the 4Runner as it begins to pass us on the right. Its windows are down, and at least four helmeted enemies are staring out, ready for action.

Then I see something extremely worrying.

The front passenger in the 4Runner is holding a grenade.

"Grenade!" I yell just as it begins flying in an arc toward the limo.

Adrenaline makes the flight of the cursed object seem glacial, like slowed footage shot with a high-speed camera.

If my boost-assisted calculations are correct, this grenade is going to land in the middle of the limo… and blow up next to Ada.

CHAPTER THIRTY

As the grenade flies, I mentally scream for Mitya to adjust our course, though I know there isn't enough time.

I reflect on the cruelty of thinking fast without being able to move proportionally fast. If I could move like the Flash, I would jump on the grenade and cover it with my vest-clad body. But I know I won't make it in time, so I don't even try. Instead, I put the aim-assist app's line in the center of the helmet of the guy who threw the grenade and, without a single qualm, pull the trigger.

The guy's head begins to explode inside his helmet just as the grenade flies through our broken window.

I consider saying some last words to Ada but decide against it on the off chance she doesn't realize we're about to die. I figure if I didn't know our situation, I wouldn't want it explained to me either. Besides, even if Ada could see the grenade, what would I say?

Then I notice something happening in the path of the grenade's trajectory—something that gives me faint hope. Gogi's hands are closing in on the exact location where the grenade is about be. He's about to pull a maneuver that looks like a slowed-down replay of a catcher getting the baseball after a strike out—though being an immigrant from baseball-less Russia, I might have this analogy wrong.

"Could they have taught him a move like this in the Georgian Special Forces?" I manage to ask in the chat as Gogi grabs the grenade and tosses it right back at the 4Runner. Even his throw reminds me of a high-speed pitch from baseball.

The grenade's flight seems to go much quicker on its way back, and I watch without blinking, still adjusting to the idea of continued existence. When the grenade lands on the floor of the 4Runner—meaning no one in that car possessed Gogi's skills—I allow myself to blink. As soon as I open my eyes again, the 4Runner turns into a big fireball, and chunks of silver SUV fly in every direction.

Simultaneously, I hear gunfire coming from both in front and behind us. The Hummer and the red Hilux are still far enough behind us not to be a cause for concern, but the same can't be said about the four bikers in front.

Just when I thought things couldn't get worse, I see that the bikers are toting AK-47s.

We didn't blow up just so we could get shot a moment later instead.

The rattle of machine guns gets louder, and shattered glass rains onto the floor in the front of the limo.

When I glance at Eli, the guy behind the wheel, I see his left arm covered with blood, but that isn't preventing him from shooting at the motorcyclists with his right as bullets cut through the divider on the passenger side. Two bullet holes appear in the TV screen that Mitya and Muhomor have been using, and Mr. Spock's aura is now a color I've never seen.

Maybe I was wrong when I thought black was the worst mood a rat could be in.

Though I know our exit ramp is coming up soon, I fear it won't arrive soon enough. Still, I check the satellite view, and what I see makes no sense.

There's a small dark cloud heading straight for us.

"Guys, am I having an LSD flashback?" I ask, my heart rate speeding up further as I examine the low-flying cloud that's getting closer to us.

"It looks like something out of an American antidepressant commercial," Muhomor quips. "Like your personal rainy day."

"You must be talking about my work," Ada says. "The only way we'll make this exit is if we get rid of these bikers in our way."

I'm about to complain about her lack of explanation, when I realize the cloud is close enough to see through the limo's front camera.

Now that I can see it, I realize that, of course, this isn't a cloud.

It's a swarm.

A swarm of drones—as in unmanned aerial vehicles, not to be confused with male wasps.

"Babe," I mentally say, "please tell me your big idea was to take control of all the drones at Mitya's LAR facility and fly them toward us?"

If Ada says no and the drones belong to the bad guys, we'll be beyond screwed—and until a few moments ago, I didn't think our situation could get any worse.

Ada doesn't answer, but I can see my supposition was spot on, because the swarm dives, and the drones hit the first biker. He does a one-eighty in the air before landing on his neck.

There is a new, more frantic round of AK-47 fire, and a bullet hits Luke in his bulletproof vest, causing the poor guy to yelp in pain.

Ada's answer is instant. Five drones hit the second motorcyclist, two from the front and three from the back. The resulting cartwheel looks like something people do in extreme sports, except stunt people don't usually fly out of their seats like this guy does—nor do they go splat against the road like that.

The third and fourth bikers stop shooting at the limo and open fire at the descending drones.

Many drones get damaged, but even with automatic weapons, the motorcyclists don't stand a chance against the number of drones Ada has under her command.

A single drone, with delivery package still attached to its bottom, lands under the tire of the third biker. The bike flies into the air and does a half rotation before the driver cannonballs onto the asphalt.

I guess Ada got especially bloodthirsty, because she hits the fourth biker with a dozen drones all at once. They all fall in a heap of plastic and metal as the motorcycle draws the number eight in the air.

"Well," I message Mitya. "The good news is all the bikers are gone. The bad news is all these broken bikes and damaged drones have created unsafe road conditions."

"You're right, but I'm taking the exit anyway," Mitya says from the broken screen on the wall. "It's going to get bumpy again, so hold on."

Remembering what happened the last time Mitya said this, I clutch the seat in front of me and hold on as though my life depends on it—since it might.

Taking the turn at 150 miles per hour is bad enough, but when we hit the bike and drone debris, we begin to skid.

Since we didn't die the last few times I thought we would, I remain optimistic. If we hit the wall, though, this could be it.

We don't hit the wall—not exactly. We crash into a yellow, water-filled barrel, a device placed on highways to lessen the impact of such hits, though I doubt the barrel was designed to help at our insane speed.

My heartbeat feels hypersonic, and that's with all my perceptions slowed by the boost.

Water sprays the limo in a fountain, and the impact makes my hands slip.

I fly across the limo, trying my best not to land on Ada.

Gogi manages to grab me by the leg mid-flight. It's the only thing that prevents me from flying out the window.

My head hits the seat so hard I'd have a cracked skull if it weren't for the cushion. As is, I see white stars dance around my vision. The real world blurs in my eyes, but the AROS screens remain as sharp as ever.

"Ada," I shout telepathically. "Are you okay?"

"Busy," she replies. "Have a look at this."

The link Ada gives me leads me to a strange camera view, one that resembles something a fly or a spider would see. It's the world seen through hundreds of eyes, all of which are looking at the Hummer and the red Hilux truck, but also into the distance.

"See that black Chevrolet Suburban speeding through the lanes up there?" Ada's mental tone is tense. "I'm worried about it."

"Yeah, probably more bad guys, but I wouldn't worry about them," I reply. "They'll be too late to kill us, since the guys in the Hummer and Hilux will surely beat them to it."

"Not if I have anything to say about it," Ada counters, and dozens of drone views go into dive mode.

The ground rushes toward each drone. I quickly get dizzy, so I look through one of the limo's back cameras.

From this vantage point, what Ada is doing to the yellow Hummer looks like a scene from Alfred Hitchcock's *The Birds*, only with drones attacking.

"Ada, don't forget to send some toward the red Hilux," I say, but it's clear she's already on it. It's just that the helmeted driver of the Hilux is insane. Though he must have zero visibility due to the diving drones, the red truck still speeds up.

Ada must be desperate, because the swarm separates into two halves, and each group drops onto one of the cars.

For a moment, I can't even see the Hilux or the Hummer under the mess made by the drones.

Then, to my relief, the drone-covered Hummer hits the freeway wall.

Unfortunately, the Hilux ignores the drone parts scattered across the asphalt in front of it, the drones sticking out of its broken windshield, and the drones diving at it.

Then my boosted mind calculates the truck's trajectory and reveals its driver's intent. I scream out loud, "We need to get out of this car!"

For the first time, I take in the wreckage inside the limo. The place looks like that grenade did explode in here.

My cousin begins to move, as do Gogi and Luke. Based on the drones' behavior, I know Ada is conscious, as is Mr. Spock, because I can see his horrified aura. No one else is conscious enough to move, yet that's what we must do and fast. In the camera view, the red truck is getting closer, and I'm a hundred-percent certain it intends to ram into our stopped limo from behind.

Ada is my biggest worry, so I get up and instantly have to enable the Relief app to mask the pain spreading through my body.

The Hilux looms closer.

"The people in the Hummer are getting out," Mitya says mentally. The wall TV is too busted for him to say it from there.

"Let's hope we live long enough to worry about them," I grimly reply.

"And don't forget about the black Suburban," Muhomor chimes in.

"They'll need to take a number." I wish I felt as confident as my mental replies suggest. Out loud, I say, "Gogi, Luke, let go of Ada and try to get out of the car."

The men separate, and when I see how pale Ada is, I want to kill someone again. Only there isn't time. The Hilux is seconds away from turning us into a pancake.

Ada tries to stand up, but yelps and crouches again. "I've been sitting on my leg, and it's completely asleep. All pins and needles." She tries to get up again but nearly twists her ankle. "Go. I'll follow you."

"Help her," Luke grits out, his face twisted in pain. "I got Gogi." Matching action to words, he begins dragging the Georgian out of the car.

"Lean on me," I tell Ada and put my arm around her slim back.

"No," Joe says with an intensity that brooks no objection. "Grab her legs. I'll take her arms."

Ada mumbles something about the indignity of the situation, but Joe and I grab her like a sack and scramble for the door.

In the camera view, I see the truck is about to slam into us.

CHAPTER THIRTY-ONE

My foot is still in the doorframe when the Hilux rips into the limo, destroying our car with the enthusiasm of a competitive eater chomping on his first hotdog.

It feels as though it's the sound wave of the impact that pushes me the rest of the way out. I stumble and nearly drop Ada's legs, but I recover and grab on to her tighter.

"At least we're done with Vincent Williams," Ada comments in the virtual chat.

"Afraid not," Mitya replies. "Whoever built the Toyota Hilux must've been inspired by tanks."

He's right. The red truck is just slightly bent in the front—completely disproportionate to the totaled state of our ride. If the Hilux had airbags—a safe bet—and if the riders wore seatbelts, which I think I recall seeing, they could easily still be alive.

"I have one more operational drone," Ada says. "Should I crash it into someone's head?"

"Let's use it for reconnaissance," I suggest. "Can you raise it up a bit so it can check on both the Hummer and the Suburban? Since we're still alive, we need to worry about them now." While the mental conversation is happening, Joe and I carry Ada to the grass by the road and gently put her down next to Gogi and Luke. Out loud, I say, "Gogi, Luke, please get back into your earlier position in case bullets start flying."

"No," Ada says out loud. "Give me a gun. I can use the aiming app same as you."

"Shit, that reminds me." I pat myself down. "I don't have a gun."

As though taunting me, Joe reloads his weapon at that very moment, and Gogi and Luke check their weapons as well.

"I guess going to a gun range is one thing, but being a professional is something else entirely," Muhomor comments sardonically. "How could you not grab a gun on your way out?"

"Here." Gogi hands me his pistol. "You and Joe should draw fire away from us."

Joe is already running back toward the limo, and I follow while frantically trying to add Gogi's Makarov Pistol to my aiming app.

"Crap," I say after a frustrating moment. "Mitya, why is this gun not in the gun database?"

"I'm not sure," Mitya responds. "Maybe because it's of Russian design? Do you even need the aiming app anymore? You got all that practice."

"I practiced at the shooting range, not in the field." I weigh the unfamiliar weapon in my hand as I approach the limo. "Plus, I did it with a Glock."

"Hey, Mike." Mitya's Zik message is full of worry. "I don't like what I'm seeing from the drone."

As though to highlight Mitya's concerns, a gunshot rings out, and a bullet zings by my head.

Joe and I duck under the limo's carcass, and when I look through the drone's view, my feet freeze to the ground. While we were busying ourselves with surviving the crash, the fourteen people sitting in the wrecked Hummer left it. They're running toward us, their shiny black helmets unmistakable.

Even worse, the black Suburban is just a few feet behind the fourteen new attackers. Assuming there are eight people in that car, Joe and I don't have enough bullets, even if we put each bullet directly into each person's brains. And that's without the two people in the red truck who might be coming to their senses, if they haven't already.

My depressing math is interrupted when I spot the attacker closest to us aiming a scoped rifle at where Ada, Gogi, and Luke are.

He must not see Joe and me hiding behind the car and probably thinks the trio on the grass is what remains of the resistance.

My heart leaps into my throat as the rifle fires.

Ada gasps and then screams.

Since her Share app is still running for Mitya's and Muhomor's benefits, I try to look through it and succeed, which means Ada's brain is intact. Shaking with relief, I realize the reason for Ada's screaming.

The rifleman shot Luke in the head, making it explode, and the gore is covering Ada's entire body.

The already slow-moving time crawls for me now, and I can see Luke's gun begin to fall to the grass and Ada's hand reach out to catch it.

I comprehend what's about to happen.

Ada is going to grab that gun and start shooting.

"Ada, no!" I scream at her from my hiding place. Mentally, I frantically add, "If you start shooting, you might as well draw a target on your forehead."

Ada catches the gun, and I see no evidence that she heard me or that she's willing to listen.

An insane plan flits through my mind.

I know how to draw fire away from Ada… at a steep price to myself.

The guy with the rifle begins to reload, and I attempt my crazy idea.

The world takes on a surreal quality as I leap from my hiding spot and shoot at the rifleman.

Without the aim-assist app, and with the unfamiliar gun in my hand, I miss.

The rifleman finishes reloading, but instead of aiming at me, he points the barrel in Ada's direction again. My heart threatens to burst out of my chest, but I climb onto the limo's ruins, take careful aim at him, and squeeze the trigger again. I must be getting used to my new gun, because my shot fells the rifleman.

His thirteen still-alive allies turn their guns in my direction.

Strong hands push me from behind, and it takes an unimaginable feat of coordination for me to land on my feet.

Joe must've pushed me, I realize. Then I hear thirteen shots ring out like a firing squad.

Their bullets are going toward the top of the limo—toward Joe.

I shoot back once, twice, and each bullet reaches its designated helmet.

Something falls on top of the limo, making my heart sink.

I'm reluctant to learn the horrible truth, but I force myself to switch to Ada's Share view. Her vantage point is getting closer, enabling me to see what the sound was about, and my stomach grows cold as the otherworldly quality of my surroundings intensifies.

It was indeed Joe. A couple of the thirteen bullets reached his head, and what's left of his skull is barely recognizable as having belonged to a human being.

I instantly regret all my snide thoughts about my cousin. Despite everything, I've grown to care about Joe, and I know this loss will devastate our family.

Before grief can warp my mind, another shot rings out, the bullet tearing through my chest.

Despite the Relief app, the pain is worse than anything I've felt—though my grief could be intensifying it. The agony is at least a thousand times worse than when the sharp object was stuck under my fingernail.

My knees buckle, and I sink to the ground.

Something tells me I'm only alive because the bullet-proof vest saved my life, but this won't be the case for long, as my enemies take aim at me again.

Through Ada's Share app, I see her vantage point is getting even closer to the limo, and I finally understand what it means.

Gun in hand, Ada is running to save me—which means she's running toward the shooters.

"No, Ada," I scream mentally. "Don't get any closer!"

To my horror, the gunmen stop aiming at me and turn their sights onto Ada, who must, at this moment, seem like the more dangerous target.

"Drop to the ground!" I scream at her.

Thirteen shots ring out.

Ada's view is a swirl of motion that indicates she's falling.

"Ada?" I frantically message in Zik. "Ada, are you okay?"

She doesn't reply.

My grief for my cousin morphs into a terrifying black hole as Ada's Share app begins to show static, like an ancient out-of-tune TV.

Mindlessly, I leap to my feet and turn.

I have to see this for myself.

I have to see her.

As I feared, Ada is on the ground, blood pooling around her face.

The shots ring out again, and I know I'll no longer feel this horrible grief in a moment.

It's a relief I welcome.

In the instant before I die, something clicks in my head. It could be wishful thinking, but I have to try.

Out loud, as though I'm addressing someone other than myself, I ask, "Is this really happening?"

CHAPTER THIRTY-TWO

The surreal quality of the world dissipates, and I snap out of the pre-cog moment—just like every other time I've asked myself this question when experiencing those nightmare scenarios.

The brain-boost vision short-circuits, and I find myself back behind the limo—effectively back in time to a few fateful seconds ago, before Joe and Ada got killed.

I understand what just happened. When I came up with that insane plan to draw fire away from Ada, my brain showed me what might happen as a result. During our last Brainocytes Club meeting, Mitya provided us with the new brain boost, and I didn't get a chance to adjust to it. I was also offline for a number of days. I'm probably lucky this is the first pre-cog moment I've experienced—if you can call that scare lucky.

The reality of our situation sets in. The pre-cog moment happened at the speed of boosted thought, and since

I didn't jump onto the limo and no shots were fired, what's really happening is that the rifleman is still reloading his weapon.

The problem is that I'm running out of options. The pre-cog moment convinced me not to execute that desperate maneuver, but I also know if Ada fires the gun she just caught, she won't be alive for long.

"Ada—" I begin to scream at her again, but then in her Share view, I see I wasn't the only one worried about her. I forgot Gogi and his Special Forces background, not to mention his years of bodyguard experience. Since Gogi is already almost hugging Ada, he just makes his hug tighter and falls on top of her the way bodyguards have done since time immemorial.

Ada's gun falls out of her hand, and she spouts mental curses about being sandwiched between a dead body and a wounded Georgian.

"Better that than dead," I reassure her mentally.

Either Gogi's action or my screaming did the trick. After the rifleman finishes reloading, he doesn't aim for Gogi or Ada, since a flat target is too difficult to hit. He focuses on me, since I've been kind enough to scream and announce my location.

Suddenly, Joe jackknifes to his feet, takes quick aim, and pulls the trigger.

The rifleman falls, but that only seems to anger the other dozen attackers running toward us. They begin to fire at the limo.

"The black Suburban will be between you and those people in a second," Mitya states in the chat.

I can see he's right, but with or without the black Suburban, Joe and I don't stand much of a chance.

Then Ada chimes in. "I'm looking through the Suburban's window with the drone," she tells us. "I think you might want to look, too."

CHAPTER THIRTY-THREE

The Suburban's tires screech, and it stops between us and the twelve attackers—a strange maneuver in and of itself.

I follow Ada's advice and look at the black car's windows through the drone's camera.

Unlike the rest of their helmeted allies, this group is wearing sunglasses and suits. That is, aviator sunglasses and creepily familiar black suits. I recognize a couple of people in that car. Agent Pugh is the one driving, and a couple of other task-force Suits—facial-recognition-immune men I first saw at the hospital—are here as well.

"How did I not see this sooner?" Mitya says as the same realization must hit him. "They were driving the most cliché government vehicle known to man. And it's even black."

"What I'd like to know," Ada says, "is whether they're here to hurt us or help us?"

I consider her question. Earlier in the chase, I decided that the task force wasn't behind Vincent Williams, and someone else must have hired him. Was I wrong?

In perfectly rehearsed unison, the Suits stick their guns out of the window and answer my question in the simplest way they can—they open fire at our attackers.

"They must've been tailing you," Muhomor says. "Even after all that hoopla in the media. Thank God bad habits are so hard to break."

"Not only did they follow us," I say, "but they also did it from far enough away that they didn't activate my paranoia. They must be learning from their mistakes."

Emboldened by the newfound support, Joe and I stand up and aim at any helmeted people we can spot, but it's difficult with the black car in the way.

I unload half my gun before I see movement inside the red Hilux truck next to us. Seemingly before my conscious mind even knows what I'm planning, my hand takes aim and shoots.

My bullet slices into Vincent Williams's ear but doesn't stop his escaping the car.

"Check his passenger," Joe barks at me. "Williams is mine."

What Joe doesn't say, but what I assume based on the cold glint in his alligator-like stare, is that he intends to make Williams pay dearly for every man Joe lost today.

I check the drone view to make sure it's safe for me to walk to the other side of the limo, since that's what's required to get to the passenger side of the truck. The Suits and our earlier attackers are still exchanging fire, and the

Suits are winning. Their only casualty so far is one of the dudes I saw at the hospital.

Since the drone doesn't have a good view of the damaged Hilux, I scan the limo's sensors. I'm shocked to find a semi-functional camera in the back.

Despite the cracked camera screen that blocks the view, I can still make out Williams as he exits the car. Joe meets the large man the moment his feet touch the ground. The first thing Joe does is put a bullet in Williams in his right hand, disarming his opponent and costing Williams yet another finger or two on his already digit-lacking hand. Williams's guttural scream brings a horrid smile to Joe's face—the same one he wore when I caught him beating a bird with a rock as a teenager.

"Oh no," I say inside the chat. "I'm afraid my cousin might not be thinking strategically."

No one replies, but in a moment, I'm proven right. Instead of shooting Williams in the head, as I would have done, Joe pistol-whips the man in the face.

"He might be out of bullets," Mitya suggests halfheartedly as we all see Williams's lip split and his blood spray across Joe's face in the ultimate unhygienic fountain.

Whatever the reason for Joe's decision to throw hits, Williams takes the damage with surprising stamina and tries to grapple with his enemy. Joe is ready for him and uses a move he's used on me at the gym. I call the move a kick-twister, only I see that Joe was severely pulling his punches and kicks with me. When Joe completes the kick-twister this time, Williams's right wrist breaks, and his already damaged hand hangs limply to the side.

With an animalistic roar, Williams punches Joe with his left hand. As someone who's received a punch like that before, I feel sympathy for Joe. To my shock, Joe takes the punch with that same creepy smile and leaps at Williams with a growl.

Since I'm standing in front of the passenger side door of the red truck, I focus on what's in front of me right now—the damaged truck's door—and proceed to pull.

The door creaks, but opens. I can see that the helmeted person who rode with Williams is—or was—a man, and he looks knocked out or dead. Something about this person's body or clothing seems familiar to me. I get the strong urge to lift his helmet to see the face hidden beneath.

Jutting my gun out, I say, "If you're alive and you move, I'll shoot you in the stomach."

"I say you shoot before you check him," Muhomor suggests. "This way, we'll be certain he's dead."

"That's cold, even for you, Viktor," Mitya counters, and I tend to agree with him. Though I did finally take kill shots at people in the heat of battle, killing someone who's unconscious like this is a whole other step, and one I'm not willing to take, especially considering the vague familiarity I feel when I look at this man.

Clicking the gun's safety off, I reach for the helmet's visor.

"No way." Mitya gapes at the mystery person's face. "It can't be him."

"Seriously," Ada echoes. "Isn't he dead? There was a posh funeral and everything."

"The funeral could've been faked," Muhomor says. "We're talking about Russia, after all. In any case, if he wasn't dead before, he might be dead now."

I study the man's face until I have no doubt. This is Alex—as in Alexander Voynskiy, the Russian billionaire. As in the guy who betrayed us on that rescue trip to Russia—a betrayal he paid for with his life, after Joe tortured him, or so it seemed until this very moment.

Of course, if Alex had survived, he would want revenge. He's the perfect person to hire all these people trying to kill us. Besides revenge, he might want us dead so he can stop pretending to be dead—a preventative strike since Joe would kill him if he knew of his survival. So it's no surprise that Alex wants Joe dead, though I'm sure he's equally pissed at the rest of us. He's the exact kind of person who'd put together a kill list, with Joe at the top, and give the list to someone like Williams. This would explain why Williams mentioned some kind of list.

Though I'm still reluctant to shoot him, I consider hitting Alex in the face to make sure he doesn't wake up anytime soon. Then the implications of Alex's survival hit me, and I frantically send Ada a telepathic message, saying, "Ada, ask Gogi if Joe has anyone guarding Muhomor. If he does, tell Gogi to order the guard to rush into Muhomor's room."

As though in response to my suspicions, Muhomor sends into the chat, "Crap. I shouldn't have said anything out loud to her. I need help. SOS."

I find the camera view into Muhomor's room and confirm my suspicions. Lyuba is there, and she's holding a pillow over Muhomor's face.

"Hold on, buddy," Ada says. "Gogi just passed along Mike's message."

Muhomor doesn't answer—a bad sign—but Jacob, another one of Joe's people I've seen at the gym, rushes into the room.

Jacob is very, very good at his job, and before Lyuba knows what's happening, the man unceremoniously punches her in the jaw.

Unsurprisingly, Lyuba imitates a knocked-out sack of potatoes as she crashes to the floor.

I never thought I'd see the day when Ada would cheer a man hitting a woman, but she does.

Jacob stabs at the nurse-call button and begins performing CPR on Muhomor.

In case someone hasn't already reached the conclusions I have, I say into the chat, "Muhomor left it to Lyuba to get rid of Alex. The billionaire must've convinced or bribed her to let him live, and she's been working with him ever since. This is how Williams and his people knew we'd be at that restaurant and how they knew we were at the hospital. We told Lyuba about it. Even this chase is her fault. I bet Muhomor told her what hospital I was left at and where we were going."

"Tell that brute I'm okay," Muhomor says into the chat after a moment. "I can't tell him because he's rape-kissing me."

"Hey." I feel instant relief. "At least we now know you've gotten to first base—"

"Watch out!" Ada screams, both mentally and from under Gogi.

Realizing I've been paying too much attention to the AROS views and not my real-world senses, I focus on Alex and see his eyes are open and narrowing at me.

"Shoot him," Muhomor urges. "Use your gun."

I'm about to listen to Muhomor, but before I get a chance to pull the trigger, Alex savagely kicks my legs, and my shin explodes in unbearable pain. In shock, I stumble back and trip, falling out of the tall truck.

My gun clanks on the asphalt, but I'm happy that I landed on my ass instead of breaking my neck in the fall, though my tailbone violently begs to differ.

Alex leaps out of the truck after me and stomps on my chest as he falls on top of me, causing the air in my lungs to escape with an almost audible whoosh.

Recovering quickly, he repeatedly punches me in the head.

The world grows distant, and I must use my willpower to stay conscious. In the AROS view from the limo's last camera, I can see Joe is still in the process of hitting what's left of Williams's face with something heavy. That's too bad for me, since I was hoping Joe would be done with his prey and on his way to rescue me.

"You bastard," Ada says inside the chat, and even through my haze I'm tempted to tell her Alex can't hear her cursing without Brainocytes.

Then I see Ada has a plan. Dimly, I watch as our last drone crash-lands into the side of Alex's head.

There's a satisfying crunch, though I think it's the plastic drone that breaks and not Alex's skull. Still, Alex's eyes glaze over, and his body goes slack on top of me.

I push Alex off me and struggle to my feet. Since I don't trust him to stay unconscious for long, I need to finish him off somehow. Shaking my head in an effort to further clear it, I think something I never thought I'd ask myself.

What would Joe do?

Since my legs are barely supporting my weight and my muscles are screaming for mercy, I decide that my gun is my best option. Pulling the trigger will be easier than punching or kicking in my current condition.

I look for the gun, but it seems to be under the limo wreckage. I'm not sure it's a good idea for me to climb under for it.

In Ada's Shared view, I see a flicker of movement behind me and instinctively duck.

As a result, I only lose a small piece of my scalp instead of my life.

My head is burning, and a double shot of adrenaline hits my brain as I spin around to face Alex and assess the situation.

Not only is he conscious, but he also pulled a knife on me, explaining that missing inch of skin on the crown of my head.

Alex stabs the knife at my torso, but I jump back, causing him to slice a gash into the bulletproof vest, not me. Wondering what would happen if he'd stabbed me instead,

I perform a frantic internet search and learn this lighter type of bulletproof vest doesn't have good knife protection.

For whatever reason, Gogi and I didn't think it was realistic that I'd ever get into a knife fight, so knife combat was a low priority. I practiced mostly hand-to-hand combat and gun disarm techniques in the last months. If I live, I'll tell Gogi he sucks at risk assessment.

Alex slices at my lower body, and I decide to take a gamble and treat the knife like a gun.

I catch Alex's wrist in a crisscross of my outstretched arms and begin to twist the knife out of his hand, as I would with a gun.

Then I realize this maneuver is best used on guns with trigger guards, which facilitates the twist that breaks the finger. Alex's butterfly-style knife doesn't have a trigger guard, so his finger is fine.

Realizing my twist was ineffective, Alex propels his whole body forward, like a fencer, his arm sliding between mine.

I watch, dumbfounded, as his knife slowly enters my body.

CHAPTER THIRTY-FOUR

At least an inch of steel is in my upper thigh, but I only feel a tingle of electricity, like I got Tasered with the voltage focused on a single point. Figuring I need to take advantage of the fact that I'm not in pain yet, I yank my leg back to make sure the knife doesn't go in deeper.

Paradoxically, as the knife rips out of my thigh, the nauseating pain hits me. It feels like a burn made by a thousand hot needles. I wonder what protection the Relief app is giving me at this moment, if any. It sure doesn't feel like this pain is dampened in any way. If I survive, I'll probably consider giving this app a "knife wound" setting, though something tells me the app would have to become equivalent to shooting heroin, presenting an even higher risk of addiction.

With my adrenaline spiking to inhuman levels, I chop at Alex's neck with my right hand and use the distraction to grab Alex's right wrist with my left hand.

Alex tries to pull out of my grip, but I'm holding on with the desperation of a man about to bleed to death—because that's my reality.

With the world around me sharpening, I realize that not only do I need to beat Alex, but I must also do it in the quickest way possible—ideally, two seconds ago.

A half-baked and perilous idea forms in my mind, and I wish my brain had showed it to me as a pre-cog moment so I could assess it better. Since pre-cog moments don't seem to come when you want them to, I execute my idea, which is simple.

Still holding on to the wrist of the hand that's wielding the knife, I sidestep and sweep Alex's legs.

In training, the best-case scenario for this move was Gogi and I ending up on the floor, meaning I was toast shortly after, given my lack of skills in wrestling.

In this case, my concern is that I might land with the knife in my heart.

Twisting in the air, Alex and I tumble onto the asphalt. My back hits the ground, putting me at a huge disadvantage as he lands on top of me. But the knife isn't in my heart, because I'm still holding on to Alex's wrist.

In movies, I've seen heroes twist a knife in someone's hand and then stab them with it. It usually begins with the hero stopping the knife close to his eye and turning the tables—or arms—and ends with the bad guy getting knifed.

Alex must've also seen those movies, because he grabs the knife with his other hand and pushes down frantically.

I would use two hands if I could, but my right arm is pinned under me. I was instinctively trying to protect my poor tailbone this time. With my arm pinned to the asphalt, I have one hand left to defend myself. Soon, it becomes obvious that I'm not stopping the knife's descent at all. At best, I'm slowing it down.

I feel blood seeping out of my leg wound, and with it, my energy and will to fight.

Alex's face is red with exertion, and beads of his sweat fall onto my face as he pushes the knife down another millimeter.

Something is happening in one of the AROS views, and the gunfire between the Suits and Alex's or Williams's remaining people stops, but I don't dare shift my focus away from the knife.

Suddenly, white fur flashes by my face, and a rat is biting Alex on the ear.

"Ada," I mentally shout. "Mr. Spock ran away from you. A rat is no match for a human. Once Alex is done with me, he'll hurt Mr. Spock."

Somehow, getting bitten seems to give Alex strength, because the knife descends another couple of millimeters and begins to enter the vest's material.

"No," Ada says out loud—from less than a foot away. "He won't hurt anyone anymore."

Through her Share app view, I see she's holding a gun firmly to Alex's head, and that Alex is aware of the gun.

"You will put that knife down," Ada says, her voice so cold she'd give Joe a run for his money. "Now."

Alex must read the deadly determination in Ada's eyes, because he tosses the knife aside and raises his hands in the air.

The first thing I do is grab Mr. Spock from Alex's ear and cradle the little guy, though I think the gesture comforts me more than my currently bloodthirsty pet.

"You left a permanent tooth mark," I tell Spock softly after examining Alex's ear. "Good rat."

Alex lifts his body off me, and as soon as I'm free, I try to stand. Finding that I can only get up to my knees, I stay there, swaying, and study Ada as she holds the gun aimed at Alex.

I wonder if she's going to shoot the bastard, and I think he's wondering the same thing. It makes me recall Muhomor's joke comparing Ada to a mama bear.

"It wouldn't be very vegan of you," I tell Ada mentally. "But if you pull that trigger, I'll support you one hundred percent."

Alex carefully backs away from Ada and says, "Look, Ada, I never had an issue with you—"

I'll never know if Alex had the balls to try to talk his way out of this predicament, because the sound of someone dragging their feet interrupts Alex's speech.

We all look at the source of the noise and see Joe. So much blood covers my cousin it's as if he's been through hell's meat factory. Alex's pupils grow to the size of his irises as he takes in the depth of hatred in my cousin's icy eyes. I bet Alex is reliving flashbacks of Joe torturing him in that car. He must realize his fate will now be worse.

Ada looks over Joe's shoulder, and I see Agent Pugh lumbering toward us, her own weapon raised.

"Lower your gun," the female Suit says. "There's been enough shooting already."

"Agent Pugh," I gasp out, the blood loss making it hard to speak louder than a whisper. "Think about how it'll look if you hurt one of us."

Agent Pugh looks uncertain, making me think she heard me.

Ada drops her gun on the ground and looks expectantly at Joe.

I show my hands empty of weapons—unless you count a rat as a weapon.

Joe's gaze doesn't leave Alex's face as he begins to lower his gun, but then I realize he isn't lowering it so much as aiming it at Alex's head.

I grit my teeth.

A gun goes off, the boom smacking my eardrums like a blow.

I look at Agent Pugh, worried I'll see a cloud of smoke around her weapon, but it isn't there.

It was Joe who fired his gun, and the result of his work is the gaping hole in Alex's forehead.

Lowering the weapon, Joe lets the gun slip from his fingers and hit the floor.

Agent Pugh walks up to Alex and stares at his corpse, her face unreadable.

"His people killed your colleagues," Ada tells her. "What Joe did was a preventative measure of self-defense. This guy had enough money to get out of any legal mishaps coming his way."

"Speaking of legal mishaps," I croak, swaying on my knees as I try to stay conscious. "If you agree this was self-defense, I'll consider us even and won't unleash Kadvosky and his lawyers on you."

Agent Pugh's expression is still unreadable as she moves her gun from Joe to Alex. Before I register what's happing, Agent Pugh puts a bullet in Alex's already cooling chest.

"Now I'm in the same boat as you," Agent Pugh says. "As I see it, this was self-defense."

My relief makes my exhaustion intensify, and I put down Mr. Spock so that I can lie back down on the asphalt. The rat sniffs my cheek and then scurries away as someone kneels to check my vitals, and someone else wraps a tourniquet around my leg wound.

"He'll be okay," someone says. "The first responders are almost here."

"I'm going to faint now," I tell Ada telepathically. "When the ambulance comes, please tell them to go ahead and use drugs. Lots of drugs."

CHAPTER THIRTY-FIVE

I wake up groggy but blissfully free of pain. I vaguely recall coming to my senses inside an ambulance and receiving a nice injection that knocked me out again.

Opening my eyes, I see my mom, Uncle Abe, and Ada staring at me intensely. I'm attached to a ton of medical equipment, but the room around me is nice for a change, well lit and crowded with comfortable furniture. This is as close as a hospital room can get to a suite at the Four Seasons.

"Kitten," Mom says in high-pitched Russian. "How are you feeling?"

"I feel great," I say out loud. Telepathically, I ask Ada, "How come I feel great? I should be in lots of interesting pain."

"They gave you morphine," Ada explains mentally and winks at me in the real world. "I didn't tell your mom about that, though."

"I'm glad to hear you're feeling great." Mom's worried tone doesn't change. "The doctor says you'll be fine, but you needed stiches on your head and leg, and that scar on your ear—"

"Calm down, sis," my uncle says soothingly. "Think of your blood pressure."

"Yeah, Mom," I chime in. "I'm fine. There's a perfectly good explanation for all of this."

"How much does she know?" I ask Ada telepathically. "Please tell me she didn't watch the news."

"Not so much," Ada replies in Zik. "But I think you should do your best to tell her what happened and soften some details if you must."

"Can you leave us alone, please?" I ask Ada and locate my bed's controls to raise the bed into a sitting position. "I think I have an idea that might make this conversation have a happy conclusion."

"Uh-huh." Ada's Zik message is pure mischief. "It seems you're thinking what I'm thinking." She looks down at her belly.

"Mr. Cohen," Ada says to Uncle Abe. "I'd like to check on your son if you don't mind."

"They're not going to buy your wanting to check on Joe, of all people," I mentally say.

"I could be warming up to him," Ada retorts. "It's theoretically feasible."

"But not likely." I chuckle in the real world, garnering myself strange looks from my mom and my uncle. "How is Joe, anyway?"

"Joe is doing better than you are," Ada replies. Despite her earlier assertions, her Zik message doesn't contain a single positive emotion, and it would have if she were happy that Joe is okay. "He's got a room here, but Gogi tells me that Joe is planning to leave the hospital soon. Something about some business we'd rather not know about."

It's all too easy to picture Joe leaving the hospital and initiating a deadly hunt for any survivors from Williams's organization. For the first time, I wish my cousin good luck in his sinister activities, but I don't share that sentiment with Ada, lest she think I'm becoming a monster. Because I'm not. I'd like to think I'm simply becoming more pragmatic, as I figure a future father should be.

"So, it all started after we left that lunch at your house," I begin in Russian when Ada and my uncle are out of the room. "Or maybe it started when we were rescuing you in Russia. It depends on how you look at it."

I tell Mom a version of the events that downplays the risks to me as much as I can.

Since I'm speaking out loud, I have plenty of time to check the internet for interesting developments—like news about further lynching of the officials complicit in the task force, or the excitement in the cybersecurity community over Tema. My favorite part is reading the reactions to open-source Brainocytes. People are speculating on countless uses and making plans to improve the technology in a thousand different ways.

After the internet, I check my emails. My friends sent me some ideas for future development, and my favorite one is something Ada came up with based on some initial work by an Israeli scientist named Golan Dahan. He has an MD specializing in nanomedicine and a PhD in nanoengineering. Golan's interest seems to be in nanomachines that can turn parts of people's bodies into computers. This specific paper outlines a design for nanobots that could turn bones into computing and storage substrates, making the bones stronger and lighter as a side effect.

I instantly see such "smart bones" as a solution to the problem of not having access to the internet—like what recently happened to me. Granted, no computing constrained to the human body will be as powerful as the supercomputers we can access via the cloud, but it would be a good backup option. Also, this could help us with another project—caching. Caching is a hardware (and sometimes software) component that stores data so future requests for that data can be served faster—a performance enhancement technique that tries to predict the future based on the recent past. Our earlier solution for better caching was to cram more Brainocytes inside our brains, but this opens up more interesting opportunities.

"A nice find for our nanobots collection," Mitya says after I forward him the article. "Almost as cool as the Respirocytes."

Respirocytes are nanobots that were designed by Robert A. Freitas Jr. in 1998. They can replace or supplement much of the normal respiratory system, allowing the user to take one breath per several hours. We, the Brainocytes Club, have plans to build these, along with microbivore (artificial white blood cells that will create a super-immune system) and many others.

"Stronger bones might be an awesome effect on its own," I add when I realize I got lost in thought.

"Yeah." Mitya's Zik message is only partially sarcastic as he adds, "And sharp retractable claws coming out of our hands would be nice if we were ever in a jam."

The fact that I missed the connection to Wolverine until Mitya's joke is a sign that the morphine has dulled my thinking. Mentally chuckling, I say, "In Muhomor's case, the claws will have USB plugs on the ends."

"Great idea," Mitya replies. "Okay, I'll go and try to recruit this Israeli guy."

In the slow-time world, tears are standing in Mom's eyes throughout my story, and I feel like she might have a nervous breakdown or start crying unless I finally play the proverbial ace up my sleeve, so I say, "But that isn't the most exciting thing that happened. I learned something amazing as well." When I'm sure I have Mom's undivided attention, I drop the bomb. "You're going to be a grandma."

Mom looks shell-shocked but recovers surprisingly quickly, clapping her hands in excitement. A huge smile spreads across her face, and my tired vocal cords can barely keep up as she peppers me with questions.

"No, Ada didn't tell me how far along she is," I say. "But she only missed her first period, so I guess the whole thing is just beginning."

"Did you do an ultrasound?" In her excitement, Mom begins to pace around my lavish room.

"No, Mom. I just learned about this a few hours ago. I don't carry around a portable ultrasound machine."

"Did you read any books about pregnancy?" Mom asks, and at first I think she might be kidding, but her expression is dead serious.

I take advantage of the few milliseconds between answering her questions and buy a book called, *What to Expect When Your Wife is Expecting*. I read a large chunk of the book as I reply, "Yep, Mom, I got one already and started reading it."

"Good boy," Mom says and stops pacing. "So, what are your intentions toward Ada?"

It's funny Mom asked that, because I've been thinking about this whenever I've had a free moment to think.

"Well, I've known for a while that I wanted to marry Ada someday," I say after I make sure I turn off my Share app. "Even when we were moving in together, I told you I thought she was the one, and that feeling has only gotten stronger."

"I know." Mom nods sagely, beaming with pleasure. "I can tell by watching the two of you."

"Right." The conversation is making me dizzy, so I lower the bed a few degrees. "This baby development does change the timeline."

"Why does it seem like you're about to say 'but'?" Mom walks up to the bed and sits on the edge.

"I don't want Ada to think I'm proposing for the wrong reasons." I use my IV-free hand to wipe my suddenly sweaty forehead. "Like because I knocked her up."

"Silliness," Mom says and folds her arms across her chest. "Look, kitten, I love you, and you know I think highly of your intellect, but Ada is twice as smart as you are and would never worry about such nonsense."

"There's also that 'I love you' thing," I remind Mom. "How do I know if Ada even believes in a traditional marriage? She's got radical views on so many things that—"

"It doesn't matter what the two of you call your relationship," Mom interrupts. "Whether she says 'I love you' every five minutes or once a year, that girl does love you, and you're crazy about her as well. If she's not into a traditional marriage, if she wants to call it something else, like a social union or a banana, you should remember that marriage is but a piece of paper anyway. What matters is how the two people feel about each other—and this you know."

"I guess you're right. It's just a bit scary."

"I understand," Mom says. "But you're in luck. I'll help you with at least one decision, but I have to go."

Before I can say anything, Mom gets up from the bed and almost runs out of my hospital room.

I stare at the closed door, thinking that the trick of telling Mom about the baby might've worked a little too well. I guess I wanted her to fuss over me for a little while before running off to who knows where.

"So, you're still awake," Mitya says out loud as he enters the room.

In a weird Russian tradition, Mitya brought me apples and a box of candy. He puts them on the end table near the bed and sits on one of the cushy couches.

When he catches my questioning look, he pretends to misinterpret it and says, "This isn't an avatar. My plane finally landed, so I figured I'd visit you."

"No, really? And here I thought you gave me virtual food." I feign a snarkiness I don't feel. "So, what's up?"

He tells me he already hired Golan Dahan, and he'll get him to come to the US from Israel shortly. Then he asks me about my health, and I tell him I'm feeling fine. Soon, our conversation turns to the same subject Mom and I were talking about—marrying Ada.

"Have you thought about the how of it?" Mitya asks. "I'm not an expert, but maybe a nice romantic proposal is the way to go?"

"That might be tricky for some time." I look down at my white hospital gown. "I don't know when I'll get out of this bed, and I want to talk to her about this as soon as possible." Suddenly, an idea hits me. "By the way, do you still own that virtual reality video game development company? The Samurai Ostrich or whatever it's called?"

"Penguin Ninjas," Mitya responds, his expression telling me he might already see where I'm going with this. "Yes, I still own them."

"Well," I say conspiratorially, "here's my idea."

By the time Ada mentally informs me she's close, Mitya and I are almost done coding the ideas we came up with during a conference call with Penguin Ninjas.

"I got it from here," Mitya says telepathically. "Just give me a few minutes."

The door opens, and Ada enters.

"Hi, Ada," Mitya says out loud as he gets up. "I was just leaving. I want to go check on Mr. Viktor Tsoi."

"Hey," I say out loud. "Let's not tease Muhomor too much. The guy just lost his ability to walk."

"You didn't tell him about Project Iron Fly?" Mitya asks Ada reproachfully. "It's the coolest thing we've done in the last hour."

"No." Ada walks up to my bed and sits on the edge. "I'll tell him now, though."

Mitya leaves, and Ada switches to mental communication as she explains that Project Iron Fly is a high-tech suit she and Mitya designed as a surprise gift for Muhomor. They started off by reading everything in the field of robotic exoskeletons, both military applications (what little is public) and suits designed to let paralyzed people walk. They then designed their own model that, if all goes well, will look like a pair of ski pants that the Brainocytes will seamlessly operate.

"This should allow Muhomor to run faster than a regular person," Ada concludes, "and without ever getting tired."

"You can weaponize this thing too," I say, getting into the spirit of it.

"Yeah." Ada rolls her eyes. "The first thing Mitya wanted to do was put rockets in the feet, hence the project name."

The first part of Muhomor's name means "a fly" in Russian, so Iron Fly is a pretty apt name for a superhero-type suit that Muhomor will wear.

"I want to help build this thing." I imbue my message with excitement. "But I think Muhomor will want to participate in the design too."

"He can build part two if he wishes," Ada counters. "If we left it up to him, he'd design a glorified wheelchair that sits on top of the most compact super server he can cram under his butt so he can hack things without reaching out to cloud servers."

"Not if we really turn his bones into computing substrate, but you have a point." I look at the opening door and say out loud, "Oh, hey, Mom."

Mom enters the room, smacks herself on the forehead in a theatrical gesture, and says, "Ada, I feel so absentminded. I forgot to pick up Misha's grilled vegetable sandwich."

If Ada notices Mom's glaring attempt to speak with me privately, she doesn't show it and instead offers to go pick up the sandwich.

"Okay," Mom says as soon as Ada leaves the room. "Here it is."

She walks up to my bed and extends her hand, palm up.

There's a ring box in her hand.

I reach out and grab it. Opening the box, I stare at the glorious piece of jewelry in fascination.

"Your great-great-grandfather was a jeweler," Mom explains. "Your great-great-grandmother was the most beautiful woman in Tomovka—a tiny Jewish village in Ukraine. Since he wanted to marry someone so out of his league, he managed to somehow get that rock"—she points at the two-karat, orange-colored diamond—"and it worked. This ring has been passed down in our family ever since."

"I don't even know what to say." I didn't even realize diamonds came in such colors, but the internet confirms they do and that this type is very rare. "Thank you so much, Mom."

"Of course," Mom replies and leans in for a kiss on the cheek. "I'll go find my brother. You best think of what you'll say to her when the time comes."

After Mom leaves, I finalize the app Mitya and I developed and test it out a few times. Then I do as Mom suggested and think of what I'll say when the time comes.

Ada brings the sandwich I never asked for, and I gladly munch on it as she and I speculate in Zik about the future of our planet once the Brainocyte technology is inside the heads of a large portion of the population.

"Smarter people will be in a position to eradicate the last remnants of age-old problems, like famine, diseases, and war." Ada walks up to the window and looks out at the impressive view of the Manhattan skyline. "We can also hope to solve some of the uniquely modern problems, like cancer and lack of long-term planning."

"I'm sure it won't all be so rosy." Though I share Ada's optimism, someone in our soon-to-be family needs to play devil's advocate, and it might as well be me. "It's only a matter of time before someone finds a way to use Brainocytes for something evil, like to spy on them as Muhomor fears."

"Tema makes spying difficult." Ada turns away from the window and comes toward me. "And we can always write an app to address whatever problems might arise."

I see a perfect segue way for my big surprise and say, "Speaking of apps, I designed something with Mitya's help, and I'd love to experience it with you."

I send Ada the Ninja Penguin app in question and wait for her to signal that she's launched it.

"Got it," Ada informs me. "You want me to start this app now?"

"Let's do it together," I say and activate my version of the app. "Close your eyes once the app is up and running."

Ada stops in the middle of the room and closes her eyes.

I initiate the app, and as soon it starts, I close my eyes as well. Instead of the backs of our eyelids, the app makes us see a fantastical garden all around us.

"The app takes Augmented Reality to the next level," I explain as I look around in awe. "It's safer to call it Virtual Reality."

Ada looks around, takes in the candlelight coming from every corner of the virtual environment, looks at the myriad of delicate flowers, and smiles at me—or smiles at who she thinks is me but is really my avatar.

My version of the app is a little different from Ada's. Ada's body controls her avatar, and the avatar is in the exact part of the room she's in. The only difference is that her avatar is clad in a glorious evening gown with a low-cut back. In contrast, because I'm currently bedridden, I control my avatar the way I would a video game character. My virtual self is sharply dressed in a tux, and he's standing next to me in the virtual environment, mainly because it's easier to control him that way.

Ada looks around some more, her amber eyes wide at the new marvels that appear as the sun sets behind the trees—details Mitya and I stole from one of Ninja Penguin's more popular VR games.

The garden is full of surreal luminescent plants of every variety, but I can tell Ada's favorites are the ones that remind me of cherry blossoms.

Birds that look like deep-water sea creatures float in the black-purple night sky. Behind the birds, we can see bright star constellations that don't resemble anything viewable from Earth.

"I get it. You're going for 'very romantic.'" Ada looks my avatar up and down appreciatively. "And you clean up nice—virtually."

"You look amazing yourself," I reply, a little at a loss for words. "Come here."

Ada walks under the spindly vines, brushing her fingers against the branches. A couple of shiny alien butterflies try to land on Ada's shoulder, but she shoos them away.

"If you're planning to sell this game, or whatever this is, the *Avatar* movie franchise might sue you." Ada's Zik message is teasing, but she looks serious as she stands under the luminous cherry blossoms, next to my virtual representation.

I activate the command that causes the leaves to fall, and before Ada knows what hit her, my avatar gets down on one knee and extends his hands in that classic gesture.

Ada looks at me intently, her eyes shining with unreadable emotion.

"Ada," I ceremonially say out loud. My heart rate spikes, and I worry a nurse might barge in on us in the real world. "Will you marry me?"

I open the ring box, and the virtual ring shines with an iridescent orange light that reminds me of the suitcase from *Pulp Fiction.*

"Wow," Ada says out loud. She sounds overwhelmed with emotion, but since she's talking in English and not Zik, the emotions are unclear. "I didn't think you'd actually go through with it."

"You what?" Her words catch me completely off guard.

"Oh, I'm sorry," Ada says, still out loud. "Now that I've seen it, it's incredibly romantic and almost not corny at all. I didn't mean—"

I turn off the app and look at Ada in the real world. She must do the same thing, because she's facing *me* and not my avatar.

"You knew I was going to propose?" I ask, switching to Zik.

"Again, I'm sorry. I considered acting like this was a surprise, but I didn't want to repay such a nice gesture with a lie." Ada walks up to my bed and sits on the edge again. "In my defense, if you wanted this stuff to stay secret, you and Mitya shouldn't have committed your fascinating Virtual Reality code into our shared source control repository."

She gives me an innocent smile that makes me want to smack my head.

Before I can actually do so, she gently touches my left hand just below the IV entry point and says, "Also, when you shut down your Share app, you need to remember to turn off the one running in Mr. Spock's head as well, like you did at the fake shrink's office."

At the mention of his name, Mr. Spock runs out of his hiding spot behind the large cushion in the middle of the room and gives Ada a drowsy nod.

"And finally," Ada says out loud, "if you want privacy, you need to make sure your room doesn't have any cameras." She points at the hospital security camera above the big TV on the opposite wall.

"So you knew." I find the bed remote and raise myself into a sitting position so I'm looking directly into her eyes.

She nods sheepishly.

"And yet you let me go through with it." I look at Mr. Spock for support, but he loses interest in us and goes back under the cushion.

Ada nods again.

"Well," I say and pull out my right hand from under the covers. I'm still grasping the ring box containing the real-world ring Mom gave me. "You must've heard me say I want to marry you because I want to be with you and not because you're pregnant."

"Yes, I heard that." She leans closer and studies the ring box curiously.

"And you've had time to think about your answer?" I open the box, and though this version of the ring doesn't have the otherworldly shine of its VR twin, it does sparkle in the room's halogen lights.

Ada looks at the ring for a moment and then back at me, making me feel like I'm a small prehistoric bug about to get stuck in amber for millennia.

Finally, with almost ceremonial gravity, she says, "Yes."

"Yes, you've had time to think about the answer?" I ask as my heart rate equipment starts to beep.

"No." A Mona Lisa smile plays in the corners of Ada's eyes. "I was answering your other question."

"Which one?"

"No, not 'which one.'" Ada grins. "Will you marry me?"

"Yes," I say confidently. "Of course I'll marry you."

"I wasn't asking you. You were asking me." Ada reaches out as though to touch me with her left hand, but instead of touching me, she simply spreads her fingers apart.

"And you said yes." I take the ring and slip it on her extended finger.

Without saying a word, Ada leans in for a kiss.

As our tongues begin to dance, a single Zik message from Ada reverberates through my head, a message imbued with an emotion Ada hasn't used until now—something warm and fuzzy, the Zik equivalent of a heart emoji.

I read the message attached to the feeling and deepen the kiss.

The message states, "Yes."

SNEAK PEEKS

Thank you for reading! If you would consider leaving a review, it would be greatly appreciated.

The final book of the Human++ series, *Neural Web*, is coming soon! If you'd like to be notified when it's out, please sign up for my new release email list at <u>www.dimazales.com</u>.

Other series of mine include:
- *The Last Humans* — futuristic sci-fi/dystopian novels similar to *The Hunger Games*, *Divergent*, and *The Giver*
- *Mind Dimensions* — urban fantasy with a sci-fi flavor
- *The Sorcery Code* — epic fantasy

I also collaborate with my wife on sci-fi romance, so if you don't mind erotic material, you can check out *Close Liaisons*.

If you enjoy audiobooks, please visit my website to check out this series and our other books in audio format.

And now, please turn the page for a sneak peek at *Oasis (The Last Humans: Book 1)*, *The Thought Readers (Mind Dimensions: Book 1)*, and *The Sorcery Code*.

EXCERPT FROM *OASIS*

My name is Theo, and I'm a resident of Oasis, the last habitable area on Earth. It's meant to be a paradise, a place where we are all content. Vulgarity, violence, insanity, and other ills are but a distant memory, and even death no longer plagues us.

I was once content too, but now I'm different. Now I hear a voice in my head, and she tells me things no imaginary friend should know. Her name is Phoe, and she is my delusion.

Or is she?

Fuck. Vagina. Shit.

I pointedly think these forbidden words, but my neural scan shows nothing out of the ordinary compared to when I think phonetically similar words, such as *shuck, angina,* or *fit*. I don't see any evidence of my brain being corrupted, though maybe it's already so damaged that things can't get any worse. Maybe I need another test subject—another 'impressionable' twenty-three-year-old Youth such as myself.

After all, I might be mentally ill.

"Oh, Theo. Not this again," says an overly friendly, high-pitched female voice. "Besides, the words do have an effect on your brain. For instance, the part of your brain responsible for disgust lights up at the mention of 'shit,' yet doesn't for 'fit.'"

This is Phoe speaking. This time, she's not a voice inside my head; instead, it's as though she's in the thick bushes behind me, except there's no one there.

I'm the only person on this strip of grass.

Nobody else comes here because the Edge is only a couple of feet away. Few residents of Oasis like looking at the dreary line dividing where our habitable world ends and the deserted wasteland of the Goo begins. I don't mind it, though.

Then again, I may be crazy—and Phoe would be the reason for that. You see, I don't think Phoe is real. She is, as far as my best guess goes, my imaginary friend. And her name, by the way, is pronounced 'Fee,' but is spelled 'P-h-o-e.'

Yes, that's how specific my delusion is.

"So you go from one overused topic straight into another." Phoe snorts. "My so-called realness."

"Right," I say. Though we're alone, I still answer without moving my lips. "Because I *am* imagining you."

She snorts again, and I shake my head. Yes, I just shook my head for the benefit of my delusion. I also feel compelled to respond to her.

"For the record," I say, "I'm sure the taboo word 'shit' affects the parts of my brain that deal with disgust just as much as its more acceptable cousins, such as 'fecal matter,' do. The point I was trying to make is that the word doesn't hurt or corrupt my brain. There's nothing special about these words."

"Yeah, yeah." This time, Phoe is inside my head, and she sounds mocking. "Next you'll tell me how back in the day, some of the forbidden words merely referred to things like female dogs, and how there are words in the dead languages that used to be just as taboo, yet they are not currently forbidden because they have lost their power. Then you're likely to complain that, though the brains of both genders are nearly identical, only males are not allowed to say 'vagina,' et cetera."

I realize I was about to counter with those exact thoughts, which means Phoe and I have talked about this quite a bit. This is what happens between close friends: they repeat conversations. Doubly so with imaginary friends, I figure. Though, of course, I'm probably the only person in Oasis who actually has one.

Come to think of it, wouldn't *every* conversation with your imaginary friend be redundant since you're basically talking to yourself?

"This is my cue to remind you that I'm real, Theo." Phoe purposefully states this out loud.

I can't help but notice that her voice came slightly from my right, as if she's just a friend sitting on the grass next to me—a friend who happens to be invisible.

"Just because I'm invisible doesn't mean I'm not real," Phoe responds to my thought. "At least *I'm* convinced that I'm real. I would be the crazy one if I *didn't* think I was real. Besides, a lot of evidence points to that conclusion, and you know it."

"But wouldn't an imaginary friend *have* to insist she's real?" I can't resist saying the words out loud. "Wouldn't this be part of the delusion?"

"Don't talk to me out loud," she reminds me, her tone worried. "Even when you subvocalize, sometimes you imperceptibly move your neck muscles or even your lips. All those things are too risky. You should just think your thoughts at me. Use your inner voice. It's safer that way, especially when we're around other Youths."

"Sure, but for the record, that makes me feel even nuttier," I reply, but I subvocalize my words, trying my best not to move my lips or neck muscles. Then, as an experiment, I think, "Talking to you inside my head just highlights the impossibility of you and thus makes me feel like I'm missing even more screws."

"Well, it shouldn't." Her voice is inside my head now, yet it still sounds high-pitched. "Back in the day, when it was not forbidden to be mentally ill, I imagine it made people around you uncomfortable if you spoke to your imaginary friends out loud." She chuckles, but there's more worry than humor in her voice. "I have no idea what would happen if someone thought you were crazy, but I have a bad feeling about it, so please don't do it, okay?"

"Fine," I think and pull at my left earlobe. "Though it's overkill to do it here. No one's around."

"Yes, but the nanobots I told you about, the ones that permeate everything from your head to the utility fog, *can* be used to monitor this place, at least in theory."

"Right. Unless all this conveniently invisible technology you keep telling me about is as much of a figment of my imagination as you are," I think at her. "In any case, since no one seems to know about this tech, how can they use it to spy on me?"

"Correction: no Youth knows, but the others might," Phoe counters patiently. "There's too much we still don't know about Adults, not to mention the Elderly."

"But if they can access the nanocytes in my mind, wouldn't they have access to my thoughts too?" I think, suppressing a shudder. If this is true, I'm utterly screwed.

"The fact that you haven't faced any consequences for your frequently wayward thoughts is evidence that no one monitors them in general, or at least, they're not bothering with yours specifically," she responds, her words easing my dread. "Therefore, I think monitoring thoughts is either computationally prohibitive or breaks one of the bazillion taboos on the proper use of technology—rules I have a very hard time keeping track of, by the way."

"Well, what if using tech to listen in on me is also taboo?" I retort, though she's beginning to convince me.

"It may be, but I've seen evidence that can best be explained as the Adults spying." Her voice in my head takes on a hushed tone. "Just think of the time you and Liam made plans to skip your Physics Lecture. How did they know about that?"

I think of the epic Quietude session we were sentenced to and how we both swore we hadn't betrayed each other. We reached the same conclusion: our speech is not secure. That's why Liam, Mason, and I now often speak in code.

"There could be other explanations," I think at Phoe. "That conversation happened during Lectures, and some-one could've overheard us. But even if they hadn't, just because they monitor us during class doesn't mean they would bother monitoring this forsaken spot."

"Even if they don't monitor *this* place or anywhere out-side of the Institute, I still want you to acquire the right habit."

"What if I speak in code?" I suggest. "You know, the one I use with my non-imaginary friends."

"You already speak too slowly for my liking," she thinks at me with clear exasperation. "When you speak in that code, you sound ridiculous and drastically increase the number of syllables you say. Now if you were willing to learn one of the dead languages…"

"Fine. I will 'think' when I have to speak to you," I think. Then I subvocalize, "But I will also subvocalize."

"If you must." She sighs out loud. "Just do it the way you did a second ago, without any voice musculature mov-ing."

Instead of replying, I look at the Edge again, the place where the serene greenery under the Dome meets the re-pulsive ocean of the desolate Goo—the ever-replicating parasitic technology that converts matter into itself. The Goo is what's left of the world outside the Dome barrier, and if the barrier were to ever come down, the Goo would destroy us in short order. Naturally, this view evokes all sorts of unpleasant feelings, and the fact that I'm voluntarily gazing at it must be yet another sign of my shaky mental state.

"The thing *is* decidedly gross," Phoe reflects, trying to cheer me up, as usual. "It looks like someone tried to make Jell-O out of vomit and human excrement." Then, with a mental snicker, she adds, "Sorry, I should've said 'vomit and shit.'"

"I have no idea what Jell-O is," I subvocalize. "But whatever it is, you're probably spot on regarding the ingredients."

"Jell-O was something the ancients ate in the pre-Food days," Phoe explains. "I'll find something for you to watch or read about it, or if you're lucky, they might serve it at the upcoming Birth Day fair."

"I hope they do. It's hard to learn about food from books or movies," I complain. "I tried."

"In this case, you might," Phoe counters. "Jell-O was more about texture than taste. It had the consistency of jellyfish."

"People actually ate those slimy things back then?" I think in disgust. I can't recall seeing that in any of the movies. Waving toward the Goo, I say, "No wonder the world turned to this."

"They didn't eat it in most parts of the world," Phoe says, her voice taking on a pedantic tone. "And Jell-O was actually made out of partially decomposed proteins extracted from cow and pig hides, hooves, bones, and connective tissue."

"Now you're just trying to gross me out," I think.

"That's rich, coming from you, Mr. Shit." She chuckles. "Anyway, you have to leave this place."

"I do?"

"You have Lectures in half an hour, but more importantly, Mason is looking for you," she says, and her voice gives me the impression she's already gotten up from the grass.

I get up and start walking through the tall shrubbery that hides the Goo from the view of the rest of Oasis Youths.

"By the way"—Phoe's voice comes from the distance; she's simulating walking ahead of me—"once you verify that Mason *is* looking for you, *do* try to explain how an imaginary friend like me could possibly know something like that… something you yourself didn't know."

Oasis is currently available at most retailers. If you'd like to learn more, please visit <u>www.dimazales.com</u>.

EXCERPT FROM
THE THOUGHT READERS

Everyone thinks I'm a genius.

Everyone is wrong.

Sure, I finished Harvard at eighteen and now make crazy money at a hedge fund. But that's not because I'm unusually smart or hard-working.

It's because I cheat.

You see, I have a unique ability. I can go outside time into my own personal version of reality—the place I call "the Quiet"—where I can explore my surroundings while the rest of the world stands still.

I thought I was the only one who could do this—until I met *her*.

My name is Darren, and this is how I learned that I'm a Reader.

———

Sometimes I think I'm crazy. I'm sitting at a casino table in Atlantic City, and everyone around me is motionless. I call this the *Quiet*, as though giving it a name makes it seem more real—as though giving it a name changes the fact that all the players around me are frozen like statues, and I'm walking among them, looking at the cards they've been dealt.

The problem with the theory of my being crazy is that when I 'unfreeze' the world, as I just have, the cards the players turn over are the same ones I just saw in the Quiet. If I were crazy, wouldn't these cards be different? Unless I'm so far gone that I'm imagining the cards on the table, too.

But then I also win. If that's a delusion—if the pile of chips on my side of the table is a delusion—then I might as well question everything. Maybe my name isn't even Darren.

No. I can't think that way. If I'm really that confused, I don't want to snap out of it—because if I do, I'll probably wake up in a mental hospital.

Besides, I love my life, crazy and all.

My shrink thinks the Quiet is an inventive way I describe the 'inner workings of my genius.' Now that sounds crazy to me. She also might want me, but that's beside the point. Suffice it to say, she's as far as it gets from my datable age range, which is currently right around twenty-four. Still young, still hot, but done with school and pretty much beyond the clubbing phase. I hate clubbing, almost as much as I hated studying. In any case, my shrink's explanation doesn't work, as it doesn't account for the way I know things even a genius wouldn't know—like the exact value and suit of the other players' cards.

I watch as the dealer begins a new round. Besides me, there are three players at the table: Grandma, the Cowboy, and the Professional, as I call them. I feel that now almost imperceptible fear that accompanies the phasing. That's what I call the process: phasing into the Quiet. Worrying about my sanity has always facilitated phasing; fear seems helpful in this process.

I phase in, and everything gets quiet. Hence the name for this state.

It's eerie to me, even now. Outside the Quiet, this casino is very loud: drunk people talking, slot machines, ringing of wins, music—the only place louder is a club or a concert. And yet, right at this moment, I could probably hear a pin drop. It's like I've gone deaf to the chaos that surrounds me.

Having so many frozen people around adds to the strangeness of it all. Here is a waitress stopped mid-step, carrying a tray with drinks. There is a woman about to pull a slot machine lever. At my own table, the dealer's hand is raised, the last card he dealt hanging unnaturally in mid-air. I walk up to him from the side of the table and reach for it. It's a king, meant for the Professional. Once I let the card go, it falls on the table rather than continuing to float as before—but I know full well that it will be back in the air, in the exact position it was when I grabbed it, when I phase out.

The Professional looks like someone who makes money playing poker, or at least the way I always imagined someone like that might look. Scruffy, shades on, a little sketchy-looking. He's been doing an excellent job with the poker face—basically not twitching a single muscle throughout the game. His face is so expressionless that I wonder if he might've gotten Botox to help maintain such a stony countenance. His hand is on the table, protectively covering the cards dealt to him.

I move his limp hand away. It feels normal. Well, in a manner of speaking. The hand is sweaty and hairy, so moving it aside is unpleasant and is admittedly an abnormal thing to do. The normal part is that the hand is warm, rather than cold. When I was a kid, I expected people to feel cold in the Quiet, like stone statues.

With the Professional's hand moved away, I pick up his cards. Combined with the king that was hanging in the air, he has a nice high pair. Good to know.

I walk over to Grandma. She's already holding her cards, and she has fanned them nicely for me. I'm able to avoid touching her wrinkled, spotted hands. This is a relief, as I've recently become conflicted about touching people—or, more specifically, women—in the Quiet. If I had to, I would rationalize touching Grandma's hand as harmless, or at least not creepy, but it's better to avoid it if possible.

In any case, she has a low pair. I feel bad for her. She's been losing a lot tonight. Her chips are dwindling. Her losses are due, at least partially, to the fact that she has a terrible poker face. Even before looking at her cards, I knew they wouldn't be good because I could tell she was disappointed as soon as her hand was dealt. I also caught a gleeful gleam in her eyes a few rounds ago when she had a winning three of a kind.

This whole game of poker is, to a large degree, an exercise in reading people—something I really want to get better at. At my job, I've been told I'm great at reading people. I'm not, though; I'm just good at using the Quiet to make it seem like I am. I do want to learn how to read people for real, though. It would be nice to know what everyone is thinking.

What I don't care that much about in this poker game is money. I do well enough financially to not have to depend on hitting it big gambling. I don't care if I win or lose, though quintupling my money back at the blackjack table was fun. This whole trip has been more about going gambling because I finally can, being twenty-one and all. I was never into fake IDs, so this is an actual milestone for me.

Leaving Grandma alone, I move on to the next player— the Cowboy. I can't resist taking off his straw hat and trying it on. I wonder if it's possible for me to get lice this way. Since I've never been able to bring back any inanimate objects from the Quiet, nor otherwise affect the real world in any lasting way, I figure I won't be able to get any living critters to come back with me, either.

Dropping the hat, I look at his cards. He has a pair of aces—a better hand than the Professional. Maybe the Cowboy is a professional, too. He has a good poker face, as far as I can tell. It'll be interesting to watch those two in this round.

Next, I walk up to the deck and look at the top cards, memorizing them. I'm not leaving anything to chance.

When my task in the Quiet is complete, I walk back to myself. Oh, yes, did I mention that I see myself sitting there, frozen like the rest of them? That's the weirdest part. It's like having an out-of-body experience.

Approaching my frozen self, I look at him. I usually avoid doing this, as it's too unsettling. No amount of looking in the mirror—or seeing videos of yourself on YouTube—can prepare you for viewing your own three-dimensional body up close. It's not something anyone is meant to experience. Well, aside from identical twins, I guess.

It's hard to believe that this person is me. He looks more like some random guy. Well, maybe a bit better than that. I do find this guy interesting. He looks cool. He looks smart. I think women would probably consider him good-looking, though I know that's not a modest thing to think.

It's not like I'm an expert at gauging how attractive a guy is, but some things are common sense. I can tell when a dude is ugly, and this frozen me is not. I also know that generally, being good-looking requires a symmetrical face, and the statue of me has that. A strong jaw doesn't hurt, either. Check. Having broad shoulders is a positive, and being tall really helps. All covered. I have blue eyes—that seems to be a plus. Girls have told me they like my eyes, though right now, on the frozen me, the eyes look creepy— glassy. They look like the eyes of a lifeless wax figure.

Realizing that I'm dwelling on this subject way too long, I shake my head. I can just picture my shrink analyzing this moment. Who would imagine admiring themselves like this as part of their mental illness? I can just picture her scribbling down *Narcissist,* underlining it for emphasis.

Enough. I need to leave the Quiet. Raising my hand, I touch my frozen self on the forehead, and I hear noise again as I phase out.

Everything is back to normal.

The card that I looked at a moment before—the king that I left on the table—is in the air again, and from there it follows the trajectory it was always meant to, landing near the Professional's hands. Grandma is still eyeing her fanned cards in disappointment, and the Cowboy has his hat on again, though I took it off him in the Quiet. Everything is exactly as it was.

On some level, my brain never ceases to be surprised at the discontinuity of the experience in the Quiet and outside it. As humans, we're hardwired to question reality when such things happen. When I was trying to outwit my shrink early on in my therapy, I once read an entire psychology textbook during our session. She, of course, didn't notice it, as I did it in the Quiet. The book talked about how babies as young as two months old are surprised if they see something out of the ordinary, like gravity appearing to work backwards. It's no wonder my brain has trouble adapting. Until I was ten, the world behaved normally, but everything has been weird since then, to put it mildly.

Glancing down, I realize I'm holding three of a kind. Next time, I'll look at my cards before phasing. If I have something this strong, I might take my chances and play fair.

The game unfolds predictably because I know everybody's cards. At the end, Grandma gets up. She's clearly lost enough money.

And that's when I see the girl for the first time.

She's hot. My friend Bert at work claims that I have a 'type,' but I reject that idea. I don't like to think of myself as shallow or predictable. But I might actually be a bit of both, because this girl fits Bert's description of my type to a T. And my reaction is extreme interest, to say the least.

Large blue eyes. Well-defined cheekbones on a slender face, with a hint of something exotic. Long, shapely legs, like those of a dancer. Dark wavy hair in a ponytail—a hairstyle that I like. And without bangs—even better. I hate bangs—not sure why girls do that to themselves. Though lack of bangs is not, strictly speaking, in Bert's description of my type, it probably should be.

I continue staring at her. With her high heels and tight skirt, she's overdressed for this place. Or maybe I'm underdressed in my jeans and t-shirt. Either way, I don't care. I have to try to talk to her.

I debate phasing into the Quiet and approaching her, so I can do something creepy like stare at her up close, or maybe even snoop in her pockets. Anything to help me when I talk to her.

I decide against it, which is probably the first time that's ever happened.

I know that my reasoning for breaking my usual habit—if you can even call it that—is strange. I picture the following chain of events: she agrees to date me, we go out for a while, we get serious, and because of the deep connection we have, I come clean about the Quiet. She learns I did something creepy and has a fit, then dumps me. It's ridiculous to think this, of course, considering that we haven't even spoken yet. Talk about jumping the gun. She might have an IQ below seventy, or the personality of a piece of wood. There can be twenty different reasons why I wouldn't want to date her. And besides, it's not all up to me. She might tell me to go fuck myself as soon as I try to talk to her.

Still, working at a hedge fund has taught me to hedge. As crazy as that reasoning is, I stick with my decision not to phase because I know it's the gentlemanly thing to do. In keeping with this unusually chivalrous me, I also decide not to cheat at this round of poker.

As the cards are dealt again, I reflect on how good it feels to have done the honorable thing—even without anyone knowing. Maybe I should try to respect people's privacy more often. As soon as I think this, I mentally snort. *Yeah, right.* I have to be realistic. I wouldn't be where I am today if I'd followed that advice. In fact, if I made a habit of respecting people's privacy, I would lose my job within days—and with it, a lot of the comforts I've become accustomed to.

Copying the Professional's move, I cover my cards with my hand as soon as I receive them. I'm about to sneak a peek at what I was dealt when something unusual happens.

The world goes quiet, just like it does when I phase in... but I did nothing this time.

And at that moment, I see *her*—the girl sitting across the table from me, the girl I was just thinking about. She's standing next to me, pulling her hand away from mine. Or, strictly speaking, from my frozen self's hand—as I'm standing a little to the side looking at her.

She's also still sitting in front of me at the table, a frozen statue like all the others.

My mind goes into overdrive as my heartbeat jumps. I don't even consider the possibility of that second girl being a twin sister or something like that. I know it's her. She's doing what I did just a few minutes ago. She's walking in the Quiet. The world around us is frozen, but we are not.

A horrified look crosses her face as she realizes the same thing. Before I can react, she lunges across the table and touches her own forehead.

The world becomes normal again.

She stares at me from across the table, shocked, her eyes huge and her face pale. Her hands tremble as she rises to her feet. Without so much as a word, she turns and begins walking away, then breaks into a run a couple of seconds later.

Getting over my own shock, I get up and run after her. It's not exactly smooth. If she notices a guy she doesn't know running after her, dating will be the last thing on her mind. But I'm beyond that now. She's the only person I've met who can do what I do. She's proof that I'm not insane. She might have what I want most in the world.

She might have answers.

The Thought Readers is now available at most retailers. If you'd like to learn more, please visit www.dimazales.com.

EXCERPT FROM
THE SORCERY CODE

Once a respected member of the Sorcerer Council and now an outcast, Blaise has spent the last year of his life working on a special magical object. The goal is to allow anyone to do magic, not just the sorcerer elite. The outcome of his quest is unlike anything he could've ever imagined—because, instead of an object, he creates Her.

She is Gala, and she is anything but inanimate. Born in the Spell Realm, she is beautiful and highly intelligent—and nobody knows what she's capable of. She will do anything to experience the world… even leave the man she is beginning to fall for.

Augusta, a powerful sorceress and Blaise's former fiancée, sees Blaise's deed as the ultimate hubris and Gala as an abomination that must be destroyed. In her quest to save the human race, Augusta will forge new alliances, becoming tangled in a web of intrigue that stretches further than any of them suspect. She may even have to turn to her new lover Barson, a ruthless warrior who might have an agenda of his own…

There was a naked woman on the floor of Blaise's study.

A beautiful naked woman.

Stunned, Blaise stared at the gorgeous creature who just appeared out of thin air. She was looking around with a bewildered expression on her face, apparently as shocked to be there as he was to be seeing her. Her wavy blond hair streamed down her back, partially covering a body that appeared to be perfection itself. Blaise tried not to think about that body and to focus on the situation instead.

A woman. A *She*, not an *It*. Blaise could hardly believe it. Could it be? Could this girl be the object?

She was sitting with her legs folded underneath her, propping herself up with one slim arm. There was something awkward about that pose, as though she didn't know what to do with her own limbs. In general, despite the curves that marked her a fully grown woman, there was a child-like innocence in the way she sat there, completely unselfconscious and totally unaware of her own appeal.

Clearing his throat, Blaise tried to think of what to say. In his wildest dreams, he couldn't have imagined this kind of outcome to the project that had consumed his entire life for the past several months.

Hearing the sound, she turned her head to look at him, and Blaise found himself staring into a pair of unusually clear blue eyes.

She blinked, then cocked her head to the side, studying him with visible curiosity. Blaise wondered what she was seeing. He hadn't seen the light of day in weeks, and he wouldn't be surprised if he looked like a mad sorcerer at this point. There was probably a week's worth of stubble covering his face, and he knew his dark hair was unbrushed and sticking out in every direction. If he'd known he would be facing a beautiful woman today, he would've done a grooming spell in the morning.

"Who am I?" she asked, startling Blaise. Her voice was soft and feminine, as alluring as the rest of her. "What is this place?"

"You don't know?" Blaise was glad he finally managed to string together a semi-coherent sentence. "You don't know who you are or where you are?"

She shook her head. "No."

Blaise swallowed. "I see."

"What am I?" she asked again, staring at him with those incredible eyes.

"Well," Blaise said slowly, "if you're not some cruel prankster or a figment of my imagination, then it's somewhat difficult to explain…"

She was watching his mouth as he spoke, and when he stopped, she looked up again, meeting his gaze. "It's strange," she said, "hearing words this way. These are the first real words I've heard."

Blaise felt a chill go down his spine. Getting up from his chair, he began to pace, trying to keep his eyes off her nude body. He had been expecting something to appear. A magical object, a thing. He just hadn't known what form that thing would take. A mirror, perhaps, or a lamp. Maybe even something as unusual as the Life Capture Sphere that sat on his desk like a large round diamond.

But a person? A female person at that?

To be fair, he had been trying to make the object intelligent, to ensure it would have the ability to comprehend human language and convert it into the code. Maybe he shouldn't be so surprised that the intelligence he invoked took on a human shape.

A beautiful, feminine, sensual shape.

Focus, Blaise, focus.

"Why are you walking like that?" She slowly got to her feet, her movements uncertain and strangely clumsy. "Should I be walking too? Is that how people talk to each other?"

Blaise stopped in front of her, doing his best to keep his eyes above her neck. "I'm sorry. I'm not accustomed to naked women in my study."

She ran her hands down her body, as though trying to feel it for the first time. Whatever her intent, Blaise found the gesture extremely erotic.

"Is something wrong with the way I look?" she asked. It was such a typical feminine concern that Blaise had to stifle a smile.

"Quite the opposite," he assured her. "You look unimaginably good." So good, in fact, that he was having trouble concentrating on anything but her delicate curves. She was of medium height, and so perfectly proportioned that she could've been used as a sculptor's template.

"Why do I look this way?" A small frown creased her smooth forehead. "What am I?" That last part seemed to be puzzling her the most.

Blaise took a deep breath, trying to calm his racing pulse. "I think I can try to venture a guess, but before I do, I want to give you some clothing. Please wait here—I'll be right back."

And without waiting for her answer, he hurried out of the room.

The Sorcery Code is currently available at most retailers. If you'd like to learn more, please visit www.dimazales.com.

ABOUT

Dima Zales is a *New York Times* and *USA Today* bestselling author of science fiction and fantasy. Prior to becoming a writer, he worked in the software development industry in New York as both a programmer and an executive. From high-frequency trading software for big banks to mobile apps for popular magazines, Dima has done it all. In 2013, he left the software industry in order to concentrate on his writing career and moved to Palm Coast, Florida, where he currently resides.

Please visit www.dimazales.com to learn more.